Someday the Rabbi Will Leave

BY HARRY KEMELMAN

HARRY KEMELMAN

Someday the Rabbi Will Leave

William Morrow and Company, Inc.   New York

Library of Congress Cataloging in Publication Data

Kemelman, Harry.
Someday the rabbi will leave.

I. Title.
PS3561.E398S6 1985   813'.54   84-14766
ISBN 0-688-04174-4

Printed in the United States of America

1 3 4 5 0 7 8 9 10

BOOK DESIGN BY LINEY LI

To the latest addition,

ANNE M. K. ROSSANT

Have a good life.

Someday the Rabbi Will Leave

1

FROM WHERE HE SAT in the living room, reading the afternoon paper, Rabbi David Small could hear his wife, Miriam, moving around in the kitchen. By the noise engendered—the rattle of pots and pans, and the banging of the oven door—he knew she was annoyed. And he knew why. She had been doing the monthly bills.

She came to the door of the living room. Her figure, he noted, was as slender and trim as a high-school girl's. Impatiently she brushed aside a wisp of blond hair that had fallen across her face.

"David, we need more money," she announced.

"Yes dear," he said meekly, automatically, from behind his paper.

"Maybe I'll look for a job."

He put aside his paper. "As what?"

"As a typist, maybe. No. That would mean working in an office and not enough people would see me. I'll get a job as a checkout girl in a supermarket. Then people would notice and realize that they were underpaying their rabbi."

The telephone rang and he reached for it. "Rabbi Small," he said. Then, "Oh, how are you? . . . No, we've got

nothing planned. . . . Sure. . . . Sure. . . . Around eight?
. . . Okay, anytime. . . . Good-bye." To Miriam he explained,
"That was Sam Feinberg. He wanted to know if we were
going to be in this evening. He'd like to come over."

"Good. You can ask him for more money."

"Just like that. And what does he do then? Reach into
his pocket for his wallet, or perhaps ask me for a pen so that
he can write out a check?"

"Oh, you know what I mean. I know the Finance Committee has to approve it, I suppose on the recommendation
of the Ritual Committee, and then the whole board has to
vote on it. But someone has to propose it, set the wheels in
motion. Well, what's wrong with asking Mr. Feinberg? He
likes you. You get along well together. In the couple of
years he's been president, you've never had any trouble
with him. At least, I don't remember your ever complaining about him."

"We get along all right."

"Then why not—"

"I can't ask him, Miriam."

"But why not? This inflation has cut your salary—"

"I get a cost-of-living increment."

"But it's never enough, and you don't get it until your
next contract. If at least you didn't turn in your fees—"

"I agreed to when I first came here."

"But we could use the money," she wailed. "The Beren-
son wedding, you got two hundred dollars."

He grinned. "I'm sure it wouldn't have been a quarter
of that if they thought it was going into my pocket. They
know I turn it over to the temple treasury, and they tend
to give more because everybody finds out how much."

"You could keep a record of all the money you turn over
and ask them to increase your salary by that much at least.
That would be only fair. Most rabbis keep their fees."

He remained silent, indicating he did not care to continue the discussion. Although only forty, Rabbi Small sometimes seemed like an old man with his scholarly stoop and pale face peering out through thick-lensed glasses. And sometimes, as now, he seemed like a small, stubborn boy who has been naughty and refuses to say he's sorry.

She persisted. "Aren't you ever going to ask for a raise, David?"

He smiled and said gently, "Look, Miriam, for me to ask for a raise is—is demeaning."

"But it's a business arrangement," she said. "You have a contract."

"Sure, so I'll go about it in a businesslike way. When the time comes."

"And what do you call a businesslike way?"

"When I can say that I want more money or else I leave. Don't you see, if I ask for a raise when I'm obviously planning to continue is like—like begging. I'm appealing to their charity. And what if they don't grant it? Do I sulk? I can't do it. If I establish that kind of relationship with them, I'll lose all authority."

"At the Rabbinical Conference down in Providence, Sarah Metzenbaum told me the way Jack works it when he wants something. He tips off his close friends on the board and they bring it up at the meeting."

He reflected that among the more unfortunate aspects of rabbinical conferences was that while the rabbis were meeting and listening to papers, their wives also met and compared notes. "Jack Metzenbaum is a friendly, outgoing guy who makes friends easily, practically automatically. I'm not. You've got to work at it. It means socializing with them, dining with them—"

"So what's wrong with that?"

"How many of our board members have kosher homes where we could eat? And I don't play golf."

"Chester Kaplan and his group all have kosher homes."

"That's all I need, to show partiality to Chester Kaplan," he scoffed. "As it is, most members of the board think I always side with the Orthodox group."

"Then what's the answer? You won't ask for a raise, and you don't have anyone to ask for you. If they haven't thought of giving you one on their own up till now, they're not likely to in the future."

He saw that she was worried and upset, and he thought it best to mollify her. "Oh, I'll work out something. Don't worry about it."

But she was not to be put off. "Considering the ground rules you've laid down, I'd like to know how." She was small, girlish, so that it was hard to believe that she was the mother of two teenage children. Her blue eyes, wide and normally gay, now focused sharply, even accusingly at him. Her chin was raised as if to give emphasis to her determination, and the mass of blond hair piled casually on the top of her head threatened to come down as she tilted her head back imperiously, a gesture which always put him on the defensive.

He temporized. "We-el, when my contract expires, I presume they'll send me another. And—and I just won't sign it. That's all. When they ask me why not, I'll tell them I can't continue on my present salary."

"How much would you ask for?"

He was exasperated. "I don't know. It would depend—"

"We need at least a couple of thousand more."

"So I'll ask for another two thousand."

"Twenty-five hundred."

"All right. Twenty-five hundred."

"And if they don't grant it?"

"Then I won't sign the contract and I'll start looking around for another job. Satisfied?"

She nodded slowly. "All right, but when Feinberg comes over tonight, wouldn't it be a good idea to hint about what you're planning so he can alert the board to begin thinking about it?"

He shook his head. "Or it might start them looking around for a replacement."

"Then you'd at least know where you stood, and you could start looking before your contract expires."

"Look, Miriam," he said patiently, "I don't know why he is coming over or what he wants to talk about—"

"But if the occasion arises—"

"All right. If he talks about a big surplus in the treasury that he wants my advice how to spend, I'll mention the board might consider raising my salary. Satisfied?"

The back door opened and then shut with a bang. From the kitchen came the strident voice of their daughter, Hepsibah, thirteen, rosy-cheeked, and blond but unfashionably short and stocky. "Jonathon is a pig," she announced. "He got a lift from Al Steiner and instead of stopping, they drove right past me. Jonathon even waved. Hi, Dad. Hi, Mom. Is he upstairs?"

"He hasn't come home yet," said Miriam. "You're late, and if you don't hurry, you'll be late for Hebrew school."

"Can you ride me down, Dad?"

"The walk will do you good," said her father.

"Your father is busy, Sibah. Now take a glass of milk. You've got plenty of time to get there if you don't dawdle."

"Why do I have to go to that darn old Hebrew school, anyway?"

"Because it's Wednesday," said her mother tartly, "and that's when your class meets."

There followed the sounds of footsteps going up the stairs, of books being dropped, of footsteps clumping down the stairs, and then the banging of the back door. Miriam sighed.

There was quiet for about fifteen minutes, and then the back door banged open and shut.

"Jonathon?" Miriam called.

Their son, seventeen, tall and thin and ungainly, came into the living room. "Hi, Dad. Hi, Ma."

"Why didn't you give your sister a ride home?" asked the rabbi.

"Because we weren't going home. We were going to Al Steiner's house. And she's a pest. Al Steiner just got a computer. I wanted to see it. Gee, it's neat. You can type your homework on it and make all kinds of corrections, and then you just press a button and it types out by itself with all the margins and everything. You can even press a button and it will correct all your mistakes in spelling."

"You could have given her a lift up to Main Street," Miriam pointed out.

"She would have tried to come along with us. You baking cookies?"

"There's some in the jar," said Miriam. "You're babysitting tonight for the Colemans, aren't you?"

"Oh yeah. Could you drive me over there, Dad?"

"I'm afraid not. We're expecting company tonight. Take your bike."

"I'm due there at seven, so I thought when you go to the *minyan* for the evening services—"

"In this weather, I walk, and I'm glad of the chance. Besides, how would you get home?"

Jonathon muttered something and mounted the stairs to his room. And once again, peace descended on the Small household.

2

WEARING A SPORT SHIRT, blue blazer, and gray slacks, Howard Magnuson came down to breakfast in the sunny dining room overlooking Barnard's Crossing Harbor. He bent over to give his wife, Sophia, a perfunctory kiss and then took his place across the table from her. Nodding his head toward the third place setting, he asked, "Laura?"

"Still sleeping," said his wife. "She got in late last night."

The maid, a local girl and not very well trained, brought out his bacon and eggs, drew his copy of *The New York Times* from under her arm, and then filled his coffee cup from the heavy silver pot already on the table. He took an experimental sip.

The girl hovered. "Miz Hagerstrom wants I should ask you if you want a pot of fresh coffee."

"No, this is all right."

"You don't want she should hot it up?"

"No, this is just fine."

He was a good-looking man of fifty with graying hair and friendly blue eyes. To the amusement of his wife, the girl gave him a yearning, adoring look before reluctantly returning to the kitchen.

"That girl, she hovers," he said.

"She's got a crush on you."

"Ridiculous," he said, trying to sound annoyed, although secretly pleased. "What time did Laura get in last night?"

"Two, three, who knows? I heard her come in but I didn't look at the clock. Why?"

"Why? Because she's our daughter. She's a girl—"

"She's twenty-five, Howard."

"So?"

"And she spent the last three years in England, and before that she was away at school."

"I suppose," he said sheepishly. "Still . . . Doesn't she ever tell you where she's going?"

"She might if she happened to think of it, or if I asked her. Last night she went to Cambridge. Some political thing."

"Oh, politics."

"Why not?" Sophia Magnuson was a tall woman with a long, narrow face that was handsome rather than pretty. Even now, in her dressing gown, she looked stately enough to go to an embassy ball. "You ought to get involved, too, Howard. Oh, I don't mean to run for office, but to advise, to influence. It's expected of a man in your position." She tapped the local newspaper she had been reading. "It says here that Ronnie Sykes has been asked to come down to Washington. He's going to serve on some sort of commission for the President. Why don't they ever ask you?"

He looked up. "I suppose because I'm not active in politics. Ronnie Sykes is a member of the state Republican Committee. Why are you interested? Do you want to go to Washington? What for?"

"Well, we'd meet some different people, important people, people who do things. You contribute to the party, don't you?"

"Nothing very substantial. Whenever they have a testimonial dinner I buy a bunch of tickets, but that's about it. Besides, Sykes is a Greek. His name used to be Skouros, or something like that."

"What's that got to do with it?"

"It means he's a contact with a minority, and so can be useful to the administration."

"Well, we're a minority, aren't we? Why couldn't you be a contact with the Jewish community?"

"It's not just being Greek. He's also involved with them. I think he was president of Ahepa once."

"Well, you were an officer in a temple once."

"Vice-president. And that was seven or eight years ago when we were still living in Boston. And I wasn't really involved. My grandfather practically founded the temple and was its first president. And afterwards my father was president for a couple of terms. So I was more or less expected to get involved. Frankly, one of the attractions of coming to Barnard's Crossing was that it gave me the excuse to drop it."

"Yet you joined the temple here the first year we came."

"That's different. It's the one Jewish organization in town. If I had an obviously Jewish name like Cohen or Levy or Goldstein, I might not have bothered. But Magnuson could be anything—British, Swedish. I didn't want anyone to think I was ashamed of my heritage, so I joined the temple."

"All right, but then last year you became a member of the Board of Directors. Wasn't that kind of overdoing it?" she challenged.

He chuckled. "I felt I had to. Let's see, you were in Paris when that right-of-way business came up. I don't think I ever told you what happened. My first thought was to consult my lawyers in Boston. Then I realized that approach might be all wrong. They'd make a Supreme Court case out of it. They'd come before the Board of Selectmen with affidavits, depositions, precedents. And I sensed it wouldn't work. The selectmen are local people, simple people. One is a barber, for instance. That approach might just get their backs up. So instead I went to the town hall to scout the situation on my own. There was a directory on the wall with the names of the town officers, and the name of the town counsel was Morris Halperin."

She smiled knowingly. "I see."

"He happened to be in his office at the time, so I explained the situation, and asked him to handle it for me as my lawyer."

"And?"

"He turned me down."

"He knew who you were?"

"Oh sure, but he explained that it was a conflict of interest, that he couldn't act as my attorney in a matter on which he might have to advise the selectmen. Then he told me I didn't need an attorney, that I should appear before the board and tell my story, and that it would make a better impression than if I were represented by counsel. Then he kind of winked at me and said, 'Besides, if the question is put to me by the selectmen, my opinion might be helpful.' "

"That was very friendly of him, I must say."

"Wasn't it? As it turned out, they didn't even ask his opinion. They decided unanimously in my favor. So after the decision was published in the town bulletin, which made it official, I went to see him again. I felt I owed him something for—for advising me not to engage a lawyer."

"And this time, I'd bet he was more amenable."

"You'd lose! He said he couldn't take payment for the advice since he had given it in his role of town counsel."

"How old is this man, Halperin?"

He pursed his lips as he considered. "Fortyish."

"It's refreshing to see that at least some of the younger people have a sense of ethics." She noted his quizzical look and added, "Or is there more?"

He laughed. "Well, not really. We talked, and the conversation turned to the temple. Then out of the blue he asked me if I'd mind if he proposed my name for the Board of Directors."

"Just like that?"

"M-hm. You see, he knew I owed him one."

"But you have no interest in religion, and—"

"I explained that and he wasn't fazed in the least. He said that very few members of the board were religious except for their sense of heritage, which they felt was bound up with the institution of the synagogue. He realized I might be busy and unable to attend the meetings regularly, and I gathered it wouldn't matter if I didn't attend any of them. They just wanted the prestige of my name on their stationery. So I agreed. What else could I do?"

"But you *have* attended meetings, some of them anyway."

He smiled ruefully. "A couple. I really ought to go more often. They don't seem to know how to transact business. I might be able to set them right."

"I'm sure you could. So how would you go about becoming president?"

"Of the temple? Why in the world would I want to?"

"Never mind. *Could* you if you wanted to?"

Put this way, as a problem in corporate and institutional politics, he canted his head to one side as he considered. "Well . . ."

"Would you talk to the rabbi about it?"

"Oh no." He shook his head impatiently. "He's just an employee of the temple. I suppose I might—hm—you know what I'd do? I'd talk to this Morris Halperin."

"Because he first proposed you to the board?"

"No. Because he has political know-how. Getting elected town counsel, even though he's Jewish, shows that. I'd get him to act as a sort of campaign manager."

"What makes you think he'd want to?"

"Oh, I think he would. He's young and on the make. I'm sure he'd appreciate the chance of associating himself with me."

"How do you know he's on the make?"

"Would he bother with the job of town counsel if he weren't? It pays next to nothing, and it means he has to attend the selectmen's meetings every Wednesday evening throughout the year." His face relaxed in a broad grin. "Besides, I looked up his account at the bank before I went to see him that second time."

"How could you do that?"

"It's a local branch of my bank in the city. And I'm a director. Do you think the manager would jib at showing me anything I wanted to see?"

"And?"

He shrugged. "He's making a living, but he's not setting the world on fire."

"What's he like? What's he look like?"

"Oh, he seems a decent sort of chap. He's a big man, six feet, I'd say, and kind of stocky, but he's not fat—not yet, anyway. He's got a big nose and fleshy lips. His hairline has crept back to the top of his head, but he has a nice face and he smiles easily."

"Well, that's fine," she said. "I'll invite him to dinner."

"What for?"

"Oh, because he was decent and helpful," she said airily. "And because it might be interesting to explore the possibilities. Besides, since selling off Elechtech Corporation you need a new interest. Do you mind?"

"What good would it do if I did, now you've set your mind to it?"

3

SAM FEINBERG, the president of the temple, short, stout, and balding, was a decent, considerate man with a talent for compromise. Which is why he was elected president in the first place, following the near-disastrous administration of Chester Kaplan and the Orthodox group. He had served three terms—in 1980 and again in 1981, and once again in 1982, the last time virtually unopposed. From the point of view of the Reform element, he was a modern man who did not flaunt his observance of the religious code; the ultrareligious clique found him acceptable because they knew he maintained a kosher home, and he came regularly to the Friday night and Sabbath services, even appearing at the daily minyan on occasion.

When he arrived, the rabbi inquired first after his wife, who was not well. Feinberg shook his head sadly. "It's what I came to see you about. I've decided we have to go away before the winter sets in. We're going to Arizona."

"I see. How long will you be gone?"

"I'm not coming back. We'll be moving out there permanently. To be perfectly candid with you, Rabbi, I've been planning this move for some time. I flew out to Phoenix last week. My son, Mark, as you know, is in the real estate business there. He moved out to Phoenix some years ago. He suffers from asthma, too, and he hasn't had a serious attack since he's been there. He's been after us to make the move because of his mother's condition. And to make a long story short, I bought a house there."

"Well, that was quick. I wish you the best of luck, of course. And what about your business here?"

"The younger boy, Abner, and my son-in-law have been running it for some time. I haven't had much to do with it for the last couple of years. Oh, I go in a few times a week, but that's about all. They can carry on without me."

"When are you planning to leave? Is this good-bye?"

Feinberg laughed. "Oh no, I won't be going for a month or more. There's still a lot to do. But the major thing that bothers me is the temple." He emitted a rich gurgle of laughter. "I can't very well run it by correspondence from Arizona."

"So our vice-president will—oh no, he's out. We have no vice-president. That means we'll have to hold a special election."

"The other day, Rabbi, I was looking over the by-laws. Back when the temple first started, they had about forty-five on the Board of Directors and three vice-presidents, a first, a second, and a third. I don't know what they were expecting."

The rabbi explained. "As I understand—I wasn't here at the very beginning, you know—it wasn't intended to ensure the succession, but as a kind of honor. And that's also why there were forty-five on the board. Only about fifteen ever came to a meeting, but the idea was to get as many members as possible actively involved. Then some years back—after they had cut the board down to fifteen—there was a change in the by-laws, setting up just one vice-president but permitting the president to appoint a vice-president if the office fell vacant for any reason—rather than holding a special election. I guess they felt that if they held a special meeting of the membership just to elect a vice-president, not many would show up."

"That's right. It was about the time when Agnew resigned and Nixon appointed Ford. The board figured that if the United States could do it, then our temple certainly could. 'If for any reason the office of vice-president shall fall vacant, then the president may appoint a member to the position with the approval of not less than two thirds of the directors at any regular meeting of the board.' Something like that, anyway. So I thought I'd appoint somebody, get the approval of the board, and then I'd resign. I was thinking of someone like—No?" as the rabbi shook his head.

"You'd appoint your friend Siskin, I suppose."

"Or Ely Mann, or Murray Larkin."

"Well, whomever you appointed, the board would probably approve because the position isn't considered important. But then when you announced you were resigning, the next sound you'd hear, and you'd hear it all the way to Lynn, would be Chester Kaplan crying foul. It would be seen as a trick, and his group wouldn't take it lying down. They'd hold meetings, launch a telephone campaign—it could split the congregation, and there'd be bad blood for years to come."

"But if I just resign, a special election would be held in a week or two, and Chester Kaplan would win easily," said Feinberg stubbornly.

"Why would he win?"

"Because he's got a close-knit group. They meet with each other all the time; Kaplan holds a weekly at-home. His campaign would be off and running before the Conservatives could even agree on a candidate."

"Nevertheless," said the rabbi, "it's a risk you've got to

take. When were you planning to announce your resignation?"

"I thought I'd wait until I was due to leave, in about a month that is. In the meantime, I might drop a hint to one or two of the Conservative members and they could sort of get started."

Again the rabbi shook his head. "That wouldn't be fair. Besides, it would get out."

"Then what can I do?"

The rabbi got up and began to stride back and forth, his head bowed in thought. He came to a halt in front of his visitor. "I'll tell you what: Announce it at the next board meeting, this Sunday."

"And?"

"That your resignation is to take effect in a month or six weeks, or whenever you are actually going to leave."

"Ah." Feinberg nodded and smiled. "Yes, I see. That will give the others a chance to get organized."

"Maybe," said the rabbi gloomily.

When Feinberg had left and they were alone, Miriam asked, "Would it really be so terrible if Chester Kaplan and his group got in?"

"You remember what happened the year he was president."

"You mean the business of wanting to buy the place up-country for a retreat? But he's probably learned his lesson and wouldn't do that kind of thing again."

"No? Well, only yesterday at the morning minyan while we were waiting for a tenth man, he suggested that we keep a record of attendance at the minyan and then restrict the honors on the High Holy Days to those who had been present a certain percentage of the time."

"Oh no."

"Oh yes. I'm sure he has a lot of other bright ideas that

24

he would try to introduce. Maybe restrict the choir to male voices. Maybe change the seating arrangements so that there were men on one side and women on the other."

"There'd be so much opposition that—"

"That's the point. We want to avoid opposition. We can't afford it. In a city with a large Jewish population, a Conservative synagogue is made up of people who believe in Conservative Judaism. But in a small town like Barnard's Crossing, the Conservative synagogue is essentially a compromise between the three elements, Reform, Conservative, and Orthodox. We've got to maintain a balance. If we lean too far in one direction or the other, we'll lose members. If Kaplan and his crew got in, there is a strong possibility that the Reform element would pull out and start a temple of their own. And the community is just not large enough to support two temples. That's mainly what worries Feinberg. And it worries me, too, of course. But I'm also bothered because Kaplan and his group represent what I think of as the New Orthodox."

"The *New* Orthodox?"

"That's right. They're terribly religious. They work at it, and when you work at it, religion is apt to turn into religiosity. You know, for all that my father was a Conservative rabbi, ours was what is nowadays thought of as an Orthodox home. And of course my grandfather *was* an Orthodox rabbi and all my relatives went to Orthodox synagogues. Well, their religion was easy. Actually, it was more of a way of life than an attempt to commune with the divine. Observance of the commandments was a matter of habit. They could no more eat nonkosher food than most people can eat snake meat. And using separate dishes for meat and for dairy products was as natural as—as eating from dishes at a table rather than from an old newspaper on the floor. The first time I ate in a restaurant and saw someone buttering his bread before cutting into his steak

—and, mind you, I was in college at the time—I almost retched."

"How about the Sabbath? Wasn't it restrictive?"

"Restrictive? Not at all. It was a holiday. You dressed up in your Sabbath best and went to the synagogue. Then there was a special dinner. It was a day for visiting and for guests. My grandfather quizzed me on what I had learned in the religious school during the week and sometimes augmented it with his own instruction, especially after I started studying Talmud. If no guests came, or after they left, my folks would nap in the afternoon. The day proceeded with a different rhythm. It wasn't hard, and I was never aware of any strain."

"Well, it wasn't that way with us," said Miriam.

"Of course not, because your family is Reform," he scoffed. "You went to the temple the way Christians go to church, full of solemn dignity. Well, Judaism isn't like that, at least not by tradition. You people prayed fervently, or felt a little guilty if you didn't. But normally, Jews don't really pray at all; they *daven.* That is, they mumble the set text as rapidly as they can, and since it's in Hebrew, hardly any of them understand it. That was the reason for the Reform change from Hebrew to the language of the country, English in our case."

"Doesn't it make sense to know what you're saying?"

"I'm not so sure. You remember old Mr. Goralsky?"

"You mean Ben Goralsky's father? Of course."

"Well, he once told me that he had never missed reciting his daily prayers from the time he was five years old. He was seventy-five or eighty at the time. He knew them by heart, but he didn't know what the words meant. He explained, however, that when he was engaged in praying he had different thoughts than he ordinarily had. In effect, he was meditating and the prayers, mumbled so rapidly that he finished the *Amidah* before anyone else was halfway through, they were a sort of mantra. He was an observant Jew in the sense that he observed the commandments expeditiously and then went about his business. I never thought of him as religious, that is, as someone intent on divining God's will. Now, I do think of Kaplan and his group as religious."

"And you're afraid that if they get in, they'll pervert the —the—"

"The service. Precisely. I guess, what I'm trying to say is that we Jews have always been suspicious of religiosity, in accordance with the commandment 'Thou shalt not take the name of the Lord in vain.'"

She nodded. "You want to know something, David? You didn't get around to talking to Feinberg about a raise."

"Miriam, Miriam, did you hear what I was saying?"

"Of course. You've said it before, you know. But right now, I'm concerned about your getting more money. We've got to be thinking of Jonathon's college. And Hepsibah is growing up. She's going to need dresses and shoes instead of the jeans and sneakers she's been wearing."

4

Scofield was one of the old Barnard's Crossing names like Meechum and Crosset. There was a Scofield Alley that led down to the public wharf, and a bit of grass with a couple of benches that was listed in the town records as Scofield Park. But in contrast to the dozen Meechums and the half column of Crossets, there was only one Scofield—John— listed in the telephone directory. According to town gossip, "the Scofields were cautious folk and tended to marry late, so they didn't have too many kids."

Unfortunately, this did not lead to prosperity except for a brief period in the nineteenth century when a Judge Samuel Scofield had taken a flyer in the China trade and made a lot of money from one voyage. But then his innate caution took over and he did not venture again. By the time of his death, the fortune was largely dissipated. But the good judge at least managed to establish a scholarship at both Harvard College and Harvard Law School with the stipulation that it was to be given only to someone bearing the name of Scofield. In the absence of a candidate, the money was to go to the general operating funds of the college and the law school, respectively.

Perhaps because there had been no applicants for years and the Admissions Committee felt a little guilty, John Scofield, whose marks at Barnard's Crossing High had been only fair, indeed on the low side, was admitted to the college. And four years later, he applied and was admitted to the law school.

At twenty-eight, John Scofield was a tall, blond young man with pale blue eyes and large square white teeth, and handsome in a stolid sort of way. He shared an office in Salem with four other lawyers, all young men like himself struggling to build a practice. He was a little better off, however, since they were all married, while he had only himself to support—"Scofields tend to marry late."

Across the hall was the office of the elderly trial lawyer, J. J. Mulcahey, from whom they rented. John Scofield spent a lot of time in Mulcahey's office because he had a lot of time to spend and because the old man liked to talk, especially when he had a drink or two in him. Occasionally, Mulcahey gave him some work, largely clerical, for which he paid him, usually quite generously. Now and then Mulcahey gave him a case that he was either too busy or too lazy to handle himself. Which is how Scofield became the attorney for the defense of Juan Gonzales. The morning of the trial, however, found him not in court but in Mulcahey's office. The older man glanced at the clock and asked, "Don't you go to trial this morning?"

"It's all over," said Scofield, smiling with satisfaction. "I did some plea bargaining."

"What you settle for?"

"Six months and a year's probation. I figure that's a lot better than taking a chance on three to five."

"I would have got him off," said Mulcahey.

"Cummon, J.J. He was guilty as hell."

"What's that got to do with it? That's for the jury to decide. What happened?"

"Well, Gonzales had his whole family there, and every now and then, one of them would come over to ask me a question or to give me some crazy advice. It began to get on my nerves. So after a while I went across the street for a cup of coffee. A couple of minutes later, the assistant D.A., Charlie Venturo, comes in. You know him?"

"Sure. He's one I'm careful not to turn my back on."

"Aw, cummon, he's a nice guy. Anyway, he joins me and we get to talking. He goes on and on about his case load and how the D.A. is on his back to get it down. And then he gives me that kind of funny one-sided smile of his—"

"That's when you've really got to watch out. I always reach back and clutch my wallet."

Scofield parted his lips and displayed his teeth to show he appreciated the joke. "Anyway, he says how would I like for my client to cop a plea. So we're up before Judge Prentiss, and you know how he is about blacks and Puerto Ricans, and I know he's got an open-and-shut case—"

"He didn't have a case," said Mulcahey flatly.

"Oh yes, J.J. He had a witness, a nice middle-aged guy who—"

"Who crapped out or didn't show."

"No, he showed all right. I saw him there in the corridor."

"So he crapped out. He told Venturo that he couldn't be certain it was Gonzales."

"Why would he do that?"

"Because his wife probably got to him. 'Why do you want to get involved with a bunch of crazy Puerto Ricans?' That kind of thing. Happens all the time. So Venturo, knowing he doesn't have a case, and seeing you go out for a cup of coffee, follows you and propositions you. Let me ask you, if he had an open-and-shut case and was sure of a conviction with a sentence of three to five years, why should he offer to settle for a lousy six months?"

"Well, he was busy—"

"So what? They're always busy, and the D.A. is always goosing them to reduce their case load. What did he stand to gain? The case would have been finished before the noon recess."

"You think he played me for a patsy?"

"I'll say."

"And I should have gone ahead with it?"

"You bet. Especially for your own sake."

"How do you mean?"

Mulcahey looked at the crestfallen young man sitting across the desk. What was wrong with him? What was lacking? A good-looking guy like that. He felt sorry for him and tried to explain. "Look, these Puerto Ricans have big families. Everyone has a bunch of brothers and sisters and more cousins and aunts and uncles than you can count. You would have had a sizable gallery in the courtroom if you'd pleaded. If they see a lawyer fighting for his client, getting up and making objections, bearing down on cross-examination, making an impassioned summation to the jury, they're going to think he's pretty good even if he loses the case. What happens if your client does get three to five? You don't have to serve it. But his family, they think a trial's a game—you win some, you lose some. What counts with them is whether you put up a good fight or not. And if they like you, there's business to be gained. Civil business as well as criminal. A lease, a contract, a title search—they'll come to you because they saw you fighting for your client and you seemed to care. But if you cop a plea, sooner or later the idea is going to occur to them that, maybe, if you'd gone to trial, you might have won."

"So you think I blew it?"

"You sure did," said Mulcahey. He was on the point of offering the usual words of solace and consolation, but catching sight of their reflections in the dusty office win-

31

dow, he could not help comparing his own appearance—his squat and shapeless body, his puffy face and bulbous nose—with that of the nice-looking young man on the other side of the desk. Scofield had everything, where as he had had nothing to start with, and yet . . . Suddenly he was annoyed and angry with him. It was not merely his mishandling of the Gonzales case, but his general complacency. However, he showed no sign of his annoyance as he pulled out the bottom drawer of his desk and fished out a bottle and a glass. Automatically, he made an offering motion with the bottle.

Scofield shook his head.

Mulcahey poured himself a drink, took a sip, and then, glass in hand, tilted back in his chair and jammed his foot against the side of the extended drawer for balance. "Have you ever thought," he asked lazily, "that you might be in the wrong profession?"

"You think I'm that bad, huh?"

The older man spread his arms in resignation. "You don't think things through. You're impulsive. You get an idea, and sometimes it's a very good idea, but you act on it without considering the long-range effects. Like the case today, or that contract you drew up a couple of days ago. You think quick, but you don't think long. Well, that's what a lawyer is supposed to do for his client, take the long view. The client does something, or wants to do something, is all hot for it, but his lawyer is the guy that asks, 'But what if . . .?' Get it? Your mind doesn't seem to work that way."

"So what should I do?"

Mulcahey considered. "You've been out three, four years?"

"Uh-huh."

"And you're not making it, are you? You dress nice and you got that place in Waterfront Towers. On the other hand, you drive that crazy second-hand car. Tell me, are you making any money?"

32

"Not much."

The older man laughed coarsely. "Well, you could marry a rich girl. That would take care of your problem."

"Aw, rich girls don't get married these days. They have careers. They become doctors and lawyers and college professors."

"Maybe you could team up with some smart young Jew or Italian. You'd work at bringing in the business and he'd handle it. You've got the looks and with your background and all, you must know a lot of people. Any clients you brought in, you'd hand over to him—Nah." With a sweep of the hand he dismissed the idea. "He'd drop you as soon as you built up a clientele. I'll tell you what you can do. Go into politics. There, if you goof up, it doesn't matter. You get to be a representative or a state senator, and you've got it made. In addition to the salary, it brings in business. See, people think you've got an in with—well, with the D.A. and the judges and the court clerks. What's more, they don't expect you to handle their cases personally because you're busy down at the statehouse. They expect you to pass it on to someone in your office."

Scofield again showed his square white teeth. "Some Jew or Italian."

"Sure. Why not?" A sudden thought struck him. "Sa-ay, did you notice the guy who was in my office yesterday afternoon? Well, that was Jim Tulley. He's an orderly or a male nurse or whatever at the Lynn hospital. He was telling me that Joe Bradley, the senator from this district, was in the hospital with a bad heart attack. They gave it out that he went in for a checkup, but it was a heart attack, and a serious one."

"So?"

"So, the chances are he won't run for reelection. Nobody knows about it yet, so if you were to declare for it—"

"State senator? That's ridiculous. How could I hope to run for state senator first crack out of the barrel? You have to work up to something like that. I *might* run for Barnard's Crossing selectman, maybe, but—"

"Selectman wouldn't get you anything except maybe a bunch of phone calls complaining about the garbage collection. And it don't pay nothing. How many selectmen do you know who've got anywhere in politics? You want to get out of the local scene; you want to get to the statehouse. You can maneuver there." He made zigzag motions with both hands. "Afterwards, you can become a member of a commission of some sort, or you can make judge, if you like that kind of thing. Or you could stay with it and move up to congressman and go to Washington. And once there, the opportunities are . . ." He waved his hands above his head to indicate infinity.

"Yeah, but all this takes money."

"The first rule of politics," said Mulcahey portentously, "is not to use your own money. You use other people's money, campaign contributions."

"But you need some money to get started."

Mulcahey nodded. "Sure, seed money. But you must have that. The way you dress and that apartment of yours in Waterfront Towers . . ."

"I have a little," Scofield admitted. "My share from the sale of the house after Dad died. It's just a few thousand."

"Look, boy, you don't need much to get started. And you're not throwing it away. It's advertising. Don't you see? Win or lose, you're getting all this advertising free. Say you hold a rally. You begin by introducing yourself. 'I'm John Scofield, a practicing attorney with offices in Salem.' Get it? There's a shnook in your audience who's got a little legal problem. Somebody owes him some money and won't pay. Or he's got to draw up a contract of some kind. He doesn't have a lawyer. Well, here's a nice young fellow who talks sense and he's a lawyer in Salem. Why not go to *him*? Get the idea? Now what happens if you should win?"

34

"What happens?"

Mulcahey raised his arms as if he were about to embrace the heavens. "You'll be getting the big cases. We'll set up a law firm: Scofield, Mulcahey, Cohen, and Mastrangelo." He made motions with his hands to indicate the sign on the door.

"Who are Cohen and Mastrangelo?"

"The smart Jew and Italian we'd get. Might as well have them both."

"Maybe Venturo of the D.A.'s office for the Italian slot," suggested Scofield.

Mulcahey nodded. "Possible."

Scofield flashed his teeth in delight at the thought of the man who had outfoxed him working for him. Then his sense of reality asserted itself. "Oh, this is silly. I can't run for state senator."

"Why not? It's your best shot. You'd run as a Republican, and you'd be running in the primary for the nomination. The Republican nominee is sure to win the election in these parts, no matter who he is. So it's the primary you're interested in. How many people vote in the primary? Twenty percent? Twenty-five, tops. You get a hard core of Barnard's Crossers behind you, and you've got it made. Now here's the beauty part of it. You'd be alone. You'd be the only one running for the Republican nomination."

"Why would I be the only one?"

"Because no one, no one in his right mind is going to challenge Joe Bradley for the nomination. He's been senator for the district for the last I don't know how many years. So you declare for it. Then when he finally gets around to announcing that he's not seeking reelection, you're the only one in the field."

"Yeah, and the minute he does, half a dozen others jump in."

"So what? You were the first in the field. You'll be known before the others can get rolling."

"And if your friend the orderly is wrong, and Bradley runs again?"

"So you'll get beat. But you will have had all that free advertising, all that exposure."

"We-el . . ."

5

WHEN ASKED WHAT HE DID for a living, Tony D'Angelo was apt to be evasive, saying only that he was in politics. But he never ran for office, nor did he campaign for anyone else's election. Instead, he made deals. His stock-in-trade was knowing the pressure points of various key members of the state legislature and the administration. Recently, he had devoted himself almost exclusively to the needs of the Majority Whip, and the connection had not gone unnoticed, which was why he was meeting the administrative assistant in an obscure café in the South End rather than in the usual restaurant on the Hill.

"Right now, Tony, you're poison," said the administrative assistant. "His Nibs would be sore if he knew I was even talking to you."

Tony D'Angelo nodded. He wasn't bitter, not even offended. The Majority Whip was simply notifying him through his administrative assistant that he did not want him seen around. There was nothing personal in it. It was merely politics, at least that aspect of politics in which Tony was involved. "So what do I do?" he asked.

The administrative assistant spread his fat, fleshy hands.

He was a heavy, pinkish young man in his thirties, very aware of his power and importance. "You've been seen around too much, Tony. The reporter for the *Globe* has begun to snoop. Word got back to us that he's lining up the other statehouse reporters, including the TV guys, to watch for you, what offices you come out of and what offices you go into. So His Nibs thinks you ought to take a vacation for a while. Two, three months, then after the election things will cool down a little. Get yourself a girl and take a trip to Florida."

"I got a girl."

"All the better, so you can start earlier."

"You telling me I'm hot?"

"Maybe just lukewarm. But why take chances? Even if you just stick close to home—where is it? Lynn? Revere?"

"Revere."

"So Revere. Take it easy for a while. Walk along the promenade there and get some of the good salt air in your lungs, or go to the racetrack, or to one of those bingo parlors—"

"Yeah, and what do I do for eating money?"

"Live on capital."

"And where do I get this capital?"

The administrative assistant smiled as though Tony were pulling his leg. "With all the deals you've been on? What happened to that money?"

"Ask the bookies."

"Oh? Well, you ought to be able to get some kind of job. I'm sure with your connections—"

"I don't have any connections in Revere. I'm careful not to mess with local politics. Nobody knows me there."

"How about Atlantic Dredging? Didn't you have something to do with Cash voting against the Harbor Bill?"

"I never got anywhere with Cash. He plays it close to the chest."

The administrative assistant didn't believe him, but, of course, it wouldn't be polite to say so. He nodded.

"And anyway, the bill went through," said Tony gloomily. He was a tall, thin man with a handsome albeit saturnine face. He had a curious sardonic smile that started out as a grimace. He displayed it now, to show that he knew more than he was telling. It also implied that his financial situation was not so dire, but that he was owed one next time they had to do business together.

As he reached for the check, he said, "You people know anyone at Atlantic Dredging?"

"Well, there's always Fowler."

"Yeah, that's right, there's always Fowler." Hell, everyone knew Fowler. He was president of the company. You could get his name from the telephone book. As he slid out of the booth and headed toward the cashier, he looked back over his shoulder. "All right. I'll be hanging around home awhile."

"If His Nibs wants to get in touch with you . . ."

Again the sardonic smile. "I'll get in touch with him. It's better that way." As the administrative assistant set off, Tony called to him, "Hey, you folks got anything on Fowler?"

"What kind of thing?"

"You know, something like if he knew I knew, he might be interested in talking to me."

The other shook his head. "Nothing like that. If I hear of anything . . ."

"Sure."

6

BELLE HALPERIN, flamboyant with reddish blond hair, was determined not to be overawed by the opulence of the Magnuson home, but all through dinner, indeed from the moment they had arrived, she couldn't stop thinking about how she would tell "the girls" about it. "We had dinner at the Magnusons'—he's a client of Morrie's, you know—"

The lamb chops and baked potato were disappointing only because she had assumed the main course would be something fancy and French. On the other hand, it would underline her description of Mrs. Magnuson: "She's so simple and gracious and down-to-earth."

Later as they sipped coffee, she said to her hostess, "You have some lovely paintings."

"Belle is crazy about art," her husband volunteered.

"Oh, then let me show you around," said Sophia Magnuson. "We have some things you might like to see on the second floor."

"I'd love to."

Mrs. Magnuson rose. "Will you excuse us?"

Alone with Morris Halperin, Magnuson refilled their

coffee cups and said, "You're really involved with the temple, aren't you?"

Halperin nodded. "That's right. Not that I'm particularly religious, you understand, but I guess I'm the kind of guy that gets involved if he's at all interested in something."

"I'm a little that way myself," said Magnuson. "At least I like to know all about anything I find myself connected with. Take the temple organization. As long as I'm a member of the Board of Directors, I want to know what's what. Of course, I've attended only a couple of meetings, the last one about a month ago, but it seems to me that we're not really moving in any direction. I don't get the impression of a program, if you know what I mean."

"Well—"

"Our president seems a very decent sort, and he does a good job of running the meeting, but I don't get the impression that he's directing policy. I have the feeling that he's more intent on maintaining the *status quo.*"

"Ah, you noticed."

Magnuson smiled. "I've attended enough board meetings to catch whatever signals were flying. Feinberg is what I'd call an interim president."

"Marvelous," said Halperin. "You're absolutely right. You see, we are a Conservative temple, because Conservatism is a kind of compromise between Orthodoxy and Reform. Since the community isn't big enough to support more than one temple, it pretty much has to be Conservative. And while some of our presidents have leaned towards Reform, and others have tended towards Orthodoxy, all of them have been basically Conservative. Except one. A couple of years back Chester Kaplan managed to get elected, and he's out-and-out Orthodox."

"Kaplan? That fat, little chap with the skullcap who sits down at the end of the table? Lawyer, isn't he?"

"That's right. And a successful one. He wears the *yarmulkeh* because the meeting is held in the temple. He also wears it at home. He'd wear it in court, I'm sure, if he thought the judge wouldn't object or that it might not have a bad effect on the jury. And he goes to the minyan every day, morning and evening. The year he was president, he all but split the congregation."

"So Feinberg was elected to heal the wounds, eh?"

"More or less. Anyway, to steer a middle course. And he did a very creditable job, which is why he was reelected twice."

"And next year?"

"Ah, that's the problem, Mr. Magnuson. At the last meeting of the board, Feinberg announced that he was resigning, effective next month. His wife is sick and they're moving to Arizona."

"So it's the vice-president then—"

"We have no vice-president. Abe Kahn died less than a month after he took office. It was not unexpected. He was a sick old man." In response to Magnuson's raised eyebrow, he explained. "He'd been a member from the beginning and contributed a lot of money. Folks thought some sort of recognition was due him. You know how it is on the High Holy Days. The president and the rabbi sit on one side of the Ark, and the vice-president and the cantor—when he's not actually leading the prayers—sit on the other. So they thought having Kahn sit up there beside the Ark would make him feel he was appreciated."

"I see. So with no vice-president and the president resigning, there will be another election?"

"That's right. A special election. And Kaplan is planning to run again."

"If his administration was such a fiasco, I shouldn't think he'd have much of a chance," Magnuson observed.

"That's where you're wrong. The election is held at a

meeting of the general membership. We have about three hundred and fifty members, but I don't suppose more than a couple of hundred will show up. Of those two hundred, maybe fifty know what's going on. Now Kaplan has a tight group of true believers. And they'll go to work. Some members will vote for him because his name is familiar. Others will vote for him because he's observant and they feel that the president of a synagogue should be. Oh, I'd say he's got a damn good chance."

"And who would you be running against him? I take it you're part of his opposition?"

"Well, that's the trouble. We haven't been able to decide on any one man. Feinberg's announcement took us by surprise. We're not organized behind one man. We've got too many possibles."

"How about yourself? Are you interested?"

"Oh no. It takes too much time, for one thing. It really calls for an older man, and preferably one who doesn't have to make his living from the community the way I do."

"Why is that? I should think the advertising would be useful."

Halperin shook his head. "It's essentially a political position, which means that while half the membership might be strong for you, the other half is apt to be against you. I can't afford that."

"I used to be involved with Temple Zedek in Boston. My grandfather was one of the founders," said Magnuson, seemingly apropos of nothing at all.

"I was hoping you might get interested. I'm sure your backing of our man, whoever we pick—"

"I'm not much good at staying in the background," said Magnuson. "When I get involved with an organization, I want to run it."

"Does that mean—?" Halperin had an inspiration. "Look here, would you be willing to run?"

"Well now, that's pretty sudden. I'd have to think about it."

"Well, would you think about it?" asked Halperin earnestly.

"I don't know. Of course, if I thought I had a chance of winning—"

"It's an election, so there can't be any guarantees, but—"

"Oh, I wouldn't expect a guarantee, but I wouldn't want to look silly. I'm new to the organization and unknown—"

"Unknown? Cummon, Mr. Magnuson. Who's better known around here? Who hasn't heard of Magnuson and Beck, the biggest department store in Boston?"

"In New England." Magnuson corrected him. "We're not connected with it anymore, however. We sold out back in twenty-nine, although they still use our name."

"Well, that's what I mean. The name is known."

"But I have no organization—"

"You say the word, and I'll get an organization."

Magnuson smiled. "You're very persuasive. I'll tell you what, make a few inquiries around, drop a few hints, and report back to me. Then we'll decide."

As they drove home, Belle Halperin was ecstatic, her color even higher than usual. "They've got a Chagall and a Seurat, and in the bedroom they have a real Renoir. Imagine, in a bedroom." Then abruptly, "Was it law business he wanted to see you about?"

Her husband chuckled. "No. He wants to be president of the temple."

"President? But—but he's never been an officer or anything. Can he?"

"Why not? There's no regulation against it. Any member can run. And he's a member."

"And he wants you to run his campaign?"

"Something like that."

"Can he make it? Has he got a chance? I mean nobody knows him or anything."

"No-o, but on the other hand everybody knows the name, and everybody loves a millionaire."

"Is he going to pay you for your work?"

"There was nothing said about it."

"Then what will you get out of it?"

"Oh well, I figure when you hang around people with the kind of money Howard Magnuson has, some of it rubs off."

7

LAURA MAGNUSON AT TWENTY-FIVE was nice-looking, even handsome if not pretty. Her mouth was a shade too wide, her nose a little too long for contemporary taste, judging by models on magazine covers. Her eyes were alert and penetrating, and her chin showed determination and resolve. Her brown shoulder-length hair was parted in the middle and brushed back behind her ears in a style that required the least amount of fussing.

She had graduated from Bryn Mawr *magna cum laude* in political science and gone on to the London School of Economics for three years, only to return without a degree. As she explained to her father who adored her and to her mother who understood her, "I had the feeling that if I got a doctorate, then sooner or later, I'd find myself teaching. And I don't want that."

"What *do* you want to do?" asked her father.

"Oh, I don't know. Something in government, maybe."

She had been home a couple of months now, doing nothing, at least from the point of view of her parents. She had visited New York several times, to buy clothes, to go to the theater, to visit friends and former classmates. The

Magnusons had given a couple of parties for her in Barnard's Crossing so that she could meet new people, sons and daughters of their own acquaintances who came down from Boston. During the day, if the weather was good, she would get into her car and drive about the countryside, up to Rockport to wander about the picture galleries, or to Gloucester to lunch on the wharf and watch the seagulls. Evenings she was apt to go into Boston or Cambridge, where there might be a lecture or a meeting she thought might be of interest.

This night she decided to drive downtown with the vague idea that she might go to a movie, or perhaps just wander about the streets in order to renew her acquaintance with the old town. As she passed the Unitarian church, she noticed a sign announcing, "Candidates' Night, A Chance to Meet the Candidates."

She drove another block to find a parking place and then walked back. The meeting was being held in the vestry, which seated a couple of hundred people. But the room was less than half full when Laura arrived, a few minutes before the meeting was scheduled to begin.

In the wide aisle that encircled the room, small folding tables had been set up, each displaying the campaign material of a particular candidate. Beside them sat campaign workers offering plastic buttons, auto bumper stickers, and the like to those interested. On the platform a row of fifteen chairs had been set up for the candidates. The chairman of the evening was one of the selectmen of the town, Herbert Bottomley, a tall, gaunt, stoop-shouldered man with unruly, grizzled hair and bushy eyebrows. In his loose-hanging suit and steel-rimmed spectacles, he looked like a retired schoolteacher presiding at a Golden Age Club meeting, but he was actually a successful contractor in his fifties and was very popular in the town.

Bottomley banged on the lectern with his gavel and

called out, "All right, let's settle down and come to order. I'm going to have the candidates come in now and have them sit in these chairs behind me so's you can get a good look at them." He walked over and opened the door and announced ceremoniously, "Ladies and gentlemen, the candidates." They trooped in, some diffident, some strutting to reflect confidence, some smiling, some thoughtful, each concerned with showing the attitude that would be most likely to create a good impression and thereby garner votes. They had evidently been lined up in the adjacent room, so they walked onstage in single file, the first taking the chair on the extreme right, the rest taking the successive seats to the left.

When they were all seated, Chairman Bottomley said, "I'm sorry that we don't have any of the candidates for statewide office—governor, lieutenant governor, and attorney general—but we have their representatives who will speak for them. Now, we want to keep this part of the meeting short, so that we can spend the greater part of the evening in getting to know the candidates informally. So I'm going to ask the speakers to limit their talks to about four minutes. Let's see, fifteen times four is sixty minutes, just an hour. That seems to me about right." He turned to face the speakers. "Now, I'm not going to hold a stopwatch on you and cut you off in the middle of a sentence. But I'll just get up and stand beside you, and you'll take that as a signal to finish up. Okay? Okay, then we'll start off with the statewide offices first. Ladies and gentlemen, the first speaker is—" he consulted a paper—"Charles Kimborough. Mr. Kimborough."

Kimborough was a middle-aged man, smiling and self-assured, perhaps because he was truly at ease. The governor, a Democrat, whom he was representing had little to gain or lose with this audience, which was overwhelmingly Republican. "I am here to convey to you the greetings of

48

His Excellency and to convey his regrets that he was unable to be with you tonight because of a previous engagement. I am here tonight to urge you to support him in his candidacy for the high office which he now holds and in which he has demonstrated his ability and his concern . . ." and so on for his full four minutes of speaking time. When Bottomley appeared at his side, he seemed startled but with good grace said, "I could go on for the rest of the evening listing His Excellency's accomplishments during his four years of office, but with Herb at my elbow I had better close by expressing my thanks for your kind attention and courtesy and hospitality. Thank you."

The next half dozen were like the first, stand-ins for candidates for Republican and Democratic statewide offices, but all took their full time, expatiating on their principals' achievements. It was dull to the point of tedium, and several in the audience left. Laura Magnuson was tempted to follow them, but John Scofield, sitting there on the platform, had piqued her curiosity and interest. He was young and good-looking, to be sure, but even more, he had had the courage—or the foolhardiness—to challenge the incumbent, Josiah Bradley. The others had entered the race only after Bradley announced that he would not seek re-election. She wondered if he would make a point of it during his speech.

Bottomley came forward and raised his arms and waggled his hands at the audience to get their attention. "All right, folks," he said, "now that we've finished with the statewide offices, we can get on with the part of the program that you people are particularly interested in, the candidates for the local offices of senator and representative to the General Court. Fortunately, none of them had pressing engagements elsewhere (snickers and laughter) and they're all here in person. First we'll hear from the candidates for state senator. We have three of them and they all list themselves as Republican. I don't know why the Democratic candidates didn't show up. (laughter) We'll proceed in alphabetical order. Let's see—" a glance at his list—"that means we'll start with Thomas Baggio, who is a city councillor of Revere, then Albert Cash, who is the representative to the General Court from this district, and end up with John Scofield of Barnard's Crossing. Mr. Baggio."

Baggio was short, thick-set, swarthy, with bluish jowls, thick black hair, and a small Hitler moustache. He came forward, oozing confidence. "As city councillor of Revere, I instituted . . . I proposed . . . I caused . . ." He finished with "and what I did for my native city of Revere, I can do for all the cities and towns of the senatorial district. I will bring to the job the same devotion to duty, the same concentration I have shown as a city councillor."

He sat down to a scattering of polite applause. It occurred to Laura that he had made a mistake spending his entire time recounting his record as city councillor, if only because it involved the repetition of first-person locutions —this was always the problem in citing one's record.

Albert Cash was an older man in his late fifties. He was smooth and fluent, the words flowed easily out of his strangely impassive face, as though they were being played by a tape recorder. The gist of his speech was that he had devoted his life to service in the community, and he listed all the political jobs he had had, including the commissions and committees he had served on. And now, having served three terms as a representative to the General Court, it was only fair, he said, that he should be promoted to the Senate.

He, too, received polite applause, although someone in the audience called out, "How about the Harbor Bill?" Pretending not to hear, Cash returned to his seat, while several people in the audience turned around to glare at the heckler. Laura made a mental note to inquire about the

Harbor Bill and Cash's part in it, if only because she detected a hint of embarrassment in the overcasual way he surveyed the ceiling at the back of the hall when he sat down.

"Talk to the people who are there," Mulcahey had advised. "I mean, don't bother about those who don't show up. Know what I mean?"

"Sure." Scofield had replied.

Mulcahey fixed him with a baleful eye. "No, you don't. You're just saying that. Listen, the Essex District takes in Lynn and Revere as well as Barnard's Crossing. Right? Well, who's going to be at this Candidates' Night? Just Crossers. That's all. Maybe there'll be one or two from Lynn or Revere, but not likely, and one or two don't count anyway. So make up your mind that you're talking just to the Barnard's Crossing people. Get it? When you get around to appearing in Lynn, you'll talk just to Lynners. Same with Revere. Point is, don't try to talk to anybody who ain't there."

"Yeah, but they hear about it, don't they?"

"Sure, if you're President of the United States and you talk in Alabama, we hear about it here in Massachusetts, but if you're running for state senator, don't kid yourself, you're not going to be quoted. If there's a reporter present from the Lynn *Express,* you'll be lucky if you're even listed as having been one of the speakers. Who's your opposition? Al Cash of Lynn and Tommy Baggio of Revere. All right. Cash has been representative from Lynn to the General Court for a couple of terms. He'll talk about his record and say he deserves promotion to the Senate. That audience won't give a damn about his record. Same with Tommy Baggio who's been a city councillor. He'll talk about his record, but it was all in Revere, so why should that impress the good folks of Barnard's Crossing?"

"Yeah, but what am I going to talk about? I don't have a record."

"So go with what you have."

"But I don't have anything."

"Sure you do. You're a local boy and you're nice-looking and friendly. So you show them that you're nice and friendly. People don't listen; they look. That's why TV beats radio. You just stand there and let them see you and say anything that doesn't mean anything."

Laura could see that Scofield was nervous and felt a twinge of pity for him. He favored the audience with an embarrassed boyish grin and then a nervous chuckle. "I am John Scofield, twenty-eight. I am a practicing attorney with offices in Salem. I am unmarried," he began. "I was born right here in Barnard's Crossing and have lived here all my life. And my family has been living here ever since Colonial times. I went to the Gaithskille School and to Barnard's Crossing High. Then I went to Harvard and Harvard Law School. Maybe they were a little easier to get into a few years back. I love this town and the people in it." He went on to talk about places in the town—the Landing, Fremont Hill, Children's Island—and the special associations they had for him. Behind him, he heard the little shuffle and scrape that suggested that Bottomley was getting to his feet and would come to stand beside him. His mind cast about for some way of ending his little speech, and then as he felt the presence of the chairman beside him, it came to him. "The point is," he said, "that I like it the way it is and I don't want to change it, not any of it."

It seemed to Laura that the applause for Scofield was a little louder and a little less perfunctory than it had been for the other candidates, but then, of course, he was the only candidate from Barnard's Crossing.

Speeches of the candidates running for representative followed. Laura Magnuson had no interest in any of them, but she remained because she wanted to speak to Scofield, to see what he looked like close up. Finally, the chairman came forward and announced, "Well, there you are, folks. You've heard them and it took just over an hour, which is not bad. I guess some of them will be standing around for a while and you can talk to them informal-like, or argue with them if you've a mind to."

Laura wandered over to the campaign material, assuming that was where he would go upon leaving the platform, only to discover that there was none for Scofield. So she headed for the door, reaching it just as he approached.

"That was a very effective speech you gave," she said.

Surprised, he stopped and looked at her with interest. "It was?"

She nodded solemnly. "Very. Is that going to be the theme of your campaign?"

He wondered what he had said that could possibly be the theme for a campaign. "Er—what, I mean what part of—?"

She sensed that he had no idea of what she had in mind, and no thought of its political effect. "You said you were against change."

"Well, you know, I was just, you know, kind of expressing my feelings—"

"The point is," she went on, "that most of the people here tonight are middle-aged or older. And that's true of voters in general. Young people want changes, but older people are worried about change. They're afraid of it. So when you said you didn't want any change, most of them approved. Politicians are always telling people that they are going to change things. Well, the older people have heard these promises all their lives, and they don't believe them. So a campaign against change might actually work."

53

"You seem to know a lot about politics. You a reporter or something?"

"No, just interested."

"Look, could we go someplace and have a drink and maybe talk about it?"

"All right. Where to? The coffee shop on West Street is nearest."

"Yeah, but it's awfully crowded this time of night," he said. "How about going over to Salem? I'm parked just around the corner."

As they walked, he shot sidelong glances at her, uncertain whether she was a pickup or was seriously interested in politics.

"Here we are," he said.

She was a little startled when she saw the car, a bright, shocking pink.

"Is this your car?" she asked. "I figured you for the conservative type. It looks like an ice-cream wagon."

He chuckled. "That's because it is—or was—an ice-cream wagon—sort of. The guy I bought it from had four trucks on the road, the same color, peddling ice cream through the neighborhoods, and he used to ride around in this keeping an eye on them. Then he went broke, and I was able to buy it up cheap because of the paint job. I'm planning to have it repainted. I have to anyway. She's starting to peel there on the fender. I just haven't got around to it yet." He didn't bother to explain that he'd had the car for almost a year.

"I hope you won't until after the election. A car that stands out like that can be good for campaigning."

"You think so?"

"Of course. It gives you instant recognition. You're planning to mount a sign on top, aren't you?"

"Oh sure."

"I'd do it right away if I were you. It's recognition that

54

gets you elected, and that's the easiest way of getting recognition. You have a sign with your picture on it and your name."

"Say, you know a lot about this stuff."

"Not as much as I'd like to know."

"You interested in politics?" he asked curiously.

"I think it's the most interesting thing in the world."

8

AT THE SPECIAL MEETING of the general membership called to elect a new president of the temple, the successful candidate was not even present. Neither was Rabbi Small, since he was not, strictly speaking, a member of the temple organization. He had gone home immediately after the minyan, before the meeting had begun. He received the results from Morton Brooks, the principal of the religious school, who was not a member either, but had been present because the school was in session on Sunday mornings, and the meeting took place in the school's assembly hall.

Shortly after noon, Morton Brooks zoomed up the street in his sports car and came to a screeching halt in front of the rabbi's house. He rang the bell, and when Miriam opened the door, he struck a pose with arms spread wide and announced, "Ta-da!"

He was wearing a light-fawn herringbone sports coat with chamois patches on the elbows and a leather tab with a buttonhole on one lapel. Underneath, he wore a cream-colored sport shirt, open at the throat, which was encircled by a bright red kerchief. His short, spindly legs were encased in sand-colored slacks, and his shoes were chocolate-brown suede with fancy laces.

Miriam smiled and said, "You look very sharp, Morton. Come in."

"Sunday in the country," he said, simpering, by way of explanation.

"But the principal of a religious school—"

"Miriam, you know that's only temporary," he said reproachfully. Although he had been the principal of the Barnard's Crossing religious school for eight years and had been a Hebrew teacher in other schools for several years before that, he still considered it essentially temporary work while he awaited the call to return to his true vocation, the theater. This, on the strength of having been the bookkeeper and general factotum of a Yiddish theater group in New York, perpetually on the verge of bankruptcy, and had occasionally been given a walk-on part to save an actor's salary.

In the living room, Morton paced back and forth like a movie director sketching a scene to the actors. "Get the picture. Although the meeting was called for ten o'clock, a lot of them were already there by nine because they had to bring their kids to school. You'd think by ten o'clock they'd be anxious for the meeting to begin. But no, people keep coming in and standing around and *shmoosing*. It's like a regular Old Home Week. It's ten o'clock, a quarter past, half past. It gets to be eleven, and still nobody is impatient, nobody is calling to get the show on the road. Then I spot Kaplan, one of the candidates, in a corner— you can hardly see him—and his pals, that long drink of water, Herbie Cohen, and Harold Gestner, and Hymie Stern, they keep coming over to where he is, to whisper to him. He listens and he makes little check marks on a paper, the membership list, I suppose. And it all becomes clear to me. See, he's still campaigning. Magnuson is not around, and Kaplan is making hay, lining up the membership." He nodded his head and winked at his own perspicacity.

"And how did you see all this?" asked the rabbi. "Didn't you have classes?"

"A class I've got at ten. All right, so I come into my office at ten to get my class list and who do I see behind my desk but our president, Sam Feinberg. 'I hope you don't mind my using your office,' sezee. So what should I say? That I do mind? Well, you know how when I'm teaching, I'm always running next door to my office to get some text that will help bring out some special point. I couldn't do that with Sam Feinberg there. He'd think I was spying on him. So I gave my class some writing to do. Then eleven o'clock is my time for staying in my office to see parents who might want to talk to me about their kids. But when I come in to put the papers from my ten o'clock class in the desk drawer, he looks at me like what am I doing there, like I'm a kind of inter—inter—"

"Interloper?" Miriam offered.

"That's the word. Like I'm a kind of interloper. So I hung around the corridor near the assembly hall, figuring any parents who wanted to see me, well I was right there, wasn't I?"

"But the meeting was finally called to order," said the rabbi patiently.

"Natch. But when? At a quarter to twelve!" Brooks exclaimed triumphantly, as though he had scored a major point.

The rabbi glanced at the mantelpiece clock. It was half-past twelve. "So the meeting is still going on?" he asked.

"It's over. They started at a quarter to twelve and by noon it was adjourned."

"And the election? Did they hold the election?"

"That's what I'm trying to tell you, if you'll only let me."

"Let him tell it in his own way, David," Miriam suggested.

58

Morton Brooks gave her a quick look of gratitude, and said, "Thanks, Miriam."

"All right," said the rabbi. "Everybody was just standing around just visiting, and—"

"And Kaplan was campaigning," said Brooks, holding up an admonishing forefinger. "Don't forget that. His lieutenants were circulating all this time, whispering to this one and that one, and then reporting back to Kaplan."

"All right, I won't forget it," the rabbi good-naturedly assured him.

"So I figure," Brooks went on, "that it was Kaplan's men that were holding up the works. Why? So they could touch all bases, contact as many of the membership as they could before the voting started. And I figured he'd win in a walk, because he's been a member practically from the beginning, and he's observant and goes to the minyan every day, whereas Magnuson is a Johnny-come-lately, and who knows him? But then I notice that Kaplan's face gets more serious, like things aren't going so well. And then he and his boys all get into a huddle there in the corner and you can see that they're arguing about something, and some are on one side and some on the other. But pretty soon they come to some kind of agreement because they all nod their heads like they're on springs. Then Kaplan marches down to the front of the room where Melvin Weill, the secretary, is sitting, and leans over and whispers to him and I can see Melvin is surprised. Then he nods and he gets up and scoots out the door down the corridor. I'm standing at the door and he don't so much as say Hi, Mort to me, even though I've been at his house I don't know how many times. He goes into my office where Sam Feinberg is still sitting.

"I thought I might go in after him, like to get some papers out of my desk, but before I could make up my mind, the door opens and Feinberg comes out and goes striding down the corridor, he stops at the door of the hall and as soon as they see him, everybody begins to quiet down and find seats, like a bunch of kids in a classroom when the teacher comes back after having gone out for a few minutes. He goes to the podium and calls the meeting to order. It's a quarter to twelve now. Okay. Then Feinberg says, 'I have an announcement to make. Mr. Kaplan, one of the two candidates in this election, has authorized me to say in his behalf that for the sake of greater unity he is retiring from the race and asks that Howard Magnuson as the remaining candidate be elected by acclamation.' Well, for a couple of minutes there was regular pan—pan—what do you call it?"

"Pandemonium?" the rabbi offered.

"That's right. Regular pandemonium. Everybody shouting, arguing. You see, while Kaplan's lieutenants knew what was going to happen—they must have decided back there when they were in a huddle with Kaplan—they hadn't bothered to tip off those they had been pressuring to vote for him. Some of *them* thought Kaplan had sold out, that Magnuson had bought him off. You don't look surprised, David."

"I'm not," said the rabbi. "I figured Magnuson would win."

"You did? But why?"

"And why would Kaplan surrender without a fight?" asked Miriam.

"Oh, I think Morton is right about Kaplan counting the votes, and then he realized he was not only going to lose, but that he was going to lose badly. So he quit to avoid being embarrassed."

Morton Brooks raised his hands and shook his head. "I don't get it. Why would they vote for Magnuson?"

"No? Tell me, Morton, when you go back to New York for a visit, and you tell your friends that you are the principal of the religious school of the Barnard's Crossing Temple, are you sure you won't add that the president is Howard Magnuson, *the* Howard Magnuson?"

Brooks shrugged casually. "I suppose I might. All right, say I do, but—"

"And so will every member of the temple. Kaplan is just an ordinary, decent man, but Magnuson is a somebody. He's been written up in *Time* magazine, and the shares of Magnuson and Beck are traded on the stock exchange. Maybe it occurred to some of the members that if Magnuson were president, he would be likely to contribute to various temple projects, but I imagine that most were content to be associated with a big name."

"All right. So why would he want the job?"

The rabbi shook his head. "That I don't know."

"Maybe he got religion," suggested Brooks.

The rabbi smiled. "Maybe. I suppose that's the way a tycoon would get religion, by becoming president of the congregation."

9

Tony d'angelo's small furnished flat in Revere was curiously at odds with the dashing figure he cut. It was in a lower-middle-class neighborhood, and the sparse furniture was cheap and shabby at that. A largish room served as kitchen, living room, dining room, and bedroom, and there was a tiny bathroom. But it didn't matter—he never brought anyone important there.

Millie Hanson, who had been living with him for several months now—like being married, he thought sometimes in wonderment—was forty and blond and buxom. Originally from a small town in Nebraska, she had drifted east, maintaining herself by a succession of odd jobs—salesgirl, supermarket checkout cashier, waitress— and had finally come to Revere, where she worked as a cocktail waitress in one of the nightclubs on the promenade. She was easygoing and friendly, and it had required no great effort on Tony's part to get her to come home with him. There was no lengthy courtship. She moved in easily and although nothing was ever said, it was tacitly agreed she would simply move out, if either of them wanted a change.

She continued to work at the nightclub. Sometimes he

would drop in near closing time and take her home. When he did not, she would take a cab. If the apartment was dark when she got home, it meant he was sleeping, in which case she would undress in the bathroom, finding her way there with the aid of a pocket flashlight, and then slip into bed beside him.

Normally, he was up first and made toast and coffee for both of them. If he stayed home, she reciprocated by preparing their lunch, usually canned soup and sandwiches. In the evening they ate out at small, inexpensive Italian or Chinese restaurants, and then came back to the apartment to watch television until it was time for her to go to work.

During the day she hung around the apartment in housecoat and flapping slippers, reading the newspaper or romance novels she got at the drugstore, or watching soap operas. Sometime during the day, she would make the bed and clean the apartment, and occasionally she would go shopping for the few groceries they needed.

Sundays they both got up late, and while he lounged about in bathrobe and pajamas, she prepared a special breakfast of French toast and sausages. They ate in front of the TV set so that he could watch the political panel shows. This Sunday, when she began to dress, he asked, "Going someplace, Baby?"

"Just down to the drugstore to get the paper."

"Get me some cigarettes, will you? Got enough money?"

"Yeah, I got enough."

She was back in less than a half hour. She drew a pack of cigarettes from the paper bag she was carrying and tossed it in his lap. Then she took out a yellow envelope. "I got the pictures from that roll you gave them to develop."

"Oh yeah? Any good?"

"I haven't looked at them yet." She handed him the envelope and looked over his shoulder as he drew out the

63

photographs. "You cut off part of my head there," she said as he held up the first.

"I guess I was focusing on your legs."

The next one he had snapped as a sudden gust of wind had blown her skirt up. "Oh, that was mean," she exclaimed. "My whole whatsis is showing."

He slid his hand under her dress along her thigh to the buttock. "It's a very nice whatsis," he said and massaged it affectionately.

"Oh you." She took the package of prints from him and began to shuffle through them, commenting on each. "This is a little out of focus . . . Oh, this is a good one . . . You moved on this one . . . What's this?"

He took the print from her. "Oh, that was taken at the Blainey testimonial dinner a couple of months ago. See those five guys at the head table?" He laughed loudly. "That's Rocco Vestucci and Charlie Mayes, and that's Jim Blainey in the middle, and then on the other side of him is Frank Callahan and Whatsisname Peterson, Nels Peterson. And every single one of those guys has been indicted and is going to jail. What do you think of that?"

"Nice bunch of friends you got."

"Aw, Baby, it's business. You do business with them, so when they ask you to buy a ticket to a testimonial for a friend of theirs, you got to buy a ticket."

"But you don't have to go."

"Well, it's usually a good feed, and you've paid for it. Besides, they almost always have entertainment. That's why I took the camera with me. Know what I mean?"

"Sure, you mean naked girls."

"Not this time, there wasn't. There was a priest there, one of the guests. I bet the guy that sold him a ticket got hell when he told the committee." He dismissed the idea. "Nah, a priest wouldn't buy a ticket. He'd get one free. Maybe on Blainey's orders. He's a very religious guy, Jim Blainey. Goes to church every Sunday."

"And if he's in jail?"

"Think they ain't got a church there?"

"I suppose. Say, who's this guy at the end. He been indicted, too?"

"Lemme see. Gee, I don't remember him sitting there. Maybe he came in for a minute to talk to Nels Peterson or one of the others. He remind you of somebody?"

"Nobody I know."

"How about Tommy Baggio?"

"Who's Tommy Baggio?"

"He's a city councillor here. He's running for state senator. His picture was in the paper yesterday. You got yesterday's paper? Did you throw it out?"

"I don't think so. Just a minute, I'll see."

She went to the cabinet kitchen, rummaged in a large basket, and found the paper, which she handed him. He turned pages, scanning each page quickly. Then he exclaimed, "Ah, here it is. Now, don't he look just like the guy in the snapshot?"

Although wanting to please him, she could not help shaking her head. "No-o, Honey. This guy in the snap has no moustache."

"So we give him one. Look." He covered the lower part of the face in the newspaper with a fingernail. "Look at the eyes, the forehead, the hair."

"Ye-ah, maybe . . ."

"It's nothing to add a moustache," he mused, his eyes focused on the ceiling, his mind far off.

"But why would you want to?" she asked.

He smiled. "It could pay off, Baby."

"How could it? What would it do?"

He smiled broadly. "Make me some money, Baby."

"But how?"

"There are angles, Baby. I got to think about it."

10

"YOU GOT A MINUTE, DAVID?" It was Morton Brooks, the principal of the religious school.

"Sure."

"I'll be right up."

The rabbi replaced the receiver, wondering at the principal's politeness. Usually he didn't bother to call to inquire if the rabbi were free when he wanted to see him. His normal procedure, even if the door of the rabbi's study was closed, was to knock perfunctorily and barge in. A few minutes later, the length of time it took him to mount the stairs from his office in the vestry to the rabbi's study on the second floor, Morton Brooks entered and flung himself in the visitor's chair in front of the rabbi's desk.

He was dressed in a sober gray business suit, a blue shirt, and a knitted black tie. His outstretched feet were encased in highly polished black shoes. It was not his usual costume, which tended to be on the sporty side and ran to loud tweed jackets and even knotted kerchiefs in place of a necktie.

The rabbi raised his eyebrows and asked, "Been to a

funeral, Morton, or were you asked to read for a part in a play?"

"Nah"—with a wide sweep of the hand—"show business is lousy." Then understanding came. "Oh, you mean the square-type threads. That's on account of the new president."

"You mean Howard Magnuson suggested you wear more sober clothing? He asked you to change from your usual attire?"

"When they ask, David, it's already too late. Then it's criticism, see? It means you've done something—not wrong, maybe, but not right either. You've got to understand about these tycoon types, David. They can dress any way they please. They can come into the office in overalls, but the peasants, the underlings, they got to dress strictly square. Maybe he wouldn't say anything, but in his mind, he'd think this one is not a team player."

The rabbi's lips twitched. "And you came up to see if I was properly dressed?"

Brooks looked at him with a sort of avuncular compassion. "You'll never be dressed properly, David. That's on account of you've got no clothes sense. Maybe it's not what you wear so much as how you wear it." With a wave of the hand he dismissed the rabbi's sartorial problem. "No, I want you to take a look at this, David, and tell me what you think."

The rabbi took the paper held out to him.

The paper was headed DUTIES AND RESPONSIBILITIES OF THE PRINCIPAL OF THE RELIGIOUS SCHOOL. It was typed and ran the length of the page. The rabbi read, nodding occasionally, ". . . responsible for formulating curricula for each grade . . . recommendations to School Committee . . . budget . . . confers with Rabbi on direction . . . hires teachers . . . confers with parents . . ."

"That's pretty good," said the rabbi when he finished.

"Seems to me, though, you've put in a lot that's pretty much implied in the first sentence about overall supervision of the school."

"In this kind of thing, David, the more you put in the better. It builds up the job."

"Well, in that case, you might put in that you arrange with the cantor about special tutoring for the Bar Mitzvah boys."

"Say, that's a good idea." He reached for the paper and penciled into the margin, "Cantor—Bar Mitzvah boys." "Anything else you can think of?" He looked up, pencil poised.

"Well, when a teacher is absent, you take his class."

Morton Brooks considered as he scratched his thinning hair and then patted it back solicitously over his bald spot. Finally, he said, "Uh-uh. That might give him ideas."

"Him?"

"Magnuson. He asked for this. Didn't you get one? If I say that I cover classes for absent teachers, he's apt to get the idea that I have time to take on another class, and maybe save a teacher's salary. Guys like Magnuson worry me."

"Really? Why?"

"If he has us do job descriptions, next thing he's apt to do a time and motion study on us, maybe end up paying us piecework."

The rabbi laughed. "That's not too likely."

"No? What do you know about Howard Magnuson?"

"I understand that he's connected with Magnuson and Beck, so I assume he's in the retail business—"

"Nah." Brooks was scornful. "They sold that back in 1929. Maybe they bought it back again because Magnuson and Beck is a conglomerate, which means their business is businesses. I read all about the company in *Time* magazine, and I looked it up and read it again when he got elected. What Magnuson does is buy and sell businesses like other people buy and sell shoes or automobiles. He buys up a business. Then he brings in his team of managers and they jack up the efficiency of the company and fire all the old hands—that's called cleaning out the deadwood. Then if they show a good quarterly report and the stock goes up, they use the upgraded stock to buy another company, or maybe they milk it for a while and then unload it. They're into electronics and hotels and shoe manufacturing and a company that makes cleats for baseball shoes. The article called him a romantic on account of he's apt to buy into something that interests him. Some romantic!"

"So you think he's going to try to increase our efficiency and then trade us in for another synagogue, or maybe a church?"

"Go on, laugh, David, but I'm telling you he's going to be trouble. He's not our kind."

"And what's that supposed to mean?"

"We're all second generation or third generation. Our parents or our grandparents came from Russia, Poland, Lithuania, or wherever. I'll bet there isn't a single member on the Board of Directors who if their parents didn't talk with an accent, then their grandparents did. The smell of the *shtetl* still clings to us. But he's different. He's fifth-generation American, or maybe even sixth. His great-great grandfather, according to this article, fought in the Civil War. He don't think like us. He's a Yankee, a Wasp—"

"A WASP? A white, Anglo-Saxon Protestant?"

"Maybe not a Protestant, but you know what I mean. He's not like us, and that means trouble. You take these job descriptions he asked us to write. Now I'm not saying that Sam Feinberg, say, might not have had an idea like that when he became president. I can even imagine him sending out these forms. Then when we'd made them out, he'd read through them maybe, and toss them in a desk drawer and never think of them again. But that's not the way Howard

Magnuson is going to deal with them. He's going to go over each and every one and check one against the other. And if they don't jibe, then there'll be trouble." His tone became very easy and casual, and the rabbi sensed that now he was going to hear the real reason for his coming. "So I thought, since we both have supervision of the religious school, each of us in a separate kind of way, we ought to adjust our job descriptions so that they'll kind of mesh instead of maybe conflicting." He looked expectantly at the rabbi.

"I didn't write one."

"Didn't you get one of these forms?"

"Yes, I got one," said the rabbi, "but I assume it was a mistake."

"If they sent it to you, it was no mistake, David. Magnuson wanted you to make it out."

"It was addressed to employees of the temple," said the rabbi, "and I don't consider myself an employee."

"Yeah, I know what you mean. I know you always say you're the rabbi of the community and not just of the temple congregation, but it's the temple that pays you, and from Magnuson's point of view that makes you an employee. Remember, David"—and it was plain that he was truly concerned—"it's not Sam Feinberg you're dealing with, it's Howard Magnuson."

"What's the difference?"

"That's just the point I'm trying to make. To a Sam Feinberg, like to the rest of us, you're a rabbi, something like a priest to an Irishman. But to Howard Magnuson, you're just an employee, an underling, the kind of person he's been giving orders to all his life."

11

THE LOWER THIRD of the store window was covered by a sign which proclaimed in large letters, "Scofield for State Senator." Beneath, in italics between quotation marks, it said, *"Let's keep things the way they are."* The store contained a desk, against one wall a long table piled with campaign literature, four wooden armchairs, a couple of metal file cabinets, and a stack of folding chairs, all rented from a local office-appliance dealer. In the rear was a partition which closed off a clothes closet, the toilet, and a washstand over which hung a small mirror.

Anyone walking along High Street usually could see the head of Laura Magnuson just above the window sign if she happened to be sitting at the desk. She was there now, going through the morning's mail. She slit each envelope, glanced at the contents, and then deposited it in one of several piles on top of the desk. Sales letters from printers, manufacturers of celluloid buttons, clipping services, photographers, electronics firms that leased amplifier equipment, everything that might be necessary in the campaign were in one pile. Another pile consisted of bills, most of them from just such companies; and a third pile, the most important, was of letters containing contributions. Once there was an offering of a whole page of postage stamps. And once a check for a hundred dollars. When with poorly concealed excitement she showed it to Scofield, he glanced at the signature and nodded matter-of-factly. "Yeah, that's my brother-in-law. My sister twisted his arm, I suppose."

She recorded the name and address of each contributor and the amount of the contribution, and made a point of sending off a letter of acknowledgment and thanks usually within a day or two of receipt. For this purpose she had composed a series of three form letters, one for small donations (under five dollars), another for larger ones, and a third for contributions of more than fifty dollars. Unfortunately, she rarely had to use the third form. Occasionally, she received an anonymous contribution in cash, in which case she added to it five or ten dollars from her own purse.

She arrived about ten o'clock in the morning and stayed until noon, when she went home for lunch. She would post a sign in the window indicating that she would be back in the afternoon, and she would return around two o'clock. Frequently, there was nothing for her to do, and she would sit and read the local and Boston papers, clipping items that she felt Scofield should read. Sometimes, people would drop in to offer advice—"What Scofield ought to do is challenge his opponents to a debate. That way he could show..."; to extend invitations—"We got like a discussion group that meets once a week. We talk about all kinds of things, anything from the United Nations to the problem of crabgrass. I was thinking if he came down, we might have an evening on local politics or . . ."; to ask for information—"What's his position on the reconsideration of the Harbor Bill? That's what I want to know"; to inquire about jobs—"I was thinking you might need somebody part time. I got a couple of kids, but I'm free mornings because they're in school. I can do filing and typing although I'm not very fast," or "Would you need a good driver? You know, to drive you to meetings and such?" or "Have you lined up people to watch the polls on election day?," or—more ambitious for jobs in the future—"I'm a first-class gardener and I was wondering if Mr. Scofield would know of some government agency that needed one."

Scofield was rarely there during the day. He would come by late in the afternoon, after his regular office hours in Salem. She would report on the events of the day and show him the newspaper stories she had clipped, and they would talk about future strategy. From the beginning he had been unduly pessimistic about his chances, she thought.

Originally, when she had offered to help, he had said, "I sure can use all the help I can get, but I couldn't pay you very much, maybe nothing until after the election—if I won."

"Oh, that's all right. I don't need the money and I've got all the time in the world."

"That's very decent of you, but—"

"Look, who's your campaign manager? Who's running things for you? Where are your headquarters?"

"Well, I've been working out of my office in Salem. I haven't done much yet. You see, there's this old guy who has an office across the hall, J. J. Mulcahey. He's the one who sort of put a bee in my bonnet, and he's been giving me some advice, but—"

"You can't have your headquarters in Salem. It's not in the district. You've got to get some place in Barnard's Crossing, a vacant store."

"But that would cost quite a bit of money. Besides, I just don't have the time to go looking. And I'd need office furniture, at least a desk and a file cabinet. Maybe I could get them second-hand, but—"

"You can rent them. And as for a store, it shouldn't cost much for the few months till election."

"Oh no? When I first thought of running I called a couple of real estate people who had vacant stores. One wanted a thousand dollars a month, payable in advance."

"Suppose I do a little looking around."

"Well . . ."

Within a few days she called him at his office. "Laura Magnuson," she announced briskly. "You know that vacant store on High Street? Just beyond the market? I can get it for a hundred dollars a month, from now through November."

"Gee! A hundred dollars a month! How did you manage that?"

"By pointing out that you had a good chance of being elected senator, and that it would do them a lot of good to have a senator for a friend. You see, I did a little checking and I found they had had some trouble with the zoning authority."

"Gee, that's wonderful. Is there a lease I have to sign? Do I send them a check for the first month's rent?"

"I could give them my check and you can repay me. You see, I had to say I was your campaign manager in order to get them to talk seriously with me. I mean, if they thought I had no authority and was just some busybody looking around . . ."

"Sure, I understand. You go right ahead."

"And if you like, I'll see about renting some furniture."

"Oh sure, absolutely. We got to have some furniture."

So she signed the lease, rented furniture, then went on to arrange for printing and stationery. In some wonderment, he told Mulcahey about it.

The older man pursed his lips and then nodded slowly. "That's one of the nice things about politics, I guess. All kinds of people are eager to jump on the bandwagon, even

74

when there is no band and not even a wagon. What's she look like?"

"She's real nice-looking in a strictly business kind of way. Dressed properly and made up for a party, she might be a knockout, but as it is she's a good-looking girl."

"You ever make a pass at her?"

"Gosh, no. Didn't I tell you who she is? Her father is Howard Magnuson. You know, of Magnuson and Beck."

"So what?" Mulcahey laughed coarsely. "She still pees sitting down, don't she? Know what? You're a new toy for her, a rich girl's plaything," he said contemptuously, a little annoyed that she was replacing him as mentor, guide, director of Scofield's career. "When she gets tired of playing politics after a couple of weeks she'll just walk out on you."

"Gee, I don't think so. She seems a lot more involved in this than I am." He laughed self-consciously. He did not like to admit, even to himself, that while his reason for being in the race was that he had weakly permitted Mulcahey to persuade him, it was only Laura's interest that was keeping him in it. So far he had not succeeded in attracting the law business that Mulcahey had assured him would follow, and now he was worried about the bills that were mounting. He had a little nest egg of six thousand dollars, all that was left of his share from the sale of the parental home, and he was morbidly certain that this would be eaten up by the campaign before he was through.

At the very beginning, to be sure, he had consented to go to various political meetings, and at her urging had risen to ask a question, or to make a comment introducing himself each time as a candidate for the state senate for this district. But when nothing tangible had resulted, either political or in the way of law business, he had lost faith. And now, when Laura told him of a group that was holding a meeting on the Harbor Bill, for example, and urged that it would be a good place to appear and present his position,

75

he was apt to tell her that he was going to be busy that evening, that he had some research to do at the law library, or that he had to prepare for an appearance in court the next day. He manifested so little faith in his chances of election that she, too, had begun to wonder if she hadn't picked a loser. When the Barnard's Crossing *Courier* published a report of a telephone poll they had taken that showed that the three candidates were practically even, he showed no great enthusiasm.

"What's so wonderful about running even with two other guys?" he asked plaintively. "The poll was primarily for the statewide offices, governor, lieutenant governor, and attorney general. Then when they got down to state senator, they probably just read off the three names, Scofield, Baggio, and Cash, and asked which they liked. If they did them in alphabetical order, my name was the last one mentioned, so the average person who doesn't care too much one way or another picked the last name he heard. But those other two guys, Baggio and Cash, they're both professional. Both of them have organizations, people they've done favors for or people who hope to get favors. What chance does a new man have?"

"Well, that's where you're wrong. Do you know why Cash is running for the Senate instead of for reelection to his seat in the General Court? It's because he hasn't got a chance of reelection. That's why. Talk to any of the people around town who know. He voted against the Harbor Bill, and the Lynn people won't forgive him that. In running for the Senate, he's hoping that he can pick up votes from Chelsea and Revere and Barnard's Crossing to offset the beating he's going to get in Lynn. The point is that he doesn't expect to win. See, if he loses he's not politically dead as he would be if he lost for reelection. Because it's a higher office."

"Yeah, I heard something about that, but—"

"And Baggio has standing only in Revere. And how about the results on second choice? You're actually leading there." She thrust the paper at him.

But he didn't take it from her. Instead, he asked, "What's this second choice?"

She explained. "They asked each person they called whom they preferred and then who was their second choice. Cash's backers split between you and Baggio for second choice, but your people picked Baggio and Baggio's people picked you."

"So?"

"So it means that a lot of people are not so much for somebody as that they are against Cash. If you could pick up some of Baggio's votes, you'd be in."

"Or if he picks up some of mine, he'd be in. Unfortunately, this isn't a horse race with win, place, and show. Here it's just the win that pays off."

She was annoyed with him, and even more annoyed with herself. Had she misjudged him, completely misread his character? She began to think that perhaps she ought to withdraw since there was nothing there for her.

"I may have to be away for a while," she essayed. "Do you have someone who could take my place here?"

"For how long a while?"

"Oh, a week or maybe two, maybe even longer."

"Then that's all right. I could just keep it closed and come in in the afternoon to take care of the mail."

The man was impossible! And yet—he had all the credentials. He was tall and good-looking. He was likable and friendly. He had a name which was associated with the town. He had the right degrees from the right schools. There must be some way she could reach him, instill desire and ambition and get him moving. What was wrong with him?

12

FROM THE BEGINNING, Howard Magnuson manifested his efficiency by starting board meetings promptly at nine and bringing them to adjournment around eleven instead of at noon. Those members who hoped to take an early lunch so they could spend the afternoon on the golf course welcomed the change, but those who brought their children to the religious school for the Sunday classes and had to wait until noon, when the last class ended, in order to drive them home, were apt to find themselves at a loose end for an hour.

The rabbi did not attend the meetings and saw little or nothing of the new president. For a month or more they did not exchange a word. The president did not come to the Friday evening services, and certainly not to the daily minyan. And he did not have an office in the synagogue where Rabbi Small might have dropped in on him, if only as a matter of courtesy. Several times the rabbi had thought of calling Magnuson in the evening, suggesting that he would like to come over to talk with him but, as he explained to Miriam, "It's up to him to call me. If I call *him,* he's apt to think I'm being pushy."

"But he's been in office over a month now—"

"So what? He's probably pretty busy, and nothing has come up that immediately concerns me."

He heard about Magnuson from various board members, and it was evident that he was popular, largely because he was friendly and affable whereas they expected that he might be distant and cool. They were never unaware however of the economic and social gulfs between them, but this awareness manifested itself not in reticence on their part, but rather in a kind of filial respect they accorded Magnuson, which had the effect of eliciting from him an almost paternal concern for them.

Harry Berg, who owned a small chain of three grocery stores, reported: "I was telling Bud Green about the trouble I was having getting money from the bank here in town. Howard overheard me and said, 'Why don't you try the main bank in Boston? It could be it's a little too much for the branch to handle. I know the head of the Loan Committee. If you like I can give him a ring.' So I said, 'Sure.' And do you know, when I came in to see the guy, he treated me like I was his rich uncle from Australia."

Dr. Laurence Cohn, a dermatologist who liked to take a flyer in the stock market now and then, told of mentioning a stock that someone had put him onto as sure to double in value in a couple of months. "I was saying how there was a takeover situation, see? Howard makes a kind of face and says he doubted it. So I ask him if he knows anything and he says, flat out, that there won't be any takeover. So I didn't buy and the stock is down twenty points."

Al Rollins was sure Howard Magnuson had helped his daughter get into the college of her choice "with a partial scholarship, yet" by dropping a word in the right quarter.

The only negative view came from Chester Kaplan, whom the rabbi saw regularly at the daily minyan. "This man is a regular *goy*. He doesn't come to services on the

Sabbath. Not once has he come to the minyan. Not once since I've been here. Believe me, I would have remembered. Even on Yom Kippur, I—"

"He came to the synagogue on Yom Kippur," said the rabbi quickly. "I saw him."

"Maybe in the morning for an hour. Then he went home, I'm sure for lunch. This is what you should expect from the president of a synagogue?"

"Most of our presidents have been nonobservant," said the rabbi. "Except for Jacob Wasserman and yourself—"

"Yeah, they were nonobservant, but at least they grew up in observant homes. Their parents were observant. They didn't come to the minyan regularly, but at least you saw them when they had *Yahrzeit* and had to say *kaddish*. This one, never. Has he conferred with you, Rabbi, since he became president? Have you talked to him at all?"

"No, but—"

"There," said Kaplan triumphantly. "A man becomes president of a synagogue, and doesn't even meet with the rabbi!"

The rabbi smiled. "It doesn't bother me, so why should it bother you?"

But the following Sunday, Howard Magnuson did seek him out. Shortly after the board meeting adjourned, there was a tap on the door of the rabbi's study, and in response to the rabbi's "Come in," Magnuson entered.

"I've been expecting to see you at the board meetings, but you seem to have stopped coming to them," he said as he took the visitor's chair.

"I didn't come because I wasn't invited," replied the rabbi.

With a touch of irony, Magnuson asked, "Do you need a special invitation?"

"Not a special invitation," said the rabbi with a smile. "Just an invitation."

Magnuson looked puzzled. "I don't understand."

"Well, I'm not a member of the board and, strictly speaking, not even a member of the temple organization. So I come to the board meetings only at the invitation of the president. Usually, the new president asks me at the beginning of his term to come to the meetings. Not always, though. There have been presidents who have not extended the invitation, or have invited me to attend only particular meetings where they felt that I could be helpful with the business that was to be discussed."

"Well now, I didn't know that. I'm new to this game. I'm glad you told me. So I am now inviting you to attend the meetings of the board."

"All right. Thank you. I'll try to be present in the future."

"You know, I didn't get your job description yet." He smiled. "If I had, perhaps I would have seen that you attend board meetings only by invitation. Are you still working on it?"

"No, I wasn't planning to make it out. I didn't feel that your letter applied to me, since I am not part of the temple organization personnel."

"No? Don't we pay you?"

"Yes, but it's really in the nature of a subsidy, since I am the rabbi of the Jewish community of Barnard's Crossing and serve the needs of the entire Jewish community of the area, those who are not members of the temple organization no less than those who are."

"You mean you're a kind of consultant like our CPA or our lawyer, but that you're on a kind of retainer."

"Something like that, but they act only when called upon, whereas I can take action on my own. If the temple organization should propose something that I considered to be contrary to our law or tradition, and by the way, I'd be the one who would decide if it was, then I would forbid it."

"And what if we, that is the temple organization, chose

to ignore your edict? You couldn't go to law about it, could you?"

"Not to a secular court, but I might appeal to a rabbinical court. In all probability, I would merely disassociate myself from you by resigning. If it were something major, a matter of important principle, I might denounce you to the Rabbinical Assembly, or to the Jewish community at large."

"I see. Well now, I didn't know that. It doesn't happen very often, does it?"

The rabbi smiled broadly. "No, not often. It's very rare."

Magnuson looked at the rabbi quizzically. "Is that all there is to it, or is there more?"

"Oh, there's lots more," said the rabbi. "I maintain oversight of the school and of the religious services; I teach our tradition in lectures and sermons; I am frequently the voice of the Jewish community in its dealings with the community at large; I have on at least one occasion acted as a rabbinical court and passed judgment on the evidence in a purely secular matter; and, oh, yes, I am a sort of scholar in residence. And then, of course, there are those functions that one usually associates with the rabbi—marriage, divorce, conversion, burial."

"Hm, you're a pretty busy man, Rabbi." And although Magnuson had intended the remark to be sarcastic, it also contained a hint of respect. "I'm glad you told me. You realize that what you've been doing is giving me your job description orally."

The rabbi smiled. "You're welcome. But since we have to work together, perhaps you ought to give me your— well, not your job description, but some idea of your plans, your attitude towards the temple and the congregation."

Magnuson nodded. "Fair enough. All right, I'm a businessman by philosophy and conviction."

The rabbi smiled faintly. "Does that mean you're going to try to have the temple turn a profit?"

Magnuson returned the smile to show that he did not take offense. "No, Rabbi. I mean that I'm a businessman in the sense that I like to do things in a businesslike way, just as a scientist might want to do things in a scientific way. That's why I called for all employees to submit job descriptions. And I intend to draw up organizational charts—"

"You think that will help?"

"Believe me, it never hurts. Look here, we have a School Committee and a principal and there's you, all involved with the religious school. What happens if a pupil or his folks have a beef? Does he complain to you, or to Brooks, or to the School Committee, or maybe even to me? It helps to have all these things spelled out in advance. I once took over a company that had only three employees." He held up three fingers to emphasize the point. "Three. And it was losing money. I applied my methods, made it plain who was responsible for what, and in six months it was showing a profit and had expanded to a staff of twenty. Now, while many businessmen, maybe most businessmen, would be interested only in the profit, I was interested in other things as well, making it a better place to work, making the work more satisfying for those employees, showing them the chances for growth and advancement."

"I see."

"Actually, for me, the profit is merely a confirmation that I'm on the right track. It's a proof of the method." He settled back in his seat. "When my father and his partner sold the department store in Boston, back in twenty-nine, they were left with a load of cash. If we had been in England, my father might have bought an estate and set us up as county people, gentry. But that's not the fashion in the States. Instead, Magnuson and Beck began to buy a number of companies, and we became what is known nowadays as a conglomerate. We were lucky, not only in selling out before the Crash, but in having ready cash afterwards. We made a lot of money. By the time my brothers and I were of age, we were in a position to choose any career, do anything we wanted to. My oldest brother, Myron, chose to do nothing."

"Nothing?"

"Oh, he lives in Paris and he goes to the theater and museums. He travels. He has lots of friends whom he visits and entertains. He never married."

"It seems a hard life," the rabbi commented.

Magnuson nodded. "My thought, too. But he seems to enjoy it. He lives in France, I imagine, because that kind of life is more readily understood there than it would be here. My other brother, Lawrence, is in medicine, in New York. I chose to go into business, but I invest only in things that interest me. I own a minor-league baseball team, for example, because I like baseball. That hasn't turned a profit yet," he added ruefully, "maybe because my methods don't seem to apply to baseball."

"What happened to Beck?" asked the rabbi.

Magnuson laughed. "I married her. Marcus Beck had only one child, Sophia. We grew up together and were more or less intended for each other. That kind of thing it's assumed doesn't usually work out, but it did in our case."

"And do you have children, Mr. Magnuson?"

"One, a daughter." The pride in his voice was unmistakable as he went on, "She graduated from Bryn Mawr *magna cum laude* and then went to the London School of Economics to do graduate work in political science. She's interested in politics."

The rabbi smiled. "Somehow, I get the impression that you approve of her."

Magnuson beamed. "Soph and I—our lives are wrapped up in her."

"Does she have any interest in the temple?"

Magnuson shook his head. "Young people don't these days. Of course, she went to Sunday school as a child, but I don't think she was very much influenced by it, although she was very fond of her grandmother Beck, and the Becks were a little more traditional than we were. My mother-in-law didn't have separate meat and dairy dishes. She was not fanatic, you understand. I don't suppose her cook would have stood for it. But when we dined there, she never had butter on the table when she was serving meat. Although, when Laura was with us, she always insisted she have a glass of milk. A little inconsistent that, and Sophia used to tease her about it." He smiled self-consciously as he realized that a rabbi might not find his cavalier attitude toward the dietary laws amusing. To change the subject, he asked, "And you, Rabbi, do you have any children?"

"Two. Jonathon is going into college next year and Hepsibah is entering high school."

"Do they give you any trouble?"

"Of course. That's what they're for."

"How do you mean?"

"I was joking, of course." The rabbi chuckled. "Still, I can't help thinking that every bachelor or spinster of my acquaintance, and childless couples, too, seem to be as upset over a missing shirt button or a dirty ashtray or something equally trivial as I am when one of my children is running a fever. I suspect that there's a certain amount of annoyance and trouble that we all have to endure, and if it isn't for something reasonable like a sick child, then it's apt to be for something silly and trivial. I suspect children give us a sense of proportion."

"What kind of trouble do they give you?"

"Oh, nothing serious. Hepsibah is of an age where the opinion of her peers is terribly important, on what to wear and where to go. It's her mother who bears the brunt of that. As for Jonathon, he's concerned about his future career. Last year he wanted to be a professional baseball player—"

"Is he any good? I might be able to help him there. I own a baseball club, you know."

The rabbi smiled. "Too late. This year, or the last I heard, he wants to be a brain surgeon."

Magnuson smiled. "I see what you mean. But don't you direct him? Steer him in the direction he ought to go?"

The rabbi shook his head. "The sages maintained that a father had four duties to his son, to get him circumcised, to teach him Torah, to teach him a trade, and to marry him off. I did the first, of course, and I interpret the other three liberally. I include a liberal arts education in the provision for Torah, and a profession as a possible substitute for trade. As for choosing a wife for him, I doubt if he'd stand for it."

"But in the choice of profession, wouldn't you try to influence him? Would you like him to be a rabbi?"

"Only if he wanted to. These days you can't direct children too easily."

"Maybe you're right, Rabbi, but I keep trying. I guess I'm the authoritarian type. And now that the temple is my baby, I intend to direct that."

"And how do you plan to direct the temple?" asked the rabbi.

"I aim to make it a better place to work in and a better place to worship in. More, I'd like to attract more of our people to it. I'd like to see everyone in the Jewish community a member."

"No one could quarrel with that," said the rabbi easily.

"And I don't tolerate quarrels in any organization I'm running." Magnuson smiled. It was a friendly smile, but the rabbi sensed in both the statement and the smile a hint of challenge? Of warning?

86

13

THE PRINTER EXCHANGED his glasses for another pair which
he took from one of the slots in the rolltop desk, and examined the sheet of paper Tony D'Angelo offered him. Across
the top it said in caps, THE COMMITTEE OF CONCERNED CITI-
ZENS. Just below was stapled the snapshot taken at the
banquet and under each figure was the name and a brief
caption noting the charge—Grand Larceny, Assault with
Intent to Kill, or Conspiracy to Defraud. One, however,
showed neither name or caption.

The printer nodded to himself and looked up. "You still
working for Moriarty?" he asked.

"His Nibs? I sure as hell ain't working against him,"
said Tony genially.

"So what do you want?"

"I'd like this set up on a piece of notepaper. You know,
something you can fold over once and put in an envelope."
He looked around at the dusty shelves, and spotting a pile
of printed forms, he took one. "Something like this. Just
about this size, but good quality. You know, we don't want
it to look cheap. This 'Concerned Citizens' line, that can go
up in the right-hand corner. Understand?"

The printer nodded.

"Now all this stuff, the picture and these little captions under each guy, I'd like that on the upper part of the page just above where it would be folded. Get it? Then below, that would be below the fold, you understand, I want just one line: 'Do you care who your senator associates with?' "

"Whom," said the printer.

"What's that?"

"It should be whom. Whom your senator associates with."

"Oh yeah?" He sampled it. " 'Do you care whom your senator associates with?' Yeah, sounds more refined. Tell you what, how about, 'Do you care with whom your senator associates?' "

"That would be even better."

"Okay, do it that way." He watched as the printer penciled it in block letters. "Now these little captions under each guy, how about having like a little box with maybe an arrow pointing to the guy it applies to?"

"I can do it, but if I put it just below each figure, I don't think you'd need an arrow. It would be plain enough with just the box. Or without the box if there was a separation between them." He studied the paper and the photograph, then pointed with an inky finger. "How about this one?"

"Nothing under that one. You know him?"

The printer shook his head.

"Never heard of Tommy Baggio?"

Again the printer shook his head.

"He's running for state senator."

"And I guess you people would rather he wouldn't?"

"That's right. There's just one thing. He needs a moustache, a little Hitler moustache." From his wallet he drew the newspaper clipping with Baggio's picture. "This is what he looks like now. Question is, can you put back the moustache?"

The printer studied the clipping and the photograph for a moment, and then said, "No problem."

"Okay. What will the whole business cost me?"

"You mean with the envelopes and all?"

"Yeah, we got to have envelopes. And the envelopes got to have The Committee of Concerned Citizens in the upper left-hand corner."

"No address?"

"No. Just The Committee of Concerned Citizens. How much would it be?"

"Well, how many would you want?"

"Oh yeah. Look, I don't know right now. Could you sort of make it up and give me like a proof? Then I could tell you afterwards how many we'd want to print up."

"Yeah, I could do that."

Tony started for the door, and then stopped. "Hey, how about changing that sentence to 'Do you care?' You know, it makes it more subtle-like."

"Sure. Tell you what, I'll set it up both ways and you can see which you like best."

"Swell."

14

HOWARD MAGNUSON PATTED the papers spread out on the desk in his study and said to Morris Halperin, "I had a couple of chaps from my Boston office do a little research. I wanted to know how our salary schedule compared with those of other religious institutions. Some of the results are quite surprising. Were you aware that overall we pay our people a lot more than our Christian friends do theirs?"

Halperin nodded. He had the uneasy feeling that he was about to be treated to a display of Magnuson's business thinking: If synagogue salaries were generally higher than church salaries, obviously money could be saved by cutting back. He thought to head him off.

"It's the old business of apples and oranges," he said easily. "You can't compare the work of our teachers in the religious school, who are professionals and work a full week, with Sunday school teachers, who teach an hour or so a week. As for the job of cantor, I don't know what you'd compare him to in a church. Maybe the leader of the choir. Again, there's really no comparison."

"I was thinking primarily of the rabbi," said Magnuson. "Now there's a reasonable comparison between the rabbi on the one hand and a minister or a priest on the other."

"Only on the surface," said Halperin. "The minister or the priest has a vocation; he receives a call to preach the word of God, something like the prophet Jonah."

"So?"

"So he's in the position of somebody who's terribly anxious to sell something to someone who's not particularly interested in buying. Which makes it a buyer's market."

"And the rabbi?"

"He's under no such divine command. He goes into the rabbinate the way someone goes into law or medicine, and he goes to a congregation, not because he receives a call—unless it's a telephone call from the head of the Ritual Committee—but because he's offered a contract. So the law of supply and demand controls, and there just aren't that many rabbis available."

"You seem to know a lot about the rabbi situation," said Magnuson.

Halperin grinned. "I ought to. We've got one in the family. My kid brother is a rabbi."

"Oh yes? I see. Well, I just brought up the comparison with churches as a matter of minor interest. What I'm really concerned about is the difference among synagogues. For one thing, there seems to be a general difference between the three groups, Reform, Conservative, and Orthodox."

"Sure, because it depends on the size and wealth of the congregation. A lot of Orthodox congregations tend to be small. Sometimes, they are what remains in the city when there has been a general move to the suburbs."

"Yes, I was aware of that, but still it's a little surprising. Salaries of teachers in the religious schools—taking in differences between cities and small towns—are remarkably similar. There is, however, a wide difference in the salaries of cantors."

"There's a wide difference in voices, too," Halperin offered.

"Of course. But now rabbis' salaries, once you make adjustments for size and social status of the congregation and so on, seem to be quite level."

"Is that so?"

"Which is why I wonder at the salary we're paying Rabbi Small. It's considerably less than other rabbis in comparable situations are getting."

"Maybe it's because he never asked for a raise."

"And others do?"

"I'm sure they do, or their party does," said Halperin.

"What do you mean by their party? What party is that?"

Halperin leaned back in his chair and said, "Let me teach you something about rabbis, Mr. Magnuson. A rabbi is in a vulnerable position, like any public servant, like a mayor, or a school principal. There are always people in the congregation who don't cotton to him because they were friends of the rabbi he succeeded, or because their wives think his wife is too hoity-toity, or because they don't like the way he parts his hair, or for any other reason that people don't like other people. He has a contract, but it's a service contract which doesn't mean too much. If they should want to get rid of him, they can, contract or no contract, by making things unpleasant for him. And since he's apt to get involved in controversy just by reason of what he might say in some sermon, there's always a group who'd like to get rid of him. So the smart operator, as soon as he comes to a congregation, sets about organizing a group of friends, associates, what have you—in effect, a party—preferably from among the important members of the congregation."

"I see."

"This party backs you and stands by you in a fight. On things like salary, they go to bat for you. If the rabbi is shy about asking for a raise, or for a sabbatical year in Israel, or whatever, they are the ones who raise the matter in the board."

"I get it. And who is in Rabbi Small's party?"

"That's just it. He doesn't have a party. Oh, there are people who like him, but that doesn't prevent Rabbi Small from disagreeing with them, or fighting them on a particular question that he feels strongly about. Another rabbi would soft-pedal his opposition, compromise a little, for the sake of friendship and not to antagonize his supporters, but not Rabbi Small. You might say that he has no political sense whatsoever. Or you might say he just doesn't give a damn."

Magnuson nodded. Then, smiling, he said, "You know, I think the first thing I ought to do is see to it that Rabbi Small gets a raise."

Halperin looked his surprise.

"And not just a token raise," Magnuson continued, "but a whopping big raise that will put him on a par with other rabbis in comparable congregations. I have in mind a raise of about six thousand a year."

"But—but—I don't get it."

Magnuson smiled broadly and leaning back in his chair, he said, "Let me teach you something about business management, Mr. Halperin. When you take over a company, it's important that you get complete control of the entire management team. Anyone you sense is not devoted to you and your interests, you get rid of. The trouble with that is that you may lose some awfully good talent. So you try to convert them. Sometimes you exert a little pressure. Fine, if it works, but I have found that you get better results by giving the man a raise. If he's a gentleman, he'll always remember that he owes you one."

"You think the board will go along?"

"Oh, I think so. I can count on your vote and your support, can't I?"

"Oh sure."

"That's fine." He reached for the phone. "So now I'll call the rabbi."

"You mean you're going to tell him before we've voted on it?"

"Of course not. I'm just going to call to tell him that I'd rather he didn't come to the next meeting of the board."

15

TONY D'ANGELO WATCHED Al Cash's secretary, an estimable woman of sixty who had been with him for years, leave the Prescott Building in Lynn's Central Square. Then he mounted the stairs and entered Cash's real estate and insurance office.

Without waiting for an invitation, D'Angelo sat down in the visitor's chair. "Hullo, Al," he said genially.

"Er—hullo," Cash replied, nonplussed. "What brings you here?"

"Took the lady friend shopping. Hey, you ever go shopping with your missus? They don't just go and buy what they need, even if they see exactly what they're after. They got to go to all the other stores, and see if maybe there's something they want even better. So I said I'd meet her afterwards. Which gives me some time to kill, so I'm right in the neighborhood, and I thought I'd drop by and pass the time of day."

"Haven't seen you around the statehouse lately," Cash remarked.

D'Angelo nodded. "That's a fact. I've been taking some time off."

"Moriarty sent you?"

"His Nibs? Well, let's just say I'm here on my own." D'Angelo favored Cash with a conspiratorial smile.

"I see. He doesn't want to be involved. Okay, what is it?"

D'Angelo's smile disappeared as he leaned forward and stared hard at the man behind the desk. "You're in a three-way race. Would it help you if it were a two-way race?"

"Who's the two?"

"You and Scofield."

"You mean Baggio might drop out? You got something on him?"

D'Angelo folded his arms across his chest and remained silent.

"Why should the Majority Whip want to get involved in Republican politics?" asked Cash suspiciously.

"He don't want to get involved, but you can understand that he might be interested."

"I see. So that's why you're here"—he smiled—"on your own."

"Uh-huh."

"All right. So why does Moriarty want me to win? I voted against the Harbor Bill, and ah—he wants me to vote against reconsideration. That's the *quid pro quo*, isn't it?"

"You vote any way you want."

"I don't get it."

"What's to get?"

"I'll tell you what's to get. Why should the Majority Whip—yeah, I know you say he's not concerned, but we both know better, don't we?—why should he be interested enough in my winning the nomination to want to do something about it when it isn't even his party? And he knows I'll be voting against him most of the time. And what's more, when it was me who led the fight against the Harbor Bill and almost made it. And furthermore knows that I'm backing reconsideration and have a good chance of bring-

96

ing it off. Did he fall out with Atlantic Dredging and wants to show them that he can pass their lousy Harbor Bill or unpass it if he wants to? Is that it? He wants to show Atlantic Dredging that they don't own him?"

"Just because he backed the Harbor Bill don't mean he takes orders from Atlantic Dredging," said D'Angelo coolly, "anymore than you take orders from Northeast Fisheries because you opposed it."

"I have no connection with Northeast Fisheries," said Cash coldly.

"Sure, that's what I'm saying," said D'Angelo affably. "Just like you got no connection with Northeast Fisheries, His Nibs got no connection with Atlantic Dredging."

"Then why does he want to do me a favor for nothing?" A thought struck him. "Or is it Baggio he wants to get?"

"I didn't say it was for nothing," said D'Angelo. "It'll cost you."

"What will it cost me?"

"Oh, nothing very much. Just a few thousand dollars—for expenses."

"What do you call a few thousand?"

D'Angelo shrugged elaborately. "Three, four, five thousand at the most. Whatever it comes to."

"Ah, I'm beginning to see daylight. For some reason, you people don't want Baggio. I can't imagine what you've got against him. He's nobody. Unless it's his brother-in-law on the Election Commission you're thinking of, maybe on account of the *paisanos* he controls. So you come to me to help you ditch him. Why? Because on no account must the Majority Whip appear to be interfering with who the opposition is picking to represent them. So you come to see me not as his agent, but on your own with an offer of straightforward, honest skullduggery." He rubbed his hands. "All right, what have you got?"

"I got a snapshot."

16

SEVERAL TIMES Laura had been on the point of giving up. It was stubbornness as much as anything that made her continue. She had thought it all out so carefully, and she refused to admit that she might have been wrong. In her judgment Scofield was the right candidate and, under the conditions as she read them, he could win. Except that he didn't seem to want to. That was something she hadn't counted on.

She was also driven by curiosity. Why was he so uninterested? Not only in the campaign, but seemingly in her? True, she had held him at a distance, to keep their relationship strictly business during the campaign. Nevertheless, she was piqued that he had made no effort to get to know her better. She was sure there was no other woman. Was he then entirely normal? Was he perhaps gay? One heard so much about that sort of thing these days. Of course, if he were, then he was useless as far as her long-range plans were concerned. But although she herself was beginning to lose enthusiasm for the campaign because of his lack of interest, she was determined to continue to the election, if only because she had started.

And then one day, a few weeks before the primary, it happened. He came into their headquarters early in the afternoon and announced, "I can win this election, Laura. You just tell me what I have to do, and I'll do it."

"Swell! Look, you've got to get yourself known. Your *name* is known in town, but you're not. So you've got to go where there are people, to meetings, hearings, forums, lectures, panel discussions. If there's a question period afterwards, you get up and say something. Usually they ask you to identify yourself, so that's what you do. 'I am John Scofield. I'm a candidate for the office of state senator. I should like to point out . . .' or 'I should like to ask the speaker . . .' I can arrange for you to be invited to various private homes to speak to small groups, informally. We've had a lot of requests. Later on, you'll have to go to shopping centers and hand out cards. You might even like it."

She eyed him appraisingly. "There's one thing we've got to settle early. Are you John or are you Jack?"

"What's the difference?"

"A Jack is different from a John. He dresses differently and he talks differently. Let's try it both ways." She took on the role of chairman of a meeting, and walked to the other end of the room. "The speaker is willing to answer some questions from the audience. Yes, that gentleman in the corner. Do you have a question? Please state your name."

He grinned at the make-believe. "My name is John Scofield, and my question is—".

"Mm, no. Let's try it the other way. The gentleman in the corner. Please state your name."

Still grinning, he said, "I'm Jack Scofield, a candidate for the Senate for the Essex District—"

"That's it," she interrupted. "You'll be Jack Scofield from now on. You're a little stuffy as John." She looked at him critically. "That tie and that suit . . ."

"What's wrong with them?"

"All right if you're going to a funeral, but—"

"I was in court today before Judge Levitt who's a very conservative guy."

"All right. So in court you can be John Scofield, but afterwards you'll be Jack and dress accordingly. More informal."

"Jeans?"

"Certainly not. You're taking the conservative position, remember? 'Let's keep things the way they are.' I suggest gray flannels and a tweed jacket. And a shirt with a button-down collar."

"I get it," he said enthusiastically.

"Then let's try it out tonight. There's a hearing on voter registration at the town hall. They want to put the deadline for registration forward a couple of weeks. I think we should oppose it. There probably won't be many there. Maybe a couple of dozen at most, but it'll be good experience. Why don't you go home and change and I'll meet you there."

"What time is it called for?"

"Eight o'clock."

"Then how about having dinner someplace first?"

"I've got a dinner date," she replied quickly. She didn't have one, but it was important to show him she was not readily available. When his face fell, she relented. "We could go somewhere afterwards for a drink or for coffee."

They went to the hearing, and at one point, he did indeed get a chance to say, "I'm Jack Scofield, candidate for the Senate from this district, so I have a special interest in this hearing. I should like to point out that . . ."

Laura thought he sounded impressive. Unfortunately, there were candidates for other offices present who took issue with him, and in the interchange he did not come off as well.

Later, over coffee, he said, "I guess I didn't do so good tonight, did I?"

"Well, they were prepared and you weren't."

"You mean I'm a dope," he said bitterly.

"No such thing. But you can't depend on ideas that come to you on the spur of the moment. You have a tendency to do that. But there's no telling where they might lead to. What you need is well-thought-out positions on all major issues. I'll start to work on it tomorrow morning."

He looked at her in frank admiration. "You know, Laura, you're something else."

17

THE RABBI REPLACED the receiver, and in answer to Miriam's questioning look, he said, "That was our president, Mr. Magnuson."

"Oh? What did he want?"

"He called to tell me not to come to the board meeting Sunday. It was nice of him to call early enough in the week so that I could make other plans for Sunday morning if I cared to."

"Did he say why he didn't want you to be there?"

The rabbi shook his head. "I presume it's because he wants to discuss something he doesn't want me to hear."

"You mean you think he wants to talk about you?"

"I suppose." He returned to his seat and picked up the book he had laid down.

But Miriam was concerned. "Do you get along well with him, David?"

"With Howard Magnuson? I guess so. I haven't seen very much of him. Just that time he came to my study. Come to think of it, that was to ask me why I *hadn't* been coming to the board meetings. After that, I saw him at the few meetings that followed, but that's all."

"Anything special happen at those meetings? I mean, as far as you were concerned?"

"Nothing unusual that I can think of. Why?"

"You didn't oppose Magnuson in any discussion?" she persisted.

"I didn't take part in any discussion. Oh, in Good and Welfare, I said I thought that all members of the board ought to come to the Friday evening services, but—"

"That's it," she said decisively.

"What's it?"

"Howard Magnuson interpreted that as a personal criticism because he never attends the Friday evening services."

"Or any other."

"So there you are," she announced triumphantly. "He thinks you were critical of him."

"Well, from that point of view, I suppose I am. What of it?"

"Oh, David, don't you see? You don't criticize people like Magnuson. You do, of course, but I mean . . . What I'm trying to say is that people like Magnuson aren't used to being criticized by people they regard as subordinates. You did, and it's probably not the only time. So he's determined to do something about it."

"Like what?" he scoffed. "Get the board to pass a resolution declaring that the rabbi must never say anything that's critical of the president?"

"You may laugh," she said, "but I'm bothered. You know it's not as though you had a life contract here. It's just year to year."

"That's the way I want it. If it leaves the temple free, it also leaves me free."

"But what if they decide they won't renew?"

He shrugged. "So I go looking for another job. And from what I hear, it would probably be a better one. Maybe a larger synagogue in a larger town, or in a city with members who are more understanding. The response to my paper in the *Quarterly* was pretty flattering, and I'm still getting letters on it."

"Then why not think of moving on? I mean, why not look around—"

"Well, because I like living here in Barnard's Crossing for one thing. And for another, I feel that I'm needed here. It's harder, and there are frequent rows. There's constant pressure from one group or another to move in all sorts of undesirable directions. I feel that I'm keeping them to the tradition. Someplace else, with an older and a more established congregation, life would be easier, but less rewarding."

This was Wednesday night. Although Miriam did not bring up the matter again, he knew it was on her mind by the questions she asked. Had Mr. Kaplan been at the min-yan? Did he say anything? Had Morton Brooks said anything to him? He usually knew what was going on. Finally, he asked her outright what was bothering her.

"I'm not really bothered. Yes, I suppose I am. I'm not too worried about your being able to get another job if you have to. But I like it here, too, and I'd rather you didn't have to. But if you're in trouble with the president—"

"So what? I've been in trouble, as you put it, with presidents before. In fact, I've fought with about half of them. It's nothing new."

"But Magnuson is different, David. The others, you knew where you stood with them. It was always about some basic principle, and you were right and they were wrong. You could always rally the congregation round you if it came to a fight. You could always explain how it was contrary to our tradition and why you had to oppose it. The point is, the other presidents were concerned about the temple, about our religion. They were Jews—"

"And Magnuson isn't?"

"Well, of course he is, but he doesn't give a hang about the temple. It's just an organization to him, and because it is an organization, he wants to run it. And he can want you out of it because—because you get in his way. And if he wanted you out, he'd get you out. It wouldn't have to be about anything in particular. He'd just convince the board, and he could, not to renew your contract when it expires. And your contract expires soon, or didn't you realize it?"

"Does it? No, I hadn't realized. Then maybe that's it. Howard Magnuson is a businessman with a concern for detail. Since my contract is due to expire, he feels that it should be voted on by the board. It's only natural that he should want them to do it in my absence."

Sunday morning when Miriam woke him to go to the morning minyan, he stretched lazily and said, "I think I'll pass it up. I'll say the morning prayers at home today."

"Anything the matter, David? Are you feeling all right?"

"I'm feeling fine," he assured her, "just lazy. I just thought I'd indulge myself a little."

Later at breakfast, after he had recited the morning prayers, he explained, "The meeting comes right after the minyan. The board members who are present at the minyan drift down the corridor to the boardroom where those who didn't come to the minyan are waiting, Magnuson usually among them. Then after a few minutes, he calls the meeting to order. All right, so after the minyan, if I go in the other direction, towards the stairs to my study, someone is sure to ask me if I'm not planning to go to the meeting. And of course, I'll have to say that I'm not. Then, most likely they'd ask why not, and I'd find it a little embarrassing to say that I was requested to stay away."

"But if it's just what you think it is, a formal vote on the renewal of your contract, wouldn't they get it out of the way the first thing and then maybe call up to your study to have you come down to participate in the rest of the meeting?"

"Possibly. But then I don't want to appear to be at their beck and call. Anyway, our board meetings don't work like that even under Magnuson who tries to keep them businesslike. They do a lot more talking than transacting business. If Magnuson brought it up right after committee reports, say, in an effort to get it out of the way, they'd still spend the whole time discussing it, even though it's purely routine. He'd call for discussion, and every one of them would take the opportunity to say something about me, how I had shown bad judgment in this, or failed to do that."

"Don't you have *any* friends among the board, David?"

"Oh sure, if you mean people I get along with. Most of them, maybe all of them. But if you mean, do I have a clique, the rabbi's party, no, definitely not."

"Maybe that was a mistake, not having one, I mean. You know what Rabbi Bernstein said—"

"Saul Bernstein is a politician from way back. He was a politician at the seminary. That kind of thing comes natural to him. It means cultivating a few important people, dining with them, going places with them. I can't do it. There are only three or four at whose homes I *could* dine. The rest don't keep kosher kitchens. Besides, it works both ways, you know. If you expect them to support you in your projects, you've got to support them in theirs. I'd rather be my own man."

He spoke somewhat testily, the matter having come up before between them. Miriam thought it best to change the subject. "When do you suppose you'll hear? Will they send you a letter?"

"Well, Magnuson, being a stickler for businesslike methods, will send me written notice, I expect. But no doubt, the secretary will call me around noon or right after the meeting is over."

However, it was not the secretary who called; it was Magnuson himself. "Rabbi? Howard Magnuson speaking. I thought you'd be pleased to hear that we have just voted to increase your salary by six thousand dollars a year, to take effect immediately."

"Oh, why—why, thank you. I appreciate that. It was very kind and generous—"

"Just good business practice, Rabbi. It's been a cardinal principle with me never to underpay personnel, especially key personnel."

"It's a wonderful principle. Thank you again."

There was no need to tell Miriam for she had been standing at his side. "Oh, David, isn't it wonderful! But I feel awful after what I said about him, because I'm sure it was all his doing."

"Yes, I'm sure it was."

She eyed him searchingly. "Yet, somehow you don't appear terribly pleased."

"Oh, I am, believe me, except . . ."

"Except what?"

"Except that I'm not sure I haven't just been co-opted into being one of the president's men."

18

FOR THE WEEK before the primaries, Laura persuaded Scofield to stay away from his law office in Salem and devote himself full-time to the campaign. Early every morning she had him down at the railroad station—either in Revere or Lynn—distributing cards to the commuters going in to Boston. He would approach them on the platform with hand outstretched and say, "Hello. I'm Jack Scofield, candidate for the Republican nomination for state senator. I'd appreciate your support." Then he'd give them one of his campaign cards with his picture and the slogan underneath, "Let's keep things the way they are."

Most of the time, the people addressed merely nodded or mumbled something and took the card, only to drop it surreptitiously when they thought he wasn't looking. At first he found it disheartening, when the train pulled out, to see how many cards were littering the platform. But he got over it after a while.

And sometimes, someone would say, "I was planning to vote for you," in which case he would give the hand a little squeeze and say, "Thanks, and please tell your friends." On rare occasions, someone would say, "Sorry, but I'm voting for Cash (or Baggio)." In those cases, Laura had taught him to say, "He's a good man. As long as we get a Republican in. That's the main thing."

"If he says he's a Democrat, don't argue with him," she instructed. "Just offer him the card and say, 'In case you change your mind, I'd appreciate your support,' and let it go at that. Whatever you do, don't argue. You won't change anybody's mind and you'll be wasting time, losing the chance to speak to someone else. And keep moving. Don't stand in one place waiting for people to approach. Go after them."

After that, they went to the supermarkets and shopping centers. Here, the technique was a little different. "They'll be mostly women," she pointed out. "So you don't hold out your hand unless they offer theirs. You just give them the card. And try to approach them as they're entering the store, not when they're leaving and loaded down with bundles. And for God's sakes, keep moving. Don't get stalled."

"What do you mean, stalled?"

She gave him a curious look. "Some of these gals can be on the hungry side—emotionally."

Scofield was tempted to say—lightly, jokingly—that he himself was on the hungry side emotionally, but he hesitated and the opportunity was lost. The truth was that he was a little in awe of her. She was so assured, so self-possessed, so—so rich. He thought of the girls he had taken out at school or picked up in bars, as chicks or broads, and his interest in them was primarily sexual. But Laura was a lady. Laura was class. Of course, if he were to win the election . . .

The first couple of days she chauffeured him around in her car just to make sure he got there, and to watch and then give her opinion of his performance. In the evenings she scheduled meetings for him, sometimes two or three for the same evening. These were brief visits to people's houses, where he would make a little speech, answer a few questions, and then, in response to a signal from her, say, "I'm sorry, folks, but I'm on a tight schedule." He would smile and nod in her direction, "The boss is signaling me and I've got to run." He would drive to those meetings in his own car with the sign on the roof because, as she explained, "It does a lot of good to have your car seen outside some of these homes."

As the campaign drew to a close, Scofield was concerned about their lack of an organization. "These other guys, they've got people to stand around each of the precincts to hand out cards, and to drive people to the polls."

"Well, so have we," she assured him.

"We have? Where'd we get them?"

"I was able to sell the Barnard's Crossing Republican Committee a bill of goods," she replied airily. "I pointed out the obvious, that you were the only local person running. In theory they're supposed to be neutral until the Republican candidate is picked in the primaries, but I convinced them that it would be to their advantage if you should win. I also contacted Josiah Bradley, the former senator, or rather his people, and they contacted some of their supporters. Don't worry, we'll have troops to man the precinct stations."

He looked at her in wonder. "You know, I never thought of that."

"You're not supposed to," she assured him. "That's what a campaign manager is supposed to do. All you have to do is run."

"Like a racehorse with you as my jockey, huh?"

She smiled. "Something like that."

On Saturday before election day, Laura received in the mail a leaflet issued by The Committee of Concerned Citizens. It showed a badly reproduced photograph of a group of six men, seated at what appeared to be the head table at a banquet. Five were named, and below each name was a note to the effect that he had been indicted or convicted of a major crime. The sixth, unmistakably Thomas Baggio, was not named but circled. Below the photograph ran the single line: "Do You Care?"

She drummed on the desk with her fingers as she studied it. When Scofield came in, she showed it to him. "Have you seen one of these? It came in this morning's mail."

He looked at it and said, "That's Tommy Baggio, isn't it?"

"No doubt about it, and it's dirty pool. Have you ever heard of The Committee of Concerned Citizens?"

He shook his head slowly.

"Neither have I," she said, "and if there were such a committee, I'm sure I would have. It's obviously a phony."

"Who do you suppose put it out?"

"Maybe Al Cash's people." She stooped to retrieve the envelope from the wastebasket. "Postmarked Revere. Or it could be one of Baggio's political enemies in his own town. With the election Tuesday, the poor devil can't do much about it, either. Even if he tries to arrange a press conference for his denial, it probably wouldn't get into the local papers until Tuesday. I doubt whether Boston papers would bother with it at all."

"But it's a photograph, and pictures don't lie."

"What difference does that make?" she demanded. "This was probably some sort of benefit or testimonial. Baggio is a pol. He must get invited to all kinds of affairs of this kind. Somebody says to him, 'So-and-so just got out of the hospital, or is getting a new job on the West Coast, or has just been elected president of the Left-handed Salesmen Association, and we're giving him a benefit. Can you come and say a few words?' So he goes, says a few words of greeting, has his picture taken, and he leaves. From his point of view, there are people there who vote, and that's enough reason for going."

"Yeah, I see what you mean."

A sudden thought came to her. "Sa-ay, we should do something about this."

"How do you mean?"

"Well, we can't just ignore it. We've got to take a position on it. It might even do us some good. I tell you what, we'll repudiate it. You will issue a statement saying you deplore this kind of politics, and you believe—no, you are certain that Thomas Baggio is an honorable man. I'll call the local papers right away. Maybe we can get into the Monday paper."

He considered for a moment and then nodded. "Yeah, let's do it. Write up a statement and we can give it to them over the phone."

19

MILLIE HANSON LAID OUT half a dozen strips of sizzling bacon on a paper towel, placed another towel over them, and patted them dry. She put three strips on each plate beside the French toast, hesitated, and then transferred one of the strips to the other plate. Bacon was fattening and she had to watch her figure. She brought the two plates to the table and set the one with four strips in front of Tony.

"Thanks, Baby. Geez, I'm starved." After spreading out his paper napkin, he reached for the bottle of maple syrup and liberally doused his French toast. "What time did you get in last night?"

"After two. You know Saturday nights."

"Busy, huh?"

"Boy, was it! For a while they were running me ragged. Hey, I saw that guy. He was with a couple of other guys—"

"What guy was that, Baby?"

"You know, the guy whose picture was in the paper. You remember. You had a picture of a bunch of hoods at a banquet and one of them had his picture in the paper you said was running for something."

"Baggio? Tommy Baggio?"

"Yeah, they were calling him Tommy."

"You sure it was him?"

"Oh sure. He looked just like the picture in the paper."

"Recognize anyone else?"

"There was a redhead they called Mike. He's been in before. That's the only one."

"Kind of squinty eyes? That's Mike Springer, his campaign manager. Did you happen to hear what they were talking about?" he asked casually.

"They were talking kind of quiet-like, almost whispering. And when I'd come over to serve them their drinks, they'd stop talking. But then after they'd had a few, they weren't so careful, and once I heard this redhead say, 'So how'd they get the picture?' And this Baggio character said, 'I tell you it's a frame. I swear I was never even there.'"

"That's all you heard?"

"I told you we were busy. I was running back and forth to the bar. I had all the booths on the left and three tables, and they kept me hopping. I got snatches, mostly about some Election Commission. And once I heard Baggio say he was going to put the boots to his brother-in-law. Do you suppose that's the guy that framed him? His brother-in-law?"

Tony raised his shoulders in expressive denial of any knowledge. "These Revere pols, who knows? They'd frame their own mother."

A thought occurred to her. "You didn't have anything to do with it, did you Tony?"

"Me? What gave you that idea?"

"Well, there was that picture you took, and they were talking about a picture—"

"Listen, Baby"—Tony's face was hard—"forget about the picture I showed you. All right?"

"Sure. You know me. But—"

"No buts. Just forget you ever saw it." He smiled. "It's like this. That picture, five or ten guys must have got it. I bet there were ten or twenty guys had cameras. I told you it was a strictly stag benefit and there was entertainment promised. So everybody expected broads and some of them came prepared. When they saw there were no broads, they began snapping pictures all over the place. So let's say one of these guys tries to put the bite on Baggio, or say he goes to someone who doesn't like Baggio and thinks the guy might want to give him the leg—"

"Not you, Tony. You wouldn't, would you?"

"Me? I don't play in a hick town like Revere."

"Because working in a nightclub, you hear things. And I wouldn't want to spend all my spare time for the next few months taking care of some guy whose had both his legs broken."

"Baby!" He spread his arms in token of innocence and candor. "You heard them say something about a picture. So, more like it was a picture of him taken in some motel with a floozie who wasn't his wife. It's got nothing to do with us. So, how's about you pouring me another cup of coffee and just forgetting all about it?"

20

"Can I have the car, dad?"

The rabbi looked at his son in surprise. "On a Monday night?"

"He's got to see Alice," Hepsibah volunteered. "She called him."

"Ma!" Jonathon's protest manifested long-suffering annoyance.

"How many times have I told you, Hepsibah?" Miriam was plaintive rather than angry.

"It's not a date," Jonathon explained. "It's like an assignment for my Political Process course."

"What kind of assignment?" asked the rabbi suspiciously.

"Well, you know, it's the night before the primaries. So there's a couple of rallies downtown. And Mr. Cronin said we ought to go, and then we're going to talk about it in class, and maybe even have like a test."

"I didn't realize the election was tomorrow," said Rabbi Small. "Where are the rallies going to be held?"

"Well, there's the big one at the town hall. And then they put up like a platform at the end of Main Street. So I guess there'll be another one there."

"That might be interesting," said the rabbi. "Maybe I'll go with you."

"I want to go, too," said Hepsibah.

"No," said the rabbi automatically.

"No," said Miriam. "You've got homework to do, Sibah, and I want you in bed early. You were up late last night."

"Nothing doing," said Jonathon. "I'm not going to have that pest hanging on to me."

So around half-past seven, the rabbi and Jonathon left their house on Maple Street. And in response to Jonathon's "Can I drive?," the rabbi handed over the keys and took the passenger seat.

"Drive down Main to Foster," he directed. "There's sure to be a space there. We can walk from there."

They found a parking place and set out for the town hall, which was about a hundred yards beyond. But as they approached their destination, Jonathon said, "You want to go to the town hall, Dad? I figured on going to the other place for a while. Why don't I meet you afterwards?"

The rabbi hesitated. He assumed Jonathon had arranged to meet his friends at the rally on the platform. "All right," he said. "But as soon as the rally there is over, you come to the town hall. Or better still, let's plan on meeting here at the town hall at ten—"

"Aw . . ."

"All right, half past, but no later."

The town hall auditorium was almost full, and noisy and disorderly. People kept getting out of their seats to talk to other people, or sometimes, it seemed, just to wander around. Conversations were carried on with little or no attention paid to the speaker at the lectern, and the speakers paid no attention to the noise, not even when it came from various people on the platform. Some in the audience carried placards with a candidate's name and they expressed approval or disapproval—it was hard to tell which —by pounding the placard stakes on the floor.

"It's like a Democratic national convention, isn't it?" said a voice behind him. The rabbi turned and saw that it was Police Chief Hugh Lanigan. Lanigan was a square-shouldered man with a round, rubicund face and white hair cut whiffle-style, so short that the pink scalp showed through. He had had dealings with the rabbi over many years, and they had become good friends. On more than one occasion he had been able to inform the rabbi of matters that were of concern to the Jewish community. Nor were the benefits one-sided, for he had also found the rabbi's advice useful on numerous occasions.

"I didn't expect to see you here, David. And then again, I can see where you might come," Lanigan smiled.

"I came with Jonathon, except that he went to the other place. He said it was for an assignment in his Political Process class. Curious, the kind of courses they teach in high school these days. It *is* noisy, isn't it?"

"Yeah, it's noisy, but that's all it is. When I was a youngster, they used to parade through the streets carrying torches, red flares really, like the kind they sell in automotive stores. It was mostly the kids that carried them, and the kids joined the parades so they could carry them. But then the Board of Selectmen passed an ordinance against them —fire hazard, you know—and that ended the parades—and the fun. The same when they outlawed fireworks for the Fourth of July."

"Everyone seems to be having a good time, though," said the rabbi. "Does anyone listen to the speakers?"

"Naw. It's just a chance to do some last-minute electioneering."

"Then . . ."

"The candidates are expected to show. I suppose anyone who didn't would be thought to lack the common touch. They quiet down, though, when the candidates for state-wide office speak."

"You mean Constant and Belise will be coming here?"

"They won't because we're a strong Republican town; they can do better in some of the cities in the western part of the state. But the candidates for lieutenant governor will show, and Duffy, one of the candidates for attorney general, is expected."

It did quiet down when Jeremiah Duffy appeared. He was listened to respectfully, and roundly applauded when he finished.

The rabbi glanced at his watch and said, "It's almost half-past ten. Jonathon is either waiting for me or will be coming along any minute."

"Well, this about winds it up. I'll be going along, too," said Lanigan. "What did you think of Duffy's idea of establishing a fund for the victims of robbery, assault, and all the rest?"

The rabbi smiled. "I approve of it. You see, it's an approach to our view."

"How do you mean?"

"Well, in Talmudic law, theft, robbery, and assault and so on were not crimes; they were torts against the victim, and the perpetrator not only had to make good what he had stolen, say, but also had to pay an additional sum, sometimes several times the value of the thing stolen."

"But if it's not a crime—"

"In this country, a crime is an injury to the state, or in England where our common law comes from, it is an injury to the Crown. Well, that's obviously a legal fiction. When A steals from B, how is the Commonwealth affected, or in England, Queen Elizabeth? But it's the Commonwealth that proceeds against him, and if he's found guilty, he goes to jail. What does it cost to keep a man in jail?"

"Last I heard, about twenty thousand dollars a year," said Lanigan gloomily.

"So all of us pay through our taxes to keep each criminal

in jail, and the victim, what does he get out of it? But in Talmudic Law, it is the victim who would recover, and the perpetrator would do hard labor to make good the penalty imposed."

"You mean this is what Jews, I mean, observant Jews would do?"

"Oh no, because there is an overriding Talmudic law, *Dina Malchuta Dina*, which states that the law of the country where we reside takes precedence."

"Well, it's an interesting idea, anyway. I just wonder how it would work on something like the Brink's robbery. They'd have to work the rest of their lives. Say, how did you like Jack Scofield?"

"Which one was he?"

"The local candidate for state senator. The tall, blond fellow."

"I don't think I noticed. There were so many speakers. Why?"

"Oh, I thought you people would be pushing for him."

Before the rabbi could ask Lanigan what he meant, Jonathon appeared and called out, "Dad."

"Okay, Jonathon. Coming." And with a wave to Lanigan, he went to join his son.

21

MONDAY AFTERNOON when the local paper had come out, Laura was pleased to see their repudiation of the Committee of Concerned Citizens leaflet covered under the headline SCOFIELD DEPLORES DIRTY TRICKS; CALLS BAGGIO HONORABLE MAN. The chairman of the Barnard's Crossing Republican Committee called to say, "That was very decent of Scofield to issue that statement. We're all good Republicans and shouldn't fight amongst ourselves." There was also a call from the Baggio headquarters. "I'm calling in behalf of Thomas Baggio to express his appreciation for Mr. Scofield's statement. We've made formal complaint to the Election Commission, but I want you to know that we appreciate Scofield's support."

"Have you heard anything from the Al Cash headquarters?" she asked.

"Not a word."

"Well, maybe he didn't see the leaflet," she suggested. "We got it in Saturday's mail."

"Maybe," was the skeptical reply.

Scofield had come in late in the afternoon, and Laura could see by the way his eyes glittered that he had had a drink or two. When she tried to fill him in on the events of the day, he cut her off with a wave of the hand. "Look, what do you say we go some place nice to eat, and—and make a night of it."

"No, not tonight," she said firmly and decisively. "Tonight, you go to the rally. Have you forgotten?"

"Oh yeah. You coming?"

"Maybe."

He could tell from her tone of voice that it was useless to argue, so he mumbled, "Okay." Without further ado, he walked out, not trusting himself to stay on in her presence.

It had come to him that afternoon that he wanted her badly. More, that he needed her. And that it might be his last chance, for the feeling was strong in him that if he lost, he would not see her again. She would say the usual, that they had put up a good fight, and maybe next time around he would do better. Then they would shake hands perhaps and say good-bye, and that would be the end of it. She had given him purpose and direction, and tomorrow, if he lost, he would be alone and wouldn't know what to do. So he had decided that it had to be tonight, and had fortified himself with a couple of drinks. But he had forgotten all about the rally and thought she was annoyed with him.

Of course, if he did win tomorrow . . .

Tuesday was a crisp, clear day. He arrived at his headquarters early, but she was there before him. "What do I do?" he demanded briskly. He had decided not to mention the rally or her failure to appear.

"Have you voted yet?"

"Gosh, no."

"Then that's the first thing you do. Then you come back here and get a load of cards, and tour the district to see if one of our people is outside each precinct station. Thank him, tell him how much you appreciate his help, and give him a supply of cards if he's running low."

"Will do." He started for the door.

She called after him, "Keep your chin up. It's our kind of weather."

He stopped. "What do you mean by that?"

"Nasty weather would have favored Cash and Baggio. They've got the organizations to bring out their people, rain or shine. But if the weather is good, then even people who are lukewarm about voting are likely to go to the polls."

"Yeah, that's right. You voted yet?"

"Naturally."

"Who'd you vote for?"

"Tommy Baggio, of course. I've been in love with that guy from the beginning."

He walked to the precinct station and wondered idly if she might not be hinting to him, trying to tell him something by her remark. As he walked along the street, he was hailed by several passers-by, who called out and wished him luck, or said they had just voted for him. One even addressed him as Senator.

He spent the whole morning touring the district, and when he got back, shortly after noon, he found that she had set up a large electric coffee urn, along with several cardboard boxes of assorted doughnuts. The wastebasket was overflowing with paper cups and wrinkled paper napkins, and there were several used paper cups rolling around on the floor under the table.

He poured himself some coffee and selected a doughnut. As he munched, he said, "Checked all the precincts. They all report the voting is slow. Only to be expected in a primary. You must have had a crowd here."

"Not too many, but people kept dropping in."

"Why don't we get the place cleaned up a little?" he suggested.

"No, leave it as it is. It makes it look as though we were busy."

"Many calls for cars?"

"Not too many. Most of them would be apt to call the offices of those running for statewide office." The telephone rang. "Just a minute."

She picked up the phone and announced, "Scofield headquarters." She listened for a moment and said, "Yes, it is a nice day for it. It looks like a good turnout. Who do you favor for governor, Constant or Belise? Yes, he is a good man. They're both good men and good Republicans. What's the address again? Okay, we'll have a car over shortly."

"What's that all about?" he asked. "What do you care who they prefer for governor?"

"So I'll know whom to call for a car. She said Constant, so I'll call the Constant headquarters. They have a lot more cars than we do."

He looked at her with admiration. "Why don't we go and get some lunch?"

"And leave the place unattended? No, you go, and bring me back a hamburger, no mustard."

"Then what do I do?"

"You make the round of the precincts again. That's the most important thing, showing your people you're interested and that you appreciate what they're doing. And only you can do it. And when you finish, you start over again."

"Okay, Sweetheart, whatever you say. But we're having dinner together tonight."

"All right, after the polls close."

"But that's not until eight o'clock," he protested.

"Well, if you're famished, you can always have a doughnut to tide you over," she said.

He left and did not reappear until half-past seven. He urged her to leave with him.

"But we can't leave before the polls close."

"How many calls have you had in the last half hour?"

"Only a couple," she admitted, "but—"

"But nothing. If they call here and get no answer, they'll call the headquarters of one of the candidates for statewide office. Chances are they'll call them first, anyhow. Besides, anyone calling now, by the time they get a car to them, and deliver them, the polls will be closed."

This seemed reasonable. And he was so surprisingly firm that she agreed. "Shall we turn the lights out? Or should we put up the Back Later sign?"

"What for?"

"Oh, you know, people come to sit around and wait for the results."

"Not here, they won't. They'll go to the committee headquarters. Turn them out." On the sidewalk, he said, "Suppose we take your car. Mine has the sign on top, and I'd like to forget about the campaign for a while. I was thinking we'd go someplace along Route 128 outside the district."

When they got to the restaurant, she discovered he had made reservations. Curiously she was not displeased. He ordered cocktails, and when the waiter asked if they wanted to order, he said, "No, after our drinks." And to Laura, "I aim to eat leisurely tonight."

It was almost ten o'clock when they finished their coffee. "The results will be broadcast on the eleven o'clock news," he said. "How about coming to my place to hear the returns?"

"All right."

He had a large studio apartment on an upper floor at Waterfront Towers, one of the few apartment buildings in Barnard's Crossing. It was sparsely furnished with a large bed, a couple of overstuffed modern chairs without arms, a businesslike desk and straight-backed chair, and a table with a TV set.

As he busied himself with ice cubes and a whiskey bottle, she turned on the TV, and then since the news wasn't on yet, she went over to the window to look out at the harbor. "Nice view," she remarked.

"Uh-huh." He handed her a tall glass and sat down in one of the armchairs facing the TV. She remained standing, sipping at her drink.

The newscast came on and the primary was the big story. In addition to the two anchormen, there were a couple of "experts," political reporters from the Boston newspapers to comment on the implications of the vote.

". . . Not all precincts in as yet . . . however, Constant appears to have a commanding lead over Belise . . . In the attorney general race . . ." It went on and on, numbers clicking on the tote board and appeals to the experts to explain the vote in this precinct or that. The turnout had been small, as it was apt to be for a primary election, and it was obvious that the anchormen were doing their best to build up a story, seizing on every change in the numbers to create suspense and excitement. It was almost midnight before one of the anchormen announced, "And now for the regional offices . . . the incumbent Democrat in the Senate was of course unchallenged in the First District, but there seems to be a horserace for the Republican nomination . . . in the Second District . . . the Third, the Essex District, usually goes Republican and nomination is regarded as tantamount to election. There were three men running for the nomination . . ."

Scofield leaned forward in his chair and Laura put her glass down on the windowsill.

". . . Winner by a sizable plurality is John Scofield. So we'll have a new face in the Senate . . ."

Scofield sat back in his seat, stunned. Laura stretched both arms ceilingward. "Wow!" she exclaimed. And then very deliberately, she sat down on Scofield's lap and pressed her lips to his.

A moment later, when she made to get up, he held her

tight, "No." It was the official Republican nominee for the Senate talking.

She did not struggle and made no further attempt to escape. When she felt his hand on her thigh, under her dress, she merely sighed contentedly.

Much later, when they were lying in bed, relaxed and at ease, he said, "You know, I'm kind of scared. I don't really know anything about politics, and I'll be one of the few new men. I'll be asked all sorts of questions—"

"I'll have to think about that. See me tomorrow."

"About what?" he asked, puzzled.

"That's what you say to them when you don't know the answer. Then we'll talk about it and decide on what position you will take."

"You'll be there?"

"Of course. I'll run your office. A couple of terms as state senator and then we take the next step."

Remembering his figure of speech of the horse and jockey, he asked, "You aiming to ride me to Washington?"

"That's right, Congressman. And maybe, after a couple of terms, if the time is right, you'll try for the Senate in Washington. Who knows, I might ride you right into the White House."

"The White House!" he chortled with delight. "Imagine me, President of these United States. And what will you be?"

"I'll be the First Lady, of course."

"You're my First Lady right now," he said soberly. "We going to make it official?"

"Of course."

"When?"

"Oh, sometime after the election."

"Why not right away? What's the point of waiting?"

"It's bad politics. I'm Jewish, so that means we'd be

married by a rabbi. There are a lot of bigots who might resent that and vote the other way just for spite."

"So why do we have to be married by a rabbi?"

"Because it's the bride's folks who make the wedding. You couldn't expect my father to arrange to get a minister and a church."

"How about a judge or a clerk of the court. I know—"

"No," she said decisively. "My folks would feel hurt and I wouldn't like it, either. I wouldn't think of us being really married."

"I'll do it any way you want, Sweetheart."

22

MORRIS HALPERIN SNEEZED, then sneezed again.

"You getting a cold, Morrie?" asked his wife.

"Nope." He sniffed deeply. "I've already got it."

"Then maybe you shouldn't go to the meeting tonight. Take a couple of those cold tablets of yours and go to bed."

"I'll take the cold tablets, but I'm going to the meeting. When I get home, I'll take a couple more and then go to bed."

"It's your funeral," she said. She went to the medicine chest. "There's only two left."

"I'll pick up another bottle at the drugstore."

The Board of Selectmen met every Wednesday evening throughout the year, and Morris Halperin as the town counsel was expected to attend. Before the public hearing in the Hearing Room, the five selectmen met in private for fifteen or twenty minutes in their office, a small room just large enough for their five desks, to discuss the agenda of the coming meeting and to agree on the order of business they would take up. Usually Morris Halperin joined them there to give whatever legal advice might be called for.

As he drove to the town hall, Halperin thought the pills had cleared his head. But no sooner was he in the enclosed atmosphere of the selectmen's office than he began to sneeze again.

"You catching cold, Morris?" asked Tom Bradshaw, the chairman.

"Or it's catching me."

"You know what you need? You need a good shot of whiskey." Bradshaw reached into the lower drawer of his desk and drew out a bottle and a glass. He poured and handed the drink to Halperin.

"Gee, I don't know. I've taken some pills."

"Go on, drink it, man. It'll do you a world of good."

It did seem to help. At least, he thought he felt better, but when they trooped into the Hearing Room, he found that he was perspiring profusely, although the room was not unduly warm. His head seemed full and his bones ached. When the meeting ended around ten o'clock, he decided not to join "the boys," that is, the selectmen and whatever senior town officials who had had occasion to be present, at the Ship's Galley for a drink. He excused himself, announcing he was going right home and getting into bed.

"You take a good shot of whiskey and maybe some more in hot tea," Tom Bradshaw urged, "and you'll feel fine in the morning."

"Right."

As he headed for home, he passed a drugstore, closed at that hour of course, but it served to remind him that he had no more cold pills. There was a drugstore in Lynn, however, that was open late, and although it was out of his way, he decided it was worth the extra fifteen-minute drive.

The druggist knew him, and when he asked for a glass of water so that he could take a couple of pills right then and there, he said, "You going home, Mr. Halperin? I mean you're not driving into Boston or anything like that, are you?"

"No, I'm going right home and going to bed. Why?"

"Well, these have antihistamine and they might make you a little drowsy."

"Oh? No, I'm going right home."

Millie Hanson looked up from the *Real Romance* she was reading as Tony D'Angelo went to the hall closet and removed his coat from its hanger.

"Where you going, Lover?" she asked.

"Going to get me some bread."

"But we got rolls, and the stores are closed— Oh, you mean money? You going to be gone long?"

He shrugged into the coat. "I don't know. Maybe not too long."

She knew better than to inquire further. She was curious, but she had a vague sense that when Tony was secretive about his activities, it was probably better that she shouldn't know. She heard the car door slam and the motor start up. Then she adjusted the pillows, stretched out on the sofa, and was soon lost in the problems Nurse Mary McTeague was having in pleasing her aged and peevish patient, Lady Haversham, and of getting her handsome son, Lord Haversham, to notice her.

Tony drove through Revere and through Lynn and then along High Street. When he came to the notice "You Are Now in Barnard's Crossing," he slowed down and eased over to the right. Then he saw the sign—Glen Lane —at a mere opening in the trees and brush that lined the road. If not for the sign, the road would be easily missed in the dark. He followed the winding, twisting lane for a hundred yards or so; then seeing an opening on one side, he steered into it and parked. He turned off his lights, lit a cigarette, and settled down to wait.

* * *

Shortly after leaving the drugstore, Morris Halperin had indeed begun feeling drowsy. Cars raced by him, and those going in the other direction blinded him with the glare of their headlights. Once or twice a car honked furiously at him, either because he had taken his foot off the gas pedal and slowed down unexpectedly, or perhaps because he had drifted out of the lane. So he decided to go home by way of Glen Lane rather than the highway—it was a short cut, but even more pertinent, he assumed there would be no traffic.

He put on his high beams and was driving along when suddenly he struck a pothole. As the front end bounced, he thought he saw a body on the road. He jammed on his brakes and brought his car to a halt. He lowered the window, stuck out his head, and looked back. There *was* someone there. He got out and walked back. He knelt down, uncertain what to do. In a low voice, almost a whisper, he called, "Hey, feller, you all right?" Then, "Can you hear me?"

If only a car would come along, he thought, he could flag it down. Then one of them could stay with the poor devil while the other went to summon help. But he realized that at this late hour it was most unlikely. Almost no one used Glen Lane at night.

He got back into his car and proceeded to the end of Glen Lane where it turned into Maple Street. He had thought he might ring someone's bell and ask to use the telephone. But all the houses were dark except for an occasional light coming from under drawn shades on an upper floor.

Down the street, almost at its end where it met Main Street, one house was lit up, Rabbi Small's. But he was reluctant to go there. He felt unsteady on his feet because of the pills or perhaps even because of the whiskey. He had

had only the one drink, and that was some hours ago, but might it not have interacted with the pills? The rabbi might think he was drunk.

He continued down Maple Street and then, just as he turned onto Main Street, he saw a police cruiser. He sounded his horn and the police car slowed down and stopped. A policeman got out and strolled over to his car.

Flashing his light, the officer said, "Oh, it's you, Counselor. Something the matter?"

"There's a body lying in the road on Glen Lane, just beyond the rise. I—I think he's dead."

"Glen Lane? Okay, we'll check it out."

Sergeant Drummond squatted down beside the figure on the road and insinuated his stubby fingers inside the collar. "He's dead, I figure, but you can't be sure. Look, I'll call in while you take some flares and set them up across the road. Better go down a ways. We don't want anyone driving into the lane and messing things up."

"Right." Officer Knowland fished in back of the cruiser. "How about the other end?"

"I'll set them up just as soon as I call in."

But when Knowland got back to the car, the sergeant was still there, sweeping the ground with his flashlight. "It's a hit-and-run, for sure. See all that glass. That's headlight glass. We better be careful not to touch anything. The lab boys can sometimes do wonders with stuff they pick up. Okay, now let's set up the flares at the other end. They'll be here in a couple of minutes."

As they proceeded down the hill, the sergeant swept the road from side to side with his flashlight. They spotted a car parked in the little siding.

"You suppose that's his car?" asked Knowland.

"Must be. Got out to take a leak, I suppose." He turned

and waved with his flashlight back toward the hill. "Probably behind that clump of trees at the top of the hill."

"Hell, Sarge, there's bushes all around. All he had to do was open the door, slew around in his seat, and let go."

Sergeant Drummond did not take kindly to disagreement from a subordinate, certainly not from the likes of Bill Knowland. "Some people," he said loftily, "are careful not to foul their own nests."

23

SOPHIA MAGNUSON SAT DOWN on the edge of the bed and watched her daughter brushing her hair at the dressing table. Addressing Laura's image in the mirror, she said, "We've seen so little of you these past weeks."

"I've been busy with the campaign," Laura admitted without turning, "but that's winding down now. There's still the election, of course, but we're not really worried now that we've won the primary. It's always been a Republican district. Of course, we can't relax, and there's still a lot of work to do, but everything is going well, and we're not running scared anymore."

"You say we as though—as though—"

She turned around to face her mother. "As though I'm standing for election myself? Well, I am. We're a team, Jack Scofield and I. He'd never have won the primary without me and he knows it. He probably would have dropped out of the race altogether if it hadn't been for me. And, of course, I couldn't get very far without him."

"I don't understand," said her mother. "When you first began this—this political work, it was our understanding, your father's and mine, that you wanted to get some practical knowledge of politics to complement the things you learned in school. That's what you told us, anyway. Your father thought you might meet some interesting young men that way and eventually you'd settle down and—and—"

"And get married?"

"There are worse careers for a woman," said her mother evenly.

"Oh, Mum, we're in the nineteen eighties."

"I said that was your father's idea. Your father is rather conservative. Most men are."

"But you don't agree?"

"Well, at least I recognize things have changed. I certainly have no objection to your going in for a career in politics, anymore than I would object to your planning a career in law or medicine. But, you must admit that politics is—is chancy. You can work and work and then if you lose the election, you're nowhere and it's all been wasted."

"Of course," said Laura eagerly. "That's why I'm going about it this way. I'm not interested in running for office myself because I'm not interested in the glory. Besides, a woman running for office is operating under a tremendous handicap. Her voice isn't suited for making political speeches. When she tries to express conviction, she's apt to scream. What's more, these days, any woman running for office can't help but get caught up in the Women's Lib movement, and I want no part of it. I just want the chance to do something important and worthwhile."

"You mean you want power and authority."

"All right. Why not? Power should go to those who can use it intelligently."

Her mother smiled. "You mean those who enjoy using it."

Laura returned the smile. "All right. So I had the idea of latching on to some political candidate that I could direct and steer. Oh, I don't mean that I planned it all out that way. I guess my original idea was that I might start by helping in a campaign, and then maybe becoming indispensable. But then I met Jack Scofield, and everything fell into place. He was perfect. For one thing, he was all alone."

"What do you mean?"

"I mean that he had no political backers, no pressure group that he was fronting for, so I had no competition. Even better, he was a bachelor, so there was no wife that I had to contend with. I could move right in and take over. And best of all, he had no position, no platform, no special ideas he was pushing, no reason for running except maybe the vague notion that it would give him some publicity that might help his law business, which isn't very lucrative right now."

"And also a desire for power and authority?" suggested Mrs. Magnuson.

Laura considered and then shook her head. "No, I don't think so, not in the sense of giving orders. He's more comfortable taking them. Oh, maybe not orders, but suggestions."

"You offered to direct his campaign, to back him—with money?"

Laura laughed. "Nothing like that. We just talked and I made suggestions, and before he knew it I had set up a headquarters. Well, that entailed his spending some money, and it worried him. You know, Mum, people who don't have much money are apt to be terribly anxious about running up bills."

"Doesn't he have any money at all?"

"Oh, a few thousand which he hoards like a miser. When I made arrangements for him to speak someplace, he agreed because it meant the possibility of campaign contributions." She chortled. "That's how I kept his nose to the grindstone."

Her mother smiled sympathetically. "But if he wins the election—"

"Almost certain, now that we've won the primary."

"Then he'll be going up to Boston, won't he. What will you do?"

"I'll run his Boston office, of course."

"You mean, you'll stay with him?"

"You bet I will. I intend to ride him to Washington as a congressman, maybe even senator eventually."

"But if he's a bachelor, he may want to marry and—"

"He'll marry me, naturally. You don't suppose I'm going to let anyone else horn in on my act."

"You mean he's asked you."

Laura smiled. "These days men don't. You sort of come to an understanding."

Her mother clenched her hands nervously. "Laura, have you been, you know—intimate with him?"

"Of course. You don't suppose I'd undertake to marry him if I hadn't."

They have no reticence these days, her mother thought. It's like trying out a car before buying. Well, maybe it *was* like that in some ways, she reflected, and perhaps it was for the best. "Do you love him?" she asked.

"Do you mean do I go all twittery when I think of him? The way I did when I was a college freshman over my math prof? No, and I wouldn't want to. But I like him a lot. We complement each other, and I expect we'll have a good marriage. And we'll have children. They're a political asset and good for campaign photographs, you know," she added impishly.

Mrs. Magnuson hesitated. Then, "He knows you're Jewish?"

"Of course."

"And it makes no difference to him?"

"Oh, Mum, it makes no difference to anyone these days."

"It might make some difference to your father now that he's president of the temple here."

"We'll have a rabbi do the ceremony, if that's what you're thinking. I made that clear to Jack from the beginning. Since it's the bride's family that makes the wedding, I felt we should do it our way."

"You mean he's willing to convert?"

"Oh no. I wouldn't let him, even if he were willing. It would handicap him politically. I wouldn't let him convert anymore than I would convert."

"Then I'm not sure the rabbi would do it," her mother said doubtfully. "I think there's some Jewish regulation against it."

"That's nonsense. Wasn't I a bridesmaid at Toby Berman's wedding a couple of years ago? The groom was Christian, and they had a rabbi, with a beard even, doing the necessary hocus-pocus. Although I do seem to remember that Toby said they had to get him from outside, from someplace in New Hampshire."

"Well, I'll talk to your father about it. Maybe you'd better have your young man come to dinner one night first."

"Will do," said Laura enthusiastically. "You'll see, you'll like him, and so will Dad."

"I hope so. I'm sure we will." Mrs. Magnuson got up to leave. At the door, she hesitated. "Did you consider the possibility of a purely civil ceremony, by a judge? Your father knows Justice Pearsall of the Massachusetts Supreme Court."

Laura pressed her lips together to form a thin line, a grimace which her mother knew meant that she had made up her mind and that there was no changing it. "It's my wedding, and I make the rules. And it's just as well that Jack recognize it from the beginning."

24

THE POLICE CHIEF OF REVERE, Cesare Orlando, Chezzie to his intimates, thought it only proper for the sake of regional harmony to report personally to Chief Lanigan. "Hugh? Chezzie Orlando. I thought I'd let you know that we took care of that hit-and-run business for you. I sent Detective Lance. You know him? He looks like an undertaker. Very good in these matters. Sympathetic, you know."

"I guess you have to use him a lot over in your town," Lanigan suggested.

"Now, now, Hugh. Remember, we're a city, not a small town like you. Anyway, Lance went to the address. It's an apartment house—residential hotel-type place. Not too clean, but fairly respectable. It isn't a place that gives us any particular trouble, you understand? Mostly transients, but there's some old people been living there for years."

"I understand."

"So there's a broad there. Looked decent enough. Not flashy. Maybe thirty-five or even a little older. They been living together for some months, she and the victim, Tony D'Angelo. These days that's practically a marriage."

"She got a name?" Lanigan reached for a scratchpad.

"Oh, I didn't give it to you? Mildred Hanson. But when the neighbors called her Mrs. D'Angelo, she didn't correct them. Lance said she seemed like a decent woman. He took her to the morgue and she identified the body all right."

"Get anything on him?"

"She said she thought he came from New York originally."

"And what he did for a living?"

"She wasn't too certain except that he was in politics."

"And you didn't know him, Chezzie?" Lanigan was frankly incredulous.

"He didn't operate local. He played with the big boys in Boston. So, for all that it's your job rather than mine, I called up a couple of pals, Italiano, as a favor to you—"

"Thanks, Chezzie, you're a sweetheart."

"Well, like I always say, one hand washes another. Anyway, he was a kind of gofer."

"For whom?"

"Sort of free lance, but he did a lot for the Majority Whip."

"Anything else?"

"Look, Hugh, it's not like it was a murder, it was a hit-and-run. Oh yeah, one thing I wanted to ask you. Your people searched him. What money did they find on him?"

"Just a few bucks. Hold it a minute. Here it is, twenty-seven dollars in his wallet, and some loose change, fifty-two cents in his right-hand trouser pocket. Why?"

"The girl hinted that he had a lot of money on him, or was supposed to have."

"I see. Where's the girl now? Where is she living?"

"She's staying on, as far as I can make out."

"She got any money? How's she going to live?"

"Well, she's a waitress. In the Blue Moon. It's a kind of cocktail lounge."

"Okay, Chezzie, thanks. Let me know if you hear any-thing."

"You know me, Hugh."

It was not that Detective Sergeant Dunstable was lazy, or a complainer, but he disliked doing useless work. So when he got his assignment, he said, "Jeez, Lieutenant, a guy would have to be out of his mind to have his headlight fixed in a local garage after he'd broken it in a hit-and-run."

"So how do you know he wasn't out of his mind? Maybe he was drunk and he hits the guy and thinks he's just gone over a bump in the road. And it's Glen Lane, remember, where there's more potholes than pavement. So he drives on home and goes to bed. And the next morning when he wakes up he sees he's got a broken headlight."

"Yeah, but—"

"So it would look pretty damn funny if we didn't bother to look, and all the time there's a gas station attendant who remembers putting in a sealed beam for a guy. And when one of the selectmen calls Hugh Lanigan on it, what's he supposed to say? 'Officer Dunstable said a guy would have to be out of his mind to have his headlight replaced if he'd been in a hit-and-run, so I didn't bother to check the local garages.'"

"It was just a thought, Lieutenant."

At the first garage, the proprietor shook his head and said, "It's about the hit-and-run, huh? Look, a guy would have to be out of his mind to replace a headlight locally where'd he'd just been involved in hit-and-run."

"How do you know about it?"

"Bill Knowland mentioned it at the coffee shop this morning."

"Oh. Well, it's routine, but we don't take any chances," the sergeant answered stiffly.

"Try Gately's," the garageman called after him.

142

On his fourth call, Sergeant Dunstable struck pay dirt. Mr. Glossop of Glossop's Automotive and Gas peered up from under sun-bleached eyebrows and said, "Yeah, I installed a sealed beam yesterday."

"You sure it was yesterday?"

Glossop removed his heels from the top of the desk and sat up, annoyance writ large on his long weatherbeaten face. "Sure, I'm sure it was yesterday. How often do I install a headlight?"

"Anyone you know?"

Glossop shook his head. "Black Chevy, a seventy-three, kind of beat up, but no one I know."

His assistant, Tom Blakely, a large, redheaded young man, who had been pumping gas came in to make out the charge slip for a credit card and volunteered, "I know him, Sergeant."

"You do? What's his name?"

"Well, I don't actually know him, but I've seen him around. Just a minute, Sarge."

He went to get the customer's signature on the charge slip, and Glossop took up the story. "He drove in sometime late in the afternoon and told me to fill her up. I noticed the broken headlight and asked him didn't he want to replace it." He looked up at the ceiling. "Maybe I used a little salesmanship on him. I kind of hinted that you guys were conducting like a campaign to see that all cars were properly equipped, and that if it got dark and he had only one headlight . . . Why should Sears get all the business?"

"Sure, keep it local."

Glossop nodded. "That's the way I feel. So he got out and came around and took a look at it and said something like he must have kicked up a rock, and sure, go ahead. So I unscrewed the rim and took out what was left of the light, the neck, you know—"

"What did you do with it, the neck, I mean?"

"In the trash barrel over there."

Tom Blakely returned. "Like I said, Sarge, I don't actually know him, but I've seen him around. I think he's new in town. He's almost as tall as me, maybe six feet, but he's on the thin side. He lives over on Maple Street, down the end, near Glen Lane. I've seen the car parked there. Last house, I think. He's got one of those stickers on the rear window, you know, Northeastern University, so I guess he goes to school in Boston."

The sergeant walked over to the trash barrel and poked a tentative hand in. Then he came back and said, "I want to use your phone to call the station house. I gotta get someone to come down here and take that trash barrel."

"What do you mean, take it?" demanded Glossop.

"Just for a little while. We'll return it. I just want them to empty it down there."

"And what'll we do in the meantime?"

"There's a carton out back we can use," said Blakely.

"What do you do on Maple Street?" Glossop asked him curiously.

Blakely grinned. "Oh, there's a girl I know lives there."

Later at the station house the sergeant reported to Chief Lanigan. "The guy lives on Maple Street, corner Glen Lane. Name is Kramer. You want me to go down and bring him in?"

"No, we'll wait until we hear from the Registry people. If it matches up with the rest of the glass, then we'll bring him in. Good job, Sergeant."

Sergeant Dunstable smirked. "Just a little straight detective work."

25

"WELL, WHAT DO YOU THINK OF HIM?" asked Mrs. Magnuson as she closed the door of their bedroom behind her.

Howard Magnuson temporized as he unknotted his tie. "He's a nice-looking fellow."

"He's obviously devoted to Laura," said Mrs. Magnuson. "He couldn't take his eyes off her all through dinner."

"Yes, I noticed that. Even when he was talking to me, he kept glancing over to her. Maybe it was devotion, but at the time it seemed to me he was looking to her for cues."

"Well, he was in a strange environment," said his wife defensively. "I can understand his not wanting to make any mistakes."

"Oh sure, I understand." He was trying hard to feel pleased. An innate reluctance to fool himself, however, made him add, "But you've got to admit he's no ball of fire."

"How do you know?"

"Well, I gathered from Laura he went into politics because he isn't making it in the law. And if it weren't for Laura, he wouldn't be making it in politics. He has a few thousand bucks that he inherited, and he puts it in a savings certificate. He buys a pink car because he was able to get it cheap. He—"

"Well, who says a ball of fire is necessary for a good marriage?" demanded Mrs. Magnuson, trying a different tack. "You take a girl like our Laura, determined, strong-minded, yes, stubborn, and if she were to marry a forceful man of determination, you know what would happen? They'd tear each other apart. Maybe Laura is smarter than you are, at least in what she needs in a husband. I'm inclined to think that Laura needs a man who is easygoing, flexible—"

"Why don't you say it?" he challenged. "Soft, weak, dumb."

"All right," she said calmly. "What of it? She'll guide him. She'll direct him. He'll know it and be grateful, and devoted. He has no money? So what? She has, and someday she will have a lot more. She wants a political career, and she'll get it through him. With her behind him, advising and directing him, my guess is that he'll make a successful state senator. After a couple of terms, he'll run for Congress, and he'll win, and they'll go to Washington. If you are interested in your daughter having a successful life, fulfilling herself, you'd be delighted with her choice."

"Sure, but dammit—"

"You know what would happen if she brought home the kind of man you think she ought to choose? A bright young doctor, or lawyer, or businessman? *He* would have a successful career, and she'd be at home, planning and arranging dinners for his friends. She'd be a housewife and that's all. He'd be doing the interesting things, and she'd be conferring with interior decorators on the color of the drapes. Look, Laura is the son we didn't have. And we brought her up that way. When all her friends were going off to finishing school, you insisted she go to college. If she were a man, you'd be delighted to have her go into politics."

"Yes, but—"

"Suppose she were a man. And he brought home a female Scofield. You'd be tickled about her putting what little money she had into a savings certificate, about her buying a pink car because it was cheap, because she kept looking to your son for proper cues before speaking."

"How about children?" he demanded.

"She'll have them."

"That's not what I mean. I'm thinking that children take after their parents. They might take after Laura, or they might take after him, or they might be a combination of the two. Are you looking forward to having grandchildren with minds and characters like Scofield's?"

She was nonplussed for a moment but recovered quickly. "Would you think of that if Laura were our son, Larry, and brought home a girl like Scofield? If you thought of children at all, you'd be thinking only if she were healthy enough to have them. Well, he certainly looks healthy enough, and for the rest, it's a matter of luck."

Magnuson sighed. "Okay, Soph, you win as usual." He smiled. "Let's hope it works out as well for them as it has for us."

She bridled. "Are you suggesting that I try to boss you? You know very well you make all the decisions."

"Yes, you only advise, but your advice is awfully persuasive. I suppose that's how Laura works it, too. Maybe all women do. Has she advised you when she's planning to get married?"

His wife shook her head. "She hasn't mentioned a specific date. I got the impression that it would be right after the election, though."

"That's only a month away. I better get cracking."

"Why, what do *you* have to do?"

"I've got to get it all set with the rabbi. Something tells me that might not be easy."

26

PAUL KRAMER OPENED the door and looked questioningly at the two men. One flipped a leather folder displaying a badge and introduced himself. "Sergeant Dunstable, Barnard's Crossing Police." He nodded to his companion. "Officer Norton. We come in?"

"Sure, I guess so. My folks aren't here if you want to see them."

"Is that your car parked on Glen Lane? The black Chevy?"

"Yes, that's my car."

"It was parked there last night?"

"Ye-es."

"And the night before?"

"Uh-huh." Then understanding came. "Oh, I know I'm not supposed to park overnight on the street from November on. But I figured Glen Lane didn't count because it's not really a street. Besides, it's sort of a little in"—he laughed nervously—"on what would be the sidewalk if there were a sidewalk."

"Why don't you park it in your garage, or in the driveway?" asked Dunstable curiously.

"Because my battery acts up sometimes, especially when it's rained during the night, and I have a hard time getting started. So I park on that little incline at the end of Glen Lane. That way I can get her started by letting her roll down."

"You lock your car when you park it for the night?"

"Yeah, sure." Again he laughed nervously. "See, I drive in every morning to school where I park on Huntington Avenue. I always lock it there because there's a lot of car theft. Around here I realize I don't have to be so careful because who would bother to pinch a beat-up seventy-three Chevy? But I got in the habit."

"Was it locked Wednesday night?"

"Yeah, I guess so." He thought a moment and then, "Yeah, I'm sure it was Wednesday night. Why? What happened Wednesday night?"

"You don't know? It was in the Lynn *Express.*"

"I don't read the *Express,* just the Boston papers."

"There was a hit-and-run on Glen Lane."

"So what's that got to do with me?"

"You had a broken headlight replaced yesterday, didn't you?"

"That's right. I was in Boston most of the day. It must have been broken there. Or I might have kicked up a stone while on my way home, or even on my way to Boston. I didn't know about it until the guy at the gas station pointed it out to me."

"And where were you Wednesday night?"

"I was right here, studying for an exam. I didn't even go out to eat. I made something right here."

"Well, suppose you come down with me to see Chief Lanigan, and you can tell him all about it."

"Okay, I'll follow you."

"No, you ride with me. Give Officer Norton your keys and he'll drive your car down."

The young man hesitated. "Is this a—are you arresting me?"

Sergeant Dunstable was elaborately casual. "I don't have no warrant. The chief just told me to ask you to come down. Of course, if you don't want to, I'll go back and report. Then he might decide to get a warrant, or have the Registry people get one."

Paul thought quickly. It was all a mistake, of course. Some guy got clipped by a drunk driver. There was probably glass found at the scene, so the police were checking up. He had had his headlight replaced, so he was one of those who were being questioned. Maybe others were also being questioned by the Lynn police and the Revere police, maybe even by the Boston police. He would explain that he had not even been on the road at the time. Maybe they would have him make a statement which would be taken down and typed up for him to sign. And that would be it.

"All right," he said, "let's go."

It was not that simple. Chief Lanigan, whom he was supposed to see, was not there when they arrived. He waited on a settee under the eye of the desk sergeant. Once or twice he got up, to stretch his legs, to get a discarded newspaper from the wastebasket in the corner. Once, when he went to the door, the sergeant asked him where he was going.

"I thought I might be able to get a cup of coffee someplace."

"The chief will be along in a minute. He wouldn't like it if you weren't here. You want a cup of coffee? Okay, I'll see what I can do."

The sergeant had someone bring coffee and even a doughnut from the wardroom. Paul did not feel that he was under restraint, and he had not been told he could not leave. But they had the keys to his car and there was no point in leaving until they were returned to him. It was after seven when Chief Lanigan finally arrived and asked him to come into his office.

He sat in the visitor's chair as Lanigan spoke on the telephone. Finally, Lanigan turned to him. With his hands behind his head, fingers intertwined, he teetered back and forth in his swivel chair. Then smiling, he said, "All right, now suppose you tell me all about it."

"I don't know what you want me to tell you."

"Just tell me what happened."

"Look, all I know is what the sergeant told me, that there was a hit-and-run on Glen Lane Wednesday night. I was home that night. I didn't go out at all."

"How did your headlight get broken?"

"I don't know. I go in to Boston every day and I park on Huntington Avenue, or the Fenway, or wherever I can find a place. Sometimes when you come back, you find your fender has been dented or scratched. You think they leave a note telling you to get in touch with them so they can make it good? They just ride off. So, somebody may have smashed my headlight Thursday, or even Wednesday, for all I know. Or while driving, I might have kicked up a stone. I don't know."

"If it happened Wednesday, wouldn't you have noticed it when you got in to drive to Boston Thursday?"

"I don't go inspecting the car every time I drive it. I just get in and drive off. I don't see the front of the car. If it was at night and I had to put on my lights, then I would have noticed it. But not in the morning."

Lanigan nodded. "That seems reasonable." He teetered for a while, his face thoughtful. "Where are your folks?" he asked.

"They're away."

"Yeah, but where?"

"I don't know right now. They're driving across the country."

"So if you want to get in touch with them, you can't?"

"Well, they said they'd call me every few days. They were supposed to tonight."

"I see. All right, let me tell you what we're up against. The victim in that hit-and-run died, which makes it vehicular homicide. That's serious. State detectives, Registry detectives, even the D.A.'s office all get involved. Now, there was glass found near the body, glass from a headlight that was broken by the impact. You know what we do with that glass?"

"Well, I saw a detective film on TV where the cops— I mean, the police match it up like—like a jigsaw puzzle."

"That's right. That's just exactly what we do. We match up the pieces and cement them together if they fit. You had your headlight replaced at Glossop's. It was the first one they'd done in days. The remains of your old light, they tossed in the trash barrel. Our man got those pieces and we put them together and cemented them the same way we did the others." Lanigan held up an admonishing forefinger. "Now, here's the situation: Those two cemented elements, with all the jagged edges, fit."

"But that's impossible."

"Just about, unless they were both parts of the same lamp."

"But I was home all that night."

Lanigan shrugged his shoulders, and then reached for the Miranda card stuck in the corner of his desk blotter.

"I want a lawyer," said Paul.

Lanigan nodded. "Yes, I think that would be a good idea." He slid his phone across the desk. "Go ahead. Call. I'll step out of the room if you like."

"I—I don't know any lawyers," said Paul sheepishly. "We're like new around here. I thought—er—I thought—"

152

"That we supply them? Well, when you're arraigned before a judge Monday, he will assign a lawyer to you if you don't have one. But—"

"Oh, I know one. That guy that just won the primary for senator."

"Scofield? You know Jack Scofield?"

"Well, I don't *know* him. But I was with my folks at a party one night and he came and talked for a few minutes. He said not to hesitate to call him if we needed help. My old man, I mean, my father, said afterwards that he seemed to be as much interested in getting customers, you know, like clients, as he was in getting votes. Maybe if I call him . . . I can't think of anyone else."

"Call him, but don't be disappointed if he refuses."

"Why should he refuse? It's law business."

"Yes, but it's a criminal charge, so he might want to talk to your folks first. Because in criminal cases lawyers usually expect to be paid in advance."

27

It was after ten when the rabbi and Miriam returned home from the Friday evening service. Even as the rabbi fiddled with the lock, they could hear the telephone ringing inside.

"It's probably a wrong number," said Miriam.

"Or it could be important," said the rabbi, "if they're calling on the Sabbath."

Still wearing his topcoat, the rabbi lifted the receiver. From the other end came the voice of a woman, hurried, breathless. "Rabbi Small? Oh, thank God, I got you. Forgive me for calling so late, but I'm—we're terribly worried. We didn't know whom to call, and then we thought of you. I'm Sally Kramer. We're neighbors. We moved into the house at the end of the street, Maple Street, right at the corner of Glen Lane. I would have called my next-door neighbor, but I don't know them. I mean, I don't even know their name. Of course, I don't really know you, either. I mean, you don't know me, but we're planning to join the temple first chance we get and—"

"What is it you want of me, Mrs. Kramer?"

The rabbi heard a male voice say, "Here, let me talk to

him." A moment later over the phone, "Ben Kramer speaking. My wife is kind of nervous, Rabbi. You see, we're taking a trip across country. I told my son, Paul, who's staying at home since he has to go to school, that we'd call him every Friday night around seven. Well, we called and there's no answer. Chances are he didn't think I'd start this Friday—we only left Wednesday morning—and he probably went out for the evening, but my wife is worried."

"What would you like me to do, Mr. Kramer?"

"Well, if you could walk down there and just look around. See if his car is there. It's a kind of beat-up black Chevy, a seventy-three, I think, and oh yes, with a Northeastern University sticker on the rear window, then it would mean he's home, and you could ask him to call us. If his car isn't there, and oh, it probably won't be in the garage or in the driveway, but right on the corner of Glen Lane, well then, it will mean he's gone away for the evening, and there's no need for my wife to worry."

"I see. And you'd like me to call you back and tell you?"

"Right. Now here's the phone number. You got a pencil and paper handy?"

"I don't write on the Sabbath, Mr. Kramer. But you give me the number and I'll repeat it, and my wife will remember it if I don't."

"That's swell, Rabbi. Believe me, we appreciate it. Now if you'll give me some idea of when you can go down there—"

"I'll leave immediately."

"Wonderful. Here's the phone number." He announced it and the rabbi repeated it aloud for Miriam to hear.

"So I'll expect to hear from you in half an hour? Three quarters?"

"Less than that, I imagine."

"Oh, that's wonderful. You'll reverse the charges, of course."

The rabbi walked to the end of Maple Street, looked around, and was back in twenty minutes. He dialed the operator and gave her the number. There was no need for him to consult Miriam about it since he had repeated it to himself over and over as he walked down and as he walked back.

It was Mrs. Kramer who answered.

"There was no car parked on the corner of Glen Lane, Mrs. Kramer. And there was no car in your driveway. I peered through the window of your garage and there *was* a car there, a small gray—"

"Oh, that's mine. Then he's probably gone off for the evening."

"There was a light in the hallway and one on the second floor," he went on. "So I rang the bell—I could hear it ringing inside—and I knocked, quite loudly, but there was no answer. Would you like me to notify—"

"No, that's fine," she said. "I told him to leave a light in the hallway and in the bedroom whenever he went out in the evening. Everything is all right, I guess. We'll call next Friday night. If—" she hesitated.

"Yes?"

"Well, if it's not too much trouble, and if you happen to think of it, we'd appreciate it if you dropped a note in the mail slot—oh, in the next day or two—telling Paul to be sure to be home for our call."

"I think I can manage that, Mrs. Kramer."

The Saturday edition of the local paper was not delivered until late in the afternoon, but the Smalls made a point of not reading it until after the Sabbath. But they went out that Saturday night, and it was not until Sunday morning before Miriam got around to leafing through it. In Police Notes, there was a short paragraph to the effect that Paul Kramer, Maple Street, had been arrested for the hit-and-run death on Glen Lane the previous Wednesday. She showed it to her husband.

"According to this he was picked up Friday afternoon. That means he was down at the station house while you were knocking at his door."

"M-hm."

"You've got to notify his folks, David."

"How?"

"Don't you remember the number they gave you?"

He shook his head. "It wouldn't do any good if I did. They're probably not there any longer."

"But the people they were staying with—"

"It was a hotel or an inn of some sort. There was a switchboard operator at their end when I called back."

"Oh, David, isn't there something we can do?"

"I suppose I could call Chief Lanigan. Since it was a hit-and-run, it may have been The Registry people who made the arrest, but he'd certainly know something about it. He's probably at home. I'll call him there."

When he got Lanigan on the phone, he asked, "Was it your people who arrested Paul Kramer?"

"That's right."

"Could you tell me about it?"

"What's your interest in the matter, David, apart from his being one of your people?"

"That in itself would be sufficient, I think, but in addition, his folks called me." He reported what had happened Friday night on their return from the temple.

"I see. Tell you what. I was on my way down to the station house. Matter of fact, you caught me just as I was leaving. Why don't I meet you there?"

28

As a member of the Executive Committee of the Police Chiefs Association, Cesare Orlando was in frequent touch with his fellow police chiefs throughout the state. He was currently engaged in promoting interest in, and more particularly attendance at, the conference scheduled to take place in Boston over Thanksgiving. Because response was usually lukewarm at best, he tended to broach the matter circuitously. So when he called Lanigan, he began by congratulating him on his success in solving the hit-and-run case so quickly.

"How'd you manage, Hugh?"

"Oh, by the good detective work that the Barnard's Crossing Police Department is noted for, Chezzie."

"Uh-huh. You might write up the case and read it at the conference in Boston."

"Yeah, I might do that if I can get hold of a pencil."

Orlando laughed. "If you're nice, maybe I'll give you one. Hey, I've got a bit of news connected with that case."

"Yeah?"

"M-hm. You remember the leaflet that some Good Government or Concerned Citizens group circulated just before the primary? Well, you know Tommy Baggio claimed it was a frame; that he was never at that dinner; and that it lost him the election. He yelled foul to the Election Commission, and they put a couple of detectives on it."

"You mean they do actually investigate these things?"

"Well, you know how it is. Usually it takes a little time before they get around to it, but Tommy has a brother-in-law on the commission, so he was able to get some pretty quick action. And do you know what they came up with? That the Concerned Citizens was none other than Tony D'Angelo, the victim of your little hit-and-run."

"Very convenient," said Lanigan.

"I know what you're thinking, Hugh. And I won't deny that occasionally a dead man is saddled with every unsolved crime on the blotter. We did the same thing during the war when I was in the Quartermaster's. Every time one of our cargo ships was sunk, we loaded it with every piece of lost or mislaid property we were accountable for. I remember one Liberty ship, ten thousand tons, mind you, that went down with about a hundred thousand tons of desks, type-writers, cranes, you name it. But this business on Tony D'Angelo is on the up-and-up. They got the printer and he named him."

"And Tommy Baggio bought it?" asked Lanigan skeptically.

"Well, he couldn't go in the face of the evidence. But he says he never even met Tony D'Angelo, wouldn't know him if he tripped over him. So he must have been working for someone else. He thinks it was the Fiore brothers on account of he managed to push through an ordinance putting a curfew of one A.M. on nightclubs. But they say why should they interfere with his election which would get him out of town, rather than staying on as a city councillor where he was a bone in their throat?"

159

"Seems reasonable. What about the woman? What does she have to say?"

"The woman? Oh, you mean Mildred Hanson, the broad he was living with? She took off. Doesn't mean anything. That kind moves around a lot."

"So the Election Commission is closing the case? Well, it's nice to know. Thanks for calling and telling me, Chezzie." Smiling, he hung up.

In less than half a minute, the phone rang. It was Orlando again. "Hey, you hung up on me."

All innocence, Lanigan said, "Why, I thought we had finished our conversation, Chezzie."

"Wise guy. Look, Hugh, you're coming to the meeting day after Thanksgiving, aren't you?"

"Why does it always have to be in Boston?"

"Where else? In Barnard's Crossing, maybe? Shall I put you and the missus down for a room?"

"What do I want a room for, Chezzie? I can get there in thirty or forty minutes' driving."

"Look, Hugh, we had to guarantee the Statler people a certain number of rooms."

"No, Chezzie. I'll try to make it, but I'll drive in."

"Well, I can put you down for the dinner, can't I?"

Lanigan relented. "All right, dinner."

29

"Kids!" Lanigan spat it out as though it were an obscenity. "You can't tell them anything. They think they know it all. We've got him dead to rights. Shattered headlight glass found at the scene matches up exactly with the broken glass taken from his car when he had his sealed beam replaced. I don't mean that it's merely the same type of glass. I mean that the pieces, the shards, match like in a jigsaw puzzle. Good enough? But he says he was home all evening and all night."

"Somebody else might have used his car," the rabbi suggested.

Lanigan shook his head. "He says no."

"I mean, without his permission."

Again Lanigan shook his head, this time smiling broadly. "He locks his car when he leaves it. And not only locks it, but attaches one of those patented gadgets that lock onto the wheel. I gather that where he usually parks during the daytime, in Boston on Huntington Avenue where the school is, there's a lot of car theft."

The rabbi nodded. "It does rather limit the possibilities, doesn't it? The victim, he was on foot, I presume. Who was he and what was he doing walking along Glen Lane at night? Was it some tramp, or—"

"That's a funny one," said Lanigan. "I just finished talking to the Revere police chief before you came. The victim was a small-time pol from Revere. According to the chief, he was the one who put out that leaflet which showed Baggio, the candidate for state senator, at some dinner with a bunch of gangsters. Did you see it? As to what he was doing in Glen Lane, our theory is that he was on his way to Salem and felt an urgent call of nature. So he swung into Glen Lane and then left his car to take a walk to relieve himself."

"I see." The rabbi thought for a moment. "I can also see that someone driving along a dark unused road like Glen Lane might not expect a pedestrian on the road—"

"That's it exactly," said Lanigan. "The guy might have even come out of the woods at that moment. Maybe, he was suddenly frightened by some animal like a—a raccoon—we have them, you know—or a skunk, and came dashing out of the woods and ran right into the car. See, in a hit-and-run there are two elements, the hit and the run. Now the hit is always an accident, of course. Nevertheless, we always start by assuming negligence on the part of the driver, and if he's had anything to drink, it becomes something more than a mere assumption. But common sense tells you that sometimes it's the victim's fault, and the most careful driver in the world couldn't have avoided an accident. But as a normal legal procedure we start on the assumption that the fault was the driver's. The Registry will suspend his license automatically, and it is the accused, the driver, who assumes the burden of proving he's innocent to get it back.

"Okay, so even where the victim dies and it's vehicular homicide, the penalty is not too severe. Usually, it's nothing more than suspension of the license for a period. But the second element—running off—now that's a conscious decision on the part of the driver, and it's criminal and reprehensible. He leaves his victim on the road, maybe in pain, and almost certainly in danger of having his condition get worse for lack of medical attention."

Lanigan leaned back in his chair, his hands folded in his lap, and stared at his visitor for some seconds. Then he sat up. "All right. We picked him up, and I told him what we've got on him. He's sitting right in that chair where you're sitting. I'm not bearing down on him, not bullying him, but telling him what we've got. And he denies it! Claims he never left his house, and says he wants a lawyer."

"It's his right," said the rabbi reasonably.

"Sure it is," Lanigan agreed. "And believe me, with all this Miranda business, I wouldn't take evidence from him without a lawyer present. But he sat there as cool as could be. When I was his age, if I found myself in a police station for any reason, I'd be in a panic no matter how innocent I was, if only about what my folks would say. But being arrested doesn't mean anything to these kids anymore. They go looking for it. You get pinched and you're a hero. It proves that you care about ecology or civil rights, or police brutality, or anything else that's high and noble. Just getting arrested implies that it's for some noble cause."

"Was he able to get a lawyer?" asked the rabbi.

"Strangely enough, he did."

"What's strange about it?"

"Well, lawyers usually ask for their money up front before they take on a criminal case. Of course, a lawyer who had done work for the family would probably take it on, but these people are new in town, and the boy didn't know of anyone local. Then he remembered that Jack Scofield had visited a house where they were guests when he was campaigning, so he called him and, to my surprise, Scofield agreed. Very decent of him, I thought. Whether he continues with him, is something else again."

"Why shouldn't he continue with him?"

"Well, Scofield didn't say anything to me, of course, but from the expression on his face, after he'd spoken to the boy, I got the impression that he wasn't too pleased. Maybe the kid tried to stonewall it, which could make it hard for his lawyer. See, in a case like this, the normal strategy is to admit the facts, giving them the best color you can—that the victim jumped out of the woods, or that you sounded your horn and he jumped the wrong way. Hell, the victim isn't around to deny it. As for running, he could say he panicked, or that he had gone home intending to call the police and then had blacked out. Almost anything. But if the boy keeps insisting that he never left the house, what can Scofield do for him?"

"So what is likely to happen to him?" asked the rabbi.

"You mean eventually?"

"No, I mean what is the procedure? I presume he'll be arraigned."

"That's right. Monday morning. We'll ask that he be held since it's a homicide, or at least we'll ask for high bail. Chances are though that the judge will release him on his own recognizance, since he's at school and not likely to run away. That's the tendency nowadays. When you come right down to it, bail never bothered the rich, only the poor."

"I'd like to see him," said the rabbi urgently, as though he expected to meet with opposition from the chief.

But Lanigan acquiesced at once. "Sure. Maybe you can talk some sense into him. Let me know how you make out."

30

"I AM RABBI SMALL, a neighbor of yours."

"Yes, I've seen you around."

"Your parents called me late Friday night when they were unable to reach you earlier."

"And you told them I'd been arrested." His tone, while not actually hostile, indicated that he felt that in the normal confrontation of the generations, parents and children, the rabbi was obviously on the side of the former.

The rabbi sensed the young man's attitude, but made no effort to mitigate it. "No-o, I didn't know at the time. I would have, of course, if I had known. They have a right to know. But I learned of your arrest only this morning when I saw the item in the newspaper."

"So you came down to—"

"To help in any way I can and to find out just what happened in case your parents decide to call me again. Do you care to tell me what happened?"

"So you can tell it to the police?"

The rabbi pursed his lips as he considered how to answer. "This is not a confessional and I am not a Catholic priest. If you told me you had committed a crime, I would certainly report it to the police. But since they feel that they have absolute proof that you did anyway, I don't see where it would make much difference. I would like to know what happened for my own interest and for your parents in the event they call me again. I'd want to put the best face possible on it."

"Nothing happened."

"All right. Then what did you do after your folks left?"

"My folks left early Wednesday morning around eight o'clock. I left for school a little after, about twenty minutes. I had classes most of the day and my last class was at three. I set out for Barnard's Crossing a little after four. I parked on Glen Lane the way I always do. There's a little incline there, like a sand and gravel pile that they may have used on the road, and if my battery acts up, as it does sometimes when it rains, I can get started by letting her roll down. My mother had left dinner for me and all I had to do was take it out of the fridge and heat it up. Then I washed the dishes and hit the books. I had a quiz the next day, and there was a lot of reading to do. I went to bed around eleven. The next morning we started out for school—"

"We?"

The young man looked nonplussed. "We?" he repeated.

"You said 'we,'" the rabbi pointed out.

"Oh, I meant me and the jalopy."

"Oh." The rabbi nodded to show he understood. "And you didn't notice that your headlight was broken?"

"Do you check the front of your car, Rabbi, before you get behind the wheel?" the young man shot back.

"I suppose not."

"Anyway, I took my exam, went to my other classes, and then headed for home around four. When I came to Barnard's Crossing, I noticed that I was low and I stopped for gas. It was while they were filling me up that one of the guys at the gas station noticed my headlight and I had him put in a new one. Then the next day a couple of cops came around and pulled me in. And that's what happened from the time my folks went off on their trip."

"You were at home on Wednesday from the time you came home from school? From about five o'clock on?"

"That's right."

"Then how do you account for the fact that glass from your headlight was found in Glen Lane?"

"How do I know it was from my headlight?" Paul countered.

"The police matched it up with the glass that was taken from your car at the gas station."

"How do I know it was my glass they got from the gas station? It could have been from another car."

"As I understand it, yours was the only sealed beam they replaced in the last few days."

"All right. How do I know it matches? You ever study anthropology, Rabbi?"

The rabbi shook his head, wondering at the sudden change in subject.

"Well, I took Anthro One last year. Somebody finds a tooth and a couple of yards away he finds a fragment of a jawbone. He fits the tooth into a hole in the jawbone. It doesn't fit well, you understand, not like a dentist would fit a tooth into a plate. It just goes in. And *voilà*, he then goes on to prove that the guy was five feet tall, walked upright, and was a hunter who lived on meat. They can draw you a picture of him and give you his whole life's history. Ever hear of Piltdown Man? Some joker planted the top of the head of a modern man together with the jaw of an ape. Or the other way around, I don't remember. And all these big-shot scientists studied it and made up all kinds of theories about it. Then, fifty years later—fifty years!—they discovered that it was a fake."

"And you think something of this sort might have happened in your case and that the police are trying to frame you? Why would they?"

"Oh, I'm not saying that they've got anything against me personally, although we are like new in town, and folks here regard you as a foreigner if you weren't actually born here. But I can see where the police might want to clear up a case and find it convenient to make things fit."

"Did you voice these objections to Chief Lanigan?"

"I thought the less talking I did, the better. Not without a lawyer present anyway."

"He's not stupid," said the rabbi when he met with Chief Lanigan. "He'd have to be exceedingly stupid to deny that his car was involved in the accident on Glen Lane in the face of the evidence you have."

"The fact is, David, when someone commits a crime and is caught, he's frequently exceedingly stupid in trying to explain it away, even though he may seem pretty smart in other matters."

"I'm afraid you're missing my point," the rabbi persisted. "If he merely wanted to disclaim responsibility for the hit-and-run, he could make out a good case to the effect that he didn't know about it. And he could make out a good case, because he parked his car right there at the end of Glen Lane, where anyone could spot it, instead of in the garage. Furthermore, he did not replace the broken headlight until the following afternoon. And even then, he replaced it at a local service station when he could easily have bought a sealed beam at someplace like Sears in Boston where he would not have been either noticed or remembered."

"Well, sure, but—"

"Now instead of that, he denies having been on Glen Lane at all, and insists he was at home the whole time."

"Then how does he explain the fact that the glass from

his headlight matches up with the glass found at the scene?"

The rabbi smiled. "He denies it. He questions whether it does match."

"Believe me, it does."

"He thinks the police are picking on him because he's a newcomer."

"That we framed him? Do you believe that, David?"

"Of course not."

"But you think he's telling the truth nevertheless. Okay, can you explain how he can be telling the truth in the face of the evidence we have?"

"Somebody else may have used his car while he was at home."

The chief shook his head vigorously. "No chance of that. He said his car was locked up and he had one of those gadgets on the steering wheel. A thief could have broken it, I suppose, but then he could not have fixed it again afterwards."

"I wasn't thinking of a thief," said the rabbi. "But suppose someone had taken it with his permission, and that person was the driver when the hit-and-run occurred."

"Then why wouldn't he say so?"

The rabbi shrugged. "Mistaken loyalty, perhaps." He thought for a moment. "Or chivalry. It might have been a girl."

"You have any reason for thinking it might have been someone else, other than Paul Kramer could not have been so stupid?"

The rabbi hesitated. "No really good reason, except for what may have been a slip of the tongue on his part. When he was telling me what he had done the last few days, he said he had stayed home all Wednesday evening to study for an exam that he was scheduled to take the next morning. Then he said, 'The next day, we went to school.' When

169

I asked him about the 'we,' he said he was referring to himself and the car."

"Could be. These kids think of their jalopies the way cowboys, at least movie cowboys, thought of their horses."

"Yes, but later he said, 'On the way home, I stopped for gas.' It seems to me that if he was accustomed to referring to himself and the car as 'we,' he would have been even more likely to use the plural when talking about getting gas."

Lanigan grinned. "I get your point, David. But it's mighty slim. What would you want me to do?"

The rabbi was troubled. "I don't know, except perhaps to keep an open mind and see if you can't check the possibility of his having had someone else with him Wednesday night."

Lanigan shook his head slowly. "I don't have the force for that kind of investigation. I can't just assign men to chase down every little possibility that might come to mind. If there is something of the sort involved, then it's up to him, because right now we've got him dead to rights."

31

HOWARD MAGNUSON HAD RETURNED any favors done him by Morris Halperin by throwing several bits of law business his way. "And remember," Magnuson had said, "you don't do yourself any good by charging the kind of fees you get locally. It's a Boston branch of a national company and they expect to pay adequately for services rendered." The connection was lucrative, and Halperin took pains to maintain it. Anytime Magnuson wanted to consult him, Halperin was available.

It was only natural for Magnuson, therefore, to confer with him before approaching Rabbi Small about Laura's wedding plans. Although the Halperins had planned to go to the movies, Morris had assured him, "No, I'm free this evening. I can come over anytime." Nor did he have to explain or apologize to his wife. She, too, was well aware of the importance of maintaining the Magnuson connection for its financial as well as social benefits. It was worth missing a movie if she could say to some friend who might phone, "We were planning to go to a movie, but Howard Magnuson—he's a client of Morrie's, you know—wanted to see him on some urgent matter that couldn't wait. And you know how Morris is about his clients. They come first."

Magnuson, although well aware that Halperin had reason to be grateful to him, always made a point of acting as if the lawyer were doing him a great favor by coming over. He greeted him effusively. "Come in, come in. Good to see you. I took a chance that you might just happen to be free."

"I was, Howard. Only too happy to come."

"I wanted to consult you—no, I'm putting it badly. This isn't a legal matter. And it's not really a temple matter either. And yet it is. But it's largely personal. I'd like your thinking on the subject, if you see what I mean."

"You'd just like to talk about it."

"That's it. That's it exactly. You see, my daughter, Laura, is planning to get married."

"Oh, congratulations. *Mazel tov.*"

"Er—yes, well, thank you. But there's a problem. The young man is not Jewish—"

"Ah, and he wants to convert?"

"No. That is, I don't think so. In fact, I'm quite sure he doesn't. I haven't spoken to him about it, but I gather from Laura that it's out of the question. She considers it bad politics. Did I say that he was in politics? Well, he is. There's no point in being secretive about it. It's John Scofield who just won the Republican primary for state senator. Laura thinks that the young man has a fine future in politics, and . . ." He looked at his guest questioningly.

Halperin nodded. "Yes, I know John slightly. And of course I know that your daughter worked very hard for him. It's harder for a Jew to get places in politics, at least in this part of the country. Maybe in New York, or in Florida, but not in Massachusetts. I can see where your daughter might think that if he converted it might hurt him politically. I suppose you would be violently opposed to her converting."

172

"*She* is. Naturally, I am too, but Laura is quite adamant about it."

"So, obviously it has to be a civil wedding."

"Well, that's just the point. Laura insists on being married by a rabbi. It isn't religion," he added as Halperin raised his eyebrows. "It's a promise she made to her grandmother, my mother-in-law, who established quite a liberal trust fund for her."

Halperin leaned forward in his chair. This was law business. "And the fund was contingent on her being married to a Jew?"

"No, not exactly. Laura was, let's see, about sixteen at the time. There was a wedding—my wife's cousin—that we all went to. She married a non-Jew, a fine man, and it's a good marriage. They have three children. The ceremony was performed by a minister, but it was really nonsectarian. I mean, there was no mention of Jesus, or anything like that, and it wasn't done in a church. It took place in the girl's house, in the garden actually. But my mother-in-law was quite upset. I gather that she spoke to Laura and made her promise that when she got married, it would be by a rabbi. Laura agreed. She was very fond of her grandmother Beck. Then her grandmother told her that she was setting up a trust fund for her that she could draw on when she was twenty-one."

"It was contingent on her being married by a rabbi?"

"Perhaps not legally, but Laura felt that she was morally obligated from the time she began to draw on the fund, five or six years ago."

"I see. Well, I don't know how much of it your daughter has drawn, but I don't suppose you'd have difficulty replacing the money."

"No, it wouldn't do. Laura is determined."

"I see. Well, there are some Reform rabbis who do occasionally consent to participate with a minister or a priest in what you might call an ecumenical wedding. Offhand, I don't know of any Conservative rabbis who have. And certainly no Orthodox rabbis."

"And Rabbi Small is of course Conservative," said Magnuson.

"With leanings towards Orthodoxy," Halperin added.

"It wouldn't have to be done in the temple, you know."

Halperin shook his head. "It wouldn't make any difference to Rabbi Small. I'm sure he wouldn't agree."

"But dammit, this kind of thing must come up every now and then."

"Of course. These days it's more common than not. My own nephew—"

"Married a Gentile?"

"Uh-huh. They had a civil wedding, so there was no problem. But my folks were pretty upset. Then there was Ben Joseph's niece, and Marty Slobodkin's sister, and Ira Lamport's brother and—you know something? I'll bet there isn't a single member of the board whose family doesn't have an intermarriage—a brother, a sister, a nephew, a niece, a cousin. I've heard that it's one in every two marriages."

"And what did they all do?"

"Different things. In some cases the Gentile gets converted. Sometimes it's the Jew who does. Or maybe it doesn't constitute an actual conversion, but some of them get married in a church by a minister or a priest. I understand the Catholics have eased up a little. They used to require a written agreement that the children would be brought up Catholic. I don't think they do now, at least not a written agreement. Most of the time, I guess, they have a civil marriage. There's a rabbi up in New Hampshire, I think, that makes quite a thing out of the intermarriage business. He goes all over New England, I've heard."

"I might want to contact him," Magnuson mused.

"I can get his name and address easily enough."

"Good. But of course I'll have to speak to Rabbi Small out of common courtesy."

"Of course."

"I'll explain the situation to him and ask him to officiate."

"He'll refuse."

"Then I'll tell him I'll get someone else."

"He won't like it," said Halperin.

"I don't like it myself. Not any part of it. Frankly, I don't like the idea of my daughter marrying John Scofield. I don't like the idea of her insisting on having a rabbi marry them when they could get some judge or clerk of the court to do it. I don't even like the jesuitical hair-splitting on my daughter's part that's involved. Because obviously when my mother-in-law made her promise that she would be married by a rabbi, she meant that she should marry a Jew, born or at least converted. But in the course of a busy life, I've run up against many things that I didn't like, but had to take anyway."

"Yeah, but the rabbi may feel that he doesn't have to take this one."

"So what can he do?"

"I don't know, except refuse."

32

PAUL KRAMER WAS ARRAIGNED Monday morning in the Salem court. Sergeant Dunstable was present, both as the arresting officer and because he had escorted the defendant from the Barnard's Crossing station house. The assistant district attorney, Charlie Venturo, argued for high bail on the ground that it was a serious crime, homicide. John Scofield, appearing for the accused, argued that Paul had no previous record, that he was in school, and there was no reason to suppose that he would not be available for trial.

The judge nodded and addressing Paul, said, "I'm setting the trial date for November twentieth. I am releasing you on your personal recognizance. You'll receive notice of the trial through the mail, but even if you don't get it, that's the date I'm putting you down for and you're to be here. Do you understand?"

"Yes, sir, I mean, Your Honor."

Scofield was extremely pleased with himself inasmuch as he had bested Venturo even though it was in a minor matter. He could not help voicing his pleasure to his rival as they left the courtroom. "I got you this time, Charlie."

Venturo, who from long experience had expected nothing else, smiled and said, "You win some and you lose some. You won, so you buy the drinks." Later as they sat in the café, he asked, "How'd you happen to get involved in this one, Jack?"

To which Scofield replied, "The kid called me. He says he met me at some party where I stopped in for a few minutes when I was campaigning."

"Did he come up with any money?"

"No, but I figure when his folks get home, I'll talk to them. I'm sure they'll pay my fee."

Venturo nodded. "I suppose in private practice, sometimes you got to work it that way."

Sergeant Dunstable returned to Barnard's Crossing and reported to Lanigan, who was neither surprised nor indignant. "Naturally. The boy is no criminal. They let them go in a lot worse cases without bail. Hell, they'd have no place to put them if they didn't."

He made a note of the trial date on his calendar, and put the case out of his mind. In spite of the doubts Rabbi Small had expressed, he felt that he had an iron-clad case.

But the next afternoon, the desk sergeant poked his head through the door of Lanigan's office and said, "Somebody here who has something on the Glen Lane hit-and-run case, Chief."

"Okay, send him in."

"It's not a him, it's a her."

"Then send *her* in."

The sergeant beckoned with his head, and then stood aside to admit a young woman in jeans and a sweatshirt, the arms of which were pushed up to the elbows. Her obviously bleached blond hair was curled Afro style, brushed back in such a way as to expose both ears from which jangled jet earrings. She was wearing a colorless lipstick which gave her lips a moist pink look. Her eyes were carefully shadowed in blue above and green below, and the edges of the eyelids were lined in black. Her jeans were worn seductively—very tight across the seat—and as she moved to the chair in front of the desk, her breasts, unhampered by a bra, jiggled underneath the sweatshirt.

"I just came to tell you that you're all wrong about Paul Kramer. He didn't do it."

"Is that so? How do you know?"

"On account I was with him that night. From around quarter past eight on. And he never left the house."

Lanigan, who had been lazing back in his swivel chair, leaned forward and sat upright. He eyed her keenly. "What's your name?"

"Fran Kimball."

"And you live . . . ?"

"On Elm Street."

"Elm Street? Tom, no, Ted Kimball?"

"He's my father. But he doesn't live with us anymore."

"About three or four years ago?"

"More like six," she said.

"All right. Now, you say you were with Paul Kramer that night. What do you mean? Until when?"

"Until next morning when we went to school together."

"You were there all night? You spent the night with him?"

"Uh-huh."

"Did your mother know?"

"Of course not. I had my friend Beth McAllister cover for me. See, I had this quiz the next day, that is, we both did, I mean Paul and I."

"You go to Northeastern?"

"That's right. I'm a senior in Business Management. Paul is just a sophomore, but we take the same course in American Literature on account of it's required. We sit next to each other because our names are close. Alphabetically, you know, Kimball, Kramer. And sometimes, I hitch a ride from him. So, that day, Wednesday, we were driving home and we talked about the quiz we had to take the next day, and he said he was prepared. He's a brain—"

"A brain?"

"I mean, he studies a lot. I was going to use the College Outline. That's a book that gives you a kind of outline of all the reading. But when I got home, I found I didn't have the book. I mean, the College Outline book. I'd left it in my locker at school. So naturally I called him and asked if I could borrow his, and he said he didn't have one, that he didn't use one. He just reads all the stuff."

"Imagine," Lanigan murmured.

"So I asked if maybe I could go over to his place and we could study it together. He'd told me his folks had started on a long trip across the country that morning, so I knew it was all right on account of he'd be alone."

"Did he suggest you spend the night with him?"

"Oh no. He's awfully young, maybe nineteen."

"And you."

"I'm twenty-two."

"Spending the night with him was your idea, then?"

"Yeah, kind of. I didn't plan to, you understand. It just happened that way. See, I didn't tell my mother I was going to his house, on account of she'd ask all kinds of questions, like who was going to be there and what time I was coming home. I told her I was going over to Beth's house. When I got there, I called Beth and asked her to cover for me—"

"Just how does that work, covering for you?"

"Oh, you know, if my mother should call, Beth would say I was in the bathroom, or that I had stepped out for a minute, and that she'd have me call her back. Then she'd call me at Paul's house—I gave her the number, see—and I'd call back."

"And did she call?"

"Uh-uh. But then around ten o'clock, I called her, I mean, my mother, and told her I was staying over at Beth's and I'd be going to school from there."

"I see. And this was around ten o'clock?"

"Just about. Yeah, because Paul wanted to turn on the TV for the ten o'clock news." Her forehead wrinkled as she concentrated. "Yeah, just before ten, on account of when I got back from the phone, the news was just starting. See, by that time, I could see there was an awful lot of work to be done, and it would take way after midnight. He was outlining all the reading for me, and I was writing it all down. He knew it all. Awesome!"

"All right. And when did you finish?"

"Must've been around one. Yeah, easily."

Lanigan leaned back in his chair and studied her. Finally, he said, "And when you were finished you offered to go to bed with him in payment, or was that understood from the beginning?"

"No such thing." She was quite indignant. "We just went to bed. Not in payment, but because he was—well—nice. He's awfully young, of course, but he's good-looking, and well—nice."

"I see. So then the next morning . . ."

"We got up, and there was some orange juice in the fridge, and he made some coffee and toast, and we went off to school."

"You went out to the car together?"

"That's right."

"The car was locked?"

Again her brow furrowed as she tried to remember. "Yeah, that's right, I went around to the passenger's side and waited until he got in and reached over to open the door for me. Then he took off this hook he has on the steering wheel, and we started off."

"I see. Now, what made you come in today?"

She looked her obvious surprise. "Well, when I heard . . . Naturally, I had to come and tell someone—"

"Did he ask you to?"

"Oh no. He was upset when I told him I was going to. He didn't want me to. He was like embarrassed. You know, he's awfully young."

Chief Lanigan pursed his lips as he thought about the situation. What did he actually have? The girl's story, which she could have cooked up with Paul Kramer. After all, they were fellow students and, by her own admission, lovers.

Lanigan got up and went over to the town map, which was pinned on the wall. He studied it for a moment and then pointed. "Here's Elm Street. And you live right about here if I remember."

"Yeah, near Laurel Street."

"And you left your house at . . . ?"

"Around eight o'clock."

"And you walked down Laurel to Maple—"

"No. I went down Elm to Main, and then turned up Main to Maple."

"Why did you go all the way around when you could have gone to the Kramer house directly by walking up Laurel?"

She made a moue of annoyance at his stupidity. "Beth lives on Gaithskille Circle, so I had to go in that direction, didn't I?"

"I see. Well, did you meet anyone you know? Did you stop to talk to anyone?"

She thought for a moment, and then shook her head vigorously so that her earrings jangled. "No."

Lanigan nodded. "Then no one knew you were at the Kramer house that night."

"Well, Beth McAllister knew," she said.

"Not really. All she had was a telephone number which she had no occasion to use. Your mother didn't know, and no one saw you go in, or come out the next morning?"

Again she shook her head and then added with a little lascivious smile, "Well, Paul knew."

"Yeah, I guess he'd know. All right. I might have you come in to make a statement which I'd have typed up and you could sign."

"Oh! Would my mother get to know about it?"

"It depends. She might."

"Because I wouldn't want her to. I mean—well, you know what I mean. On the other hand, I don't want Paul to go to jail or anything, when he didn't do it. I mean, that's good citizenship, isn't it?"

33

ALTHOUGH MAGNUSON HAD SAID he would speak to Rabbi
Small as a matter of courtesy, in back of his mind he had
the thought that the rabbi would probably agree to perform the ceremony. In his short acquaintance he had found
Rabbi Small to be a reasonable man. He had done him a
favor, an unsolicited favor, in getting him a sizable salary
increase. And the rabbi knew it. Well then . . . In Magnuson's code, if you did someone a favor, he owed you one.
In accepting a favor, one incurred an obligation, a debt, and
anyone who failed to make good was an ingrate and no
gentleman.

So when he came to see the rabbi, it was with full expec-
tation of success, and he assumed the discussion would be
on matters of detail. "I have something of a problem," he
began.

"If I can be of any help . . ."

"My daughter is getting married—"

"Oh, *mazel tov!* When is it planned for? Is it a local
boy?"

"Yes, he's local all right—"

"The reason I ask," the rabbi went on, "is because if at

all possible, I like to see both the prospective bride and groom—"

"He's the Republican nominee for state senator from this district."

"But, that's—"

"John Scofield," Magnuson supplied.

It came to the rabbi that this was why Lanigan expected Jews to be pushing for Scofield. But quietly all he said was, "I didn't realize he was Jewish."

"He's not."

"Ah, I see. He's planning to convert."

"I'm afraid not, Rabbi. Conversion is out of the question."

The rabbi was silent for a moment. "Then you're planning a civil ceremony?" he asked quietly.

"Laura insists on having the ceremony performed by a rabbi. I realize you can't do it in the temple," he went on hurriedly, "but as a matter of fact, from the beginning we planned on having it in the house, or in our garden if the weather is right."

"It can't be done at all," said the rabbi flatly.

"You mean—"

"I mean that if it's a religious wedding, then it has to be between two Jews. If one of the principals is not Jewish, then you can no more have a religious wedding, a Jewish religious wedding, than if both were non-Jews. It's a contradiction in terms."

"But—but—look here, Rabbi, I know it's religion and religion is important. But when a couple comes to see you about getting married, do you question them about their beliefs and practices, or do you say, 'Ah, congratulations, Mr. Goldstein and Miss Cohen. When do you plan to have the wedding? Will you be using the vestry?' And yet they might both be out-and-out atheists."

"True."

"Then—"

The rabbi sighed. "It's most unfortunate that outsiders, especially our worst enemies, seem to have a better understanding of the situation than do many Jews. At least they realize that it is a matter of ethnicity; that a Jew is a Jew, even if he never sets foot in a synagogue. We are a tribe, a family, if you will, the descendants of Abraham, Isaac, and Jacob. In some primitive tribes, marriage is always with someone outside the tribe. Exogamy, the anthropologists call it. Among other tribes, the practice is to marry only within the tribe. Endogamy. Well, we are endogamous. That is the tradition, the practice, the law of our tribe. Because we believe that we—as a tribe, mind you—entered into a compact with God. The requirement of this contract on our side is that we practice Judaism, our religion. When one of us marries an outsider, we require not only that he undertake to join with us in keeping our part of the bargain, but also that he become one of us—by adoption into the tribe.

"Judaism is a system of morals and ethics as well as of ceremonials, rituals, and liturgical practices, which are intended primarily to fortify us in the practice of our ethical code. The basis of this ethical code is the commandments given us by God, the result of our compact with Him at Sinai. Some Jews obey these commandments to the letter" —he smiled—"religiously, you might say. And some obey some of them and some pay no attention to them at all. But the obligation is there.

"There are also some Gentiles who obey them, but that does not make them Jews. They come by them in a different way. Perhaps they have worked them out as leading to a good life, or because they consider them sensible. But because they have worked them out on their own, they can also change them. We can't because we have made a contract with God, and these are the terms that we accepted.

When you make a business contract with someone and he fails to carry out all the terms of the contract, that doesn't mean that the contract is nullified, only that he is in default. And when it is with a group, a corporation, rather than an individual, it isn't abrogated when one member of the group leaves.

"A Catholic who does not believe in the tenets of his church and does not practice them, is not a Catholic. But a Jew who does not obey the commandments and never enters a synagogue, is still a Jew. And he might marry the daughter of the Chief Rabbi of Israel. The rabbi wouldn't like it, perhaps. He might try to prevent it. He might even disown his daughter, but he would not mourn her as dead, as he would if she were to marry a Gentile."

Magnuson shook his head. "I don't understand you, Rabbi. You'd rather have her undergo a civil marriage—"

"I'd rather have her marry a Jew."

"I know, but in the context of the present situation, does it have to be a civil marriage? And the children, I presume, would be—according to Jewish law—bastards?"

"Oh no." The rabbi was shocked. "The children would be Jews, since they would be the children of a Jewish mother. Not if it were the other way around, you understand. That is, not if the father were Jewish and the mother Gentile. Then they would be Gentile, even if they were brought up as Jews and were most observant. As a matter of fact, even if there were no marriage at all, they wouldn't be bastards, according to Jewish law. Only the issue of adultery or incest are."

"Well, in my case, it's out of the question. Laura is determined to be married by a rabbi. I don't understand you. Isn't half a loaf better than none?"

"Your half a loaf is like being a little bit pregnant," said the rabbi. "I could not participate in the wedding ceremony."

"I suspect that not all rabbis feel as you do," said Magnuson.

"No Orthodox or Conservative rabbi would perform the ceremony. I've heard that some Reform rabbis do, but none that I know of around here."

"I'm sure that I can find one who will," said Magnuson grimly, "even if I have to bring him here from some distance. What else can I do?"

"You can resign," said the rabbi quietly.

"Resign?"

"As president of the synagogue," said the rabbi firmly.

"Why should I resign?" He was angry and he had reddened.

"Because it would be the honorable thing to do," said the rabbi. "As president of the temple, you are in effect the leader of the Conservative Jewish community, and you are planning to do something that is contrary to Conservative Judaism. If your daughter were to go off to New Hampshire or Vermont, or wherever this compliant rabbi lives, and get married there, I would sympathize with you and I would understand. One cannot always control the behavior of one's children. But you are planning to bring another rabbi here to Barnard's Crossing, into my area, and into your area, I might add, to do something I consider wrong. That action I cannot pass over, not when it's done by the president of the temple. I must forbid it." He had not intended to go so far, but had been led on by his own rhetoric.

As for Magnuson, he suddenly felt at ease. In a sense, he was on familiar ground. On more than one occasion he had taken over a company and found that the previous owner, who had retained stock in the company, or the manager or some of the older employees disapproved of changes he had introduced. Sometimes it had involved a fight in the Board of Directors. He flattered himself he knew his way around in boardroom politics. He rose and reached for the door-knob. "No, Rabbi, *I* am not going to resign." He started to open the door when he had another thought. "And under the circumstances, I'd rather you didn't come to the board meetings from now on."

34

"YOU GOING TO CALL THE D.A.?" asked Lieutenant Eban Jennings lugubriously when Lanigan had finished telling him about Fran Kimball. He was tall and spare, with watery blue eyes and a prominent Adam's apple that bobbled in his neck when he was excited.

"Well, let's just think about it. How do I know she's telling the truth?"

"A girl wouldn't lie about a thing like that, Hugh. No girl is going to admit she spent the night with some guy unless she's forced to, let alone volunteer it."

"Pshaw, Eban, things have changed since you were chasing girls. It don't mean a thing to them since the pill. Women's Lib. They even lie about it the same way as men do. Take a guy who's a big shot, a movie actor, say, or a rock singer or an important pol. Well, a girl might claim she slept with him when she hadn't, just to improve her status."

"I didn't get the impression that this Paul Kramer was a big shot."

"Maybe not. But I can imagine this Kimball girl being willing to do him a favor. She said he was a brain. And he seemed like a bright kid. All right, so suppose he promises to help her with her schoolwork in exchange for her coming to see me and giving me a song and dance of having been with him all night. Remember, we can't check on her story. We can't ask her ma. She'll say she was with her friend"—he glanced at his notes—"Beth McAllister. And if we ask this McAllister, all she can tell us is that she was given a phone number to call, which, mind you, she didn't have occasion to use."

"Well, you could ask her mother."

"Ask her what?"

"You could just ask her if her daughter spent the night at home that Wednesday."

Lanigan shook his head. "Chances are she didn't. I'm sure she would have thought of that. All right, so then I see the McAllister girl. And the chances are she won't squeal unless we put some pressure on her. Then suppose she admits she covered for her friend Kimball. 'She gave me a telephone number to call.' 'What's the number?' 'I don't remember. I wrote it down someplace, but I didn't bother to save it.' "

"But suppose it's true."

"That means that the driver of that car had to continue on Glen Lane, stop at the corner, get out of his car, go over to where Kramer's car was parked, smash the headlight, and then gather up the shards, bring them back to his car, turn around, go back to where the body is lying, drop the glass, and then run off. Now, why would anyone do a fool thing like that for?"

"Well, he might have hated Kramer."

"He'd have to have hated him an awful lot. Think of the chance he was taking. And Kramer is new in town. He's been here just since school started. Probably doesn't even know anyone around here."

Jennings wiped his eyes with his handkerchief, pushing

his glasses up on his forehead to do so. "It's not that much of a chance. He drives back up Glen Lane and he stops. Well, if anyone sees him, he says he's seen the body in the road. So then if he squats down to put the glass near the body, and somebody comes along just then, well, it's only natural to squat down to see if the guy is alive." He replaced the handkerchief, rolling in his chair to reach his back pocket. "I'll admit it's a bit unusual, but—" He stopped suddenly as an idea occurred to him. His Adam's apple bobbled nervously. "Look, Hugh, what if it was the girl that the guy, the driver, I mean, was sore at? Suppose he had a thing for the girl. He's jealous, get it?"

"So why would he want to take it out on Kramer?"

"Well, you know, you see a guy with your girl and—"

"And how would he know that she was with Kramer?"

"Maybe this McAllister girl mentioned it, or maybe he saw her going into the house."

"Possible," said Lanigan.

The two sat in silence. Then Jennings said, "Hey, do you realize that if the girl's story is true, we'll have to start from the beginning again."

Lanigan nodded gloomily. "And we don't even have a lead."

"There's Morris Halperin," suggested Jennings.

"The town counsel? Go on. What have we got on him?"

"Well, he was there. He's the one who reported it," said Jennings stubbornly. Then, excitedly, "That night I was at the selectmen's meeting, and he was there. He looked pretty rocky. Had a bad cold. Then afterwards, you know, the selectmen and some of the town officials go on to the Ship's Galley for a beer, and I went along. And they were kind of laughing about Halperin. Seems that Tom Bradshaw gave him a good stiff shot of whiskey for his cold, and some of them thought he acted kind of tiddly at the meeting."

"So?"

"So, maybe that one drink got to him. Maybe he was a little drunk."

"What? One drink?"

"Sure, if it was a big one, and if he wasn't used to it, and if he wasn't feeling so good, and maybe had taken some pills. Or maybe he stopped off somewhere and had another. He didn't go right home, that's for sure, because what was he doing in Glen Lane if he was headed home? That's out of his way. So, let's say, he's a little drunk and he runs into this guy, not expecting to see anyone in the middle of the road in Glen Lane, especially at that hour."

"Yeah, but why would he want to break somebody's headlight and put the blame on him?"

"Because a thing like that could kill his career."

"Anyone can have an accident. It's my guess if Halperin had one, he'd report it to the police."

"But if he were driving under the influence—or thought he was . . ."

"Well . . . But he did report it to the police. He told the men in the cruising car."

"Sure, because he saw them and thought maybe they saw him. But he didn't get out of his car or anything. He just said there was a body on the road. And naturally they went right off to take a look."

"Hm." Lanigan chewed on his lower lip. "It won't do any harm to check it out. But I can't just confront him, not the town counsel. We'll have to set it up. I could call him in for a statement. Then while his car is in the parking lot, you could give it a good lookover."

Jennings grinned. "If I happened to be there when he drives in, and if there are a lot of cars in the lot, I could invite him to park right in the garage."

"All right, let's try to work it that way. In the meantime

I've got to call the D.A. and tell him about this Kimball girl."

"And what will he do?"

"Well, he's supposed to notify defense counsel who can then do what he pleases."

35

"I MUST ADMIT," said Howard Magnuson solemnly when Morris Halperin had taken his seat, "that I misjudged Rabbi Small. I thought he was a gentleman. I was mistaken."

"Oh?"

Magnuson nodded. "I assumed that he'd make an effort to work something out for me. But no, he was adamant. I admitted that I was in a bit of a pickle, but the man wasn't the least bit concerned. When I asked him what I could do, do you know what his answer was? He told me to resign."

"He did?" Halperin was shocked, but being a lawyer and hence used to getting garbled versions of facts, he asked, "Just exactly what did he say?"

Magnuson recounted the conversation with the rabbi. "I accepted his position that he could not himself perform the ceremony, although considering that some rabbis do it without getting unfrocked or struck off the rolls, or whatever you call it, I had reason to feel that he was being excessively dogmatic. I accepted his stricture that the ceremony could not be performed in a synagogue. But his insistence that I could not even have it done in my own house by a rabbi of my own choice because it is in his territory and within his jurisdiction, that was a bit much. This I cannot tolerate. I mean, the next thing I know he might want to inspect my kitchen to see if we use two sets of dishes."

Although Halperin's natural inclination was to agree with Magnuson, as a fair-minded man he felt that he ought to explain the rabbi's position. "I think the rabbi was trying to tell you that holding the ceremony in your house was unseemly, since you were the president of the congregation. From his point of view, it's as though—"

"I know what he was trying to tell me," said Magnuson severely. "Do you agree with him?"

Halperin realized that Magnuson was demanding that he declare himself. It occurred to him that the better part of valor was to straddle. He shrugged slightly and smiled. "As far as I'm concerned, it's just a ceremony and I'm not much of a one for ceremonies. It's the marriage that's important rather than who says what and where in order to effect it. I'm a lot more concerned with the question of who's boss, the congregation through its elected representatives or the rabbi. I'm interested in the question of whether a rabbi can ever order, or even suggest, that the president of the congregation resign. Who is supreme, the rabbi or the congregation? In other words, who can fire whom?"

Magnuson was no fool. He saw the subtle shift in direction that Halperin was suggesting. "Do you think the rest of the board are apt to look at it that way?"

Halperin thought for a moment. "I think so, if it's pointed out to them. Of course, if you go ahead as planned, and get some rabbi from outside, I presume Small would register his opposition by resigning. Then he'd explain to the congregation just why he was resigning. And that could create a stink."

"True. But we don't have to play it that way."

"No?"

"I've been in this type of situation before. When you take over a company, and you can't make some of the key people see things your way, you know what you do? You fire them."

"But you can't fire the rabbi just because he won't officiate at your daughter's wedding."

"Of course not. But we can fire him for challenging the authority of the board, by calling for my resignation. That is, if they go along."

"But he has a contract."

"No problem. We would simply continue to pay his salary until it runs out. It hasn't very long to run. We could even pay it to him in a lump sum. If we call on him to resign, he'll naturally feel it necessary to explain to the congregation, at least to that part of it that comes to the Friday evening service. What's he draw at a service? Seventy-five? A hundred? But the next week there would probably be two or three hundred attending, and he'd explain again. Then the fat would be in the fire. But if we dismiss him because—because we have lost confidence in him, my guess is that he won't say a word, except good-bye, maybe. He's pretty damn proud. I doubt if he would suggest that it was because of his refusal to officiate at my daughter's wedding, especially where there would be no mention of it in the notice of dismissal. Of course, it would be better if we had another rabbi ready to take over at the very next service. I don't know. Would that be difficult to manage? What do you think?"

Halperin sat back and crossed his legs. He tilted his head back, canted to one side, and focused on a corner of the ceiling as he appeared to give the matter considerable thought. Finally, elaborately casual, he said, "I might be able to get my brother to take the job."

"Yes, you mentioned having a brother who is a rabbi. What's he doing now? Doesn't he have a position?"

"Oh, he's got a pulpit all right, but he doesn't much care for it, and he refused to sign a contract. Ever hear of Jezreel, Kansas? Well, that's where he is and it's that sort of place."

"What's the matter with him?"

"Nothing. I think he's a damn good rabbi. I've got a videotape that he prepared as a sort of résumé for applying for a job. You could play it and judge for yourself, and of course if he came, it would be on a trial basis and it would be up to him to make good."

"Well, I'd like to see the tape. But if he's that good, how did he get stuck out there?"

"He's been unlucky. That's the only way I can explain it. When he got through at the seminary, he became a chaplain in the Navy, largely because the girl he was going with and then married was the daughter of a Navy man, a dentist. Then when his trick was up, he got a Hillel job because at the time there were no decent pulpits available. Then he took this job in Kansas because he thought he'd better get cracking on his career, and he thought any pulpit was better than none. For the experience, you know. He's been stuck there ever since."

"I see. Well, I'm inclined to believe that experience with a military outfit, especially in combination with the Hillel experience of working with young people, might be just what we need here. But what about my little problem?"

"Naturally, I'd explain to him that was part of the deal. He's three years younger than I am, and he's always looked up to me. I think I can bring him around. I'll call him, if you say the word."

"Okay. Go ahead. But first, sound out the rest of the board."

36

Morris halperin was friendly and cordial but a little puzzled. "You've got the culprit, and it was quick work, too, so I don't understand . . ."

"It's these young assistant D.A.s," said Lanigan wearily. "He wants a statement from you since you found the body. You know, how you happened to be in Glen Lane, what you saw, what you did. Damn silly, but he wants it."

"Well, I suppose if he's new at the game, he naturally wants everything just so. Okay, shoot."

Lanigan reached for a legal pad and then unscrewed the top of an old-fashioned fountain pen. "Suppose we take it from the top. Let's see, that was the night of the selectmen's meeting. You were there, weren't you?"

"Yeah. But haven't you got a stenographer for this?"

"Not right now. I'll just take it down myself and then I'll have it typed and you can look it over and sign it. Now, did you stay to the end of the meeting?"

"Yeah, but I left right after."

"That would be around ten o'clock?"

"Just about, I'd say. Maybe a little after."

"You didn't go to the Ship's Galley with the boys?"

"No, I had this cold and I thought I ought to go to bed. I could hardly keep my head up."

"So . . ."

"But there are some pills I take that have always worked for me and I was out of them. I took the last two before I left for the meeting. I was planning to buy some more but I forgot all about it. Of course, when I left the meeting, the drugstores were closed. So I decided to run over to Lynn where there's one that keeps open till midnight."

"Just a minute, Morris. 'Keeps open till midnight.' Take it a little slower, will you?"

"So I went there and bought the pills and took a couple right in the store," said Halperin, slowing down so that Lanigan could keep up with him. "Then I started back home, proceeding along High Street, of course."

"How were you feeling?"

"Oh, fine, just fine. My nose was stuffed up, but my head was perfectly clear. When I came to Glen Lane, I turned in, figuring I could save a few minutes. It's dark as a pocket there, so I turned on my high beams. Just as I came to the crest of that hill in the middle, I hit a pothole. You understand, with my high beams on, I couldn't see the road surface."

"Sure."

"But the front end jounced up and down. Maybe I need new shocks. Anyway, that's how I happened to catch a glimpse of the body. From the jouncing, see."

" 'From the jouncing.' Uh-huh. So then what did you do?"

"Well, I jammed on my brakes and came to a stop maybe twenty or thirty feet beyond. I got out of the car—"

"Did you shut off the motor?"

"I—I must have. No, I didn't. I just put her in park."

"Okay."

"Then I walked back and squatted down beside the

body. And I noticed all the glass. Boy, was I relieved. See, for a minute there, I thought maybe I had hit him. But both my lights were still shining, so I knew I hadn't."

"How could you see anything when it was so dark and with your headlights pointing the other way?"

"Just by my taillight. It wasn't much, but it was enough."

"So then what did you do?"

"I didn't do anything. Oh, I sort of called to him, asked if he could hear me, but I was careful not to touch him. I didn't want to move him or anything like that because if there were bones broken, I could make it worse. And I realized it was a hit-and-run, so I didn't want to mess up any clues. Legal training. Well, if it had been anyplace else, I would have stayed there and tried to flag down a car, but in Glen Lane . . . and late at night. So I got back into my car and headed for the nearest phone. I was going to ring someone's bell, but you know, not a single house was lit except Rabbi Small's. I guess he always stays up late."

"So why didn't you call from there?"

"I was going to, but then it occurred to me that you people might ask me to wait there, or that I might get involved with the rabbi, and I was terribly anxious to get to bed. Besides, I was only a few minutes away from home. In any case, I spotted the cruising car just as I turned into Main. I signaled them and told them."

Lanigan continued to write for a minute or two. Then he looked up and smiled at his visitor. "I guess that's about it. I'll get it typed up and you can sign it if it's all right."

Later Lanigan spoke to Jennings. "Did I give you enough time? Get anything?"

"Uh-huh. Plenty. I got a bunch of prints from the hood and fenders. Chances are they're his or his wife's or some gas station attendant's. I'll send them in on the chance that one of them might match the dead man's. I also got some fibers on the chance they might match up with those from the man's coat. There were no dents. Did he suspect anything?"

Lanigan shook his head. "No reason to."

37

Meyer andelman was aghast when Morris Halperin told him that Howard Magnuson might resign. As head of the UJA drive, he had not only counted on a large donation from Magnuson, but felt that it would serve to jack up the size of the contributions that others would make.

"You mean just from the presidency, Morris, or from the temple?" he asked anxiously.

"As far as I know, it would be just from the presidency," said Morris Halperin. "I suppose he'd continue to be a member of the board."

"Don't you believe it. If he resigns from the presidency because of some row with the rabbi, he'll resign from the board, too. And even if he doesn't, you'll never see him at a board meeting again."

"I think maybe you're right," Halperin agreed, "but the way it looks now, it's him or the rabbi."

"That's the choice? Then I'll take Magnuson any day. Rabbis are a dime a dozen, but where would we get another millionaire-type businessman like Howard Magnuson? He's a real asset to everyone on the board. I got nothing against our rabbi, even though he's a cold fish and sometimes acts like God Almighty, but if you ask me to choose between the two, it's no contest."

"But, Meyer, it isn't a case of voting one against the other."

"No?"

"Well, it is and it isn't. See, if Howard goes ahead and gets some outside rabbi to marry off his daughter, even if it's in his own house, the rabbi will resign. But"—and he held up an admonishing forefinger—"he'd explain his reason to the whole congregation. And Howard doesn't want that because he thinks it might cause a split."

"Now, that's what I call one sweet guy. He's willing to resign rather than cause trouble. So I'll tell you what we do. Why don't we fire the rabbi for—for something, inattention to his duties, or because we want a change? After all, he wouldn't take a life contract when it was offered him some years ago. He wanted to be free to leave, so why aren't we free to pick someone else? Then he wouldn't appeal to the general membership, would he? What could he say to them? The board is firing me because they're tired of me, but I don't think they are?"

Halperin inclined his head in agreement. "It's a thought. But keep it under your hat, will you, until I talk to some of the other fellows."

"Gotcha. Hey, isn't your brother a rabbi?"

"Yeah, what about it?"

"Maybe he'd be interested in the job."

Oscar Stein had a great deal of sympathy for Magnuson. "When my kid sister told me she was planning to marry a goy, naturally I was upset, but more because I knew how my folks would react. They were pretty cut up, let me tell you, especially my mother. They didn't go to the wedding. Wedding? Some wedding! I went with them to the courthouse in Salem, and then we went out to lunch. If we could

203

have had a rabbi, my folks would have made a wedding in the house, and they would have felt better about it. Because they like the fellow. He's a very decent chap. I talked to our rabbi about it, but he didn't budge. I suppose from his point of view, he couldn't. I didn't argue with him, but I couldn't help feeling that something ought to be worked out because there's an awful lot of this business going on. After all, some rabbis do it. So if some do it, there must be some leeway in the law. I mean, if it's flat out against the law, then how do these other guys get away with it? You never hear of any of them being unrabbied or anything like that. Maybe it's just that our rabbi is a stickler. Know what I mean?"

"A lot of the guys agree with you, Oscar," said Halperin. "And I heard that some of them are even planning to do something about it."

"Oh yeah? Like what?"

"Like maybe getting another rabbi. Some of the guys seem to feel that since the rabbi has always insisted on no more than a one-year contract so he can leave whenever he feels like it, what's sauce for the goose is sauce for the gander, and where our president is having this trouble with him, why don't we get someone else for a change?"

"Sounds reasonable to me."

Malcolm Kovner said, "Maybe the rabbi is right and maybe he's wrong. Whether he can marry somebody or not is his business, and I'm willing to admit that he probably knows his business. But he had no right to tell Magnuson to resign. That's not his business, and when he did, he got out of line. Now if Magnuson had taken it from him, he'd still be out of line, but it would be no concern of ours. Or maybe it would, but I can't see us doing anything about it unless we got a gripe from Magnuson. But with Magnuson saying he's going to resign—hey, that puts it right into our lap. You might say Magnuson is one of us and the rabbi isn't."

"How do you mean, Mal?"

"I mean, look here, in the good old U.S. of A., we've got three branches: the Executive, the Congress, and the Judiciary." He ticked them off on his fingers. "Right? So they're separate but equal. It's like a balance of forces. The Congress can't tell a Cabinet officer what to do. That's the President's prerogative. Just as the President can't say to the Congress, I don't like this senator and I want you to get rid of him. That's the Senate's bailiwick. Now we're the Board of Directors of the temple and the rabbi is an outsider that we hire. So he can't tell one of us to resign, anymore than Stanley the janitor can. See what I mean?"

"Sure, but what do we do about it?"

"Look, Morris, we've had how many, half a dozen presidents? So where is it written that we can have only one rabbi? Every now and then we change presidents, so maybe it's time to change rabbis."

"That's the way a lot of guys seem to feel." He chuckled. "Meyer Andelman suggested I contact my brother—he's a rabbi—and see if he'd be interested."

"Hey, how about that! Think he'd be interested?"

"I don't know. I doubt it."

"Well, why not ask him, Morris? It's only a phone call."

"I might at that."

Charlie Tanner had never liked the rabbi. "The guy was never my cup of tea. I'm not crazy about rabbis in general, but this one especially I didn't cotton to. And I'm not alone. Plenty of the guys can't stand him. Matter of fact, name me one real friend he has on the board. I mean, one guy who is known as the rabbi's friend, who stands behind him and backs him up. There's not one. And you know why? It's because he acts so damn superior. According to my old man, in the old days the rabbi was the big noise in the community. He was the one educated man and everyone used to defer to him on that account. And Rabbi Small goes on like that, like we're back in the nineteenth century and he's the only one who knows anything. But these days the community is full of doctors, lawyers, accountants, engineers. And most of the businessmen have been to college. So where does he get off looking down his nose at the rest of us and telling us what we can do and what we can't do? Yup, that's what's the matter with him. He's an old-fashioned guy in a modern world. He's an anachronism, that's what he is. Chester Kaplan tells me he knows all about Talmud. And you know what that is? It's the laws they had back in the days of the Bible. Fine, if we were living back in biblical times. But we're not. We're living in the good old USA and we're in the twentieth century, approaching the twenty-first. So who needs it? What we need is a modern man who understands what's happening in the world today and can give spiritual guidance for the problems of today."

"So you wouldn't be averse to change?"

"Morris, Morris, what have I been saying? I'm prepared to take almost anyone, a kid fresh out of the seminary, in exchange for Rabbi Small."

"That seems to be the general sentiment."

"So what do we do about it? Ask him to resign?"

"No. That would mean we'd have to give him some reason, maybe prefer charges. Then he might appeal to the general membership, and that could mean all kinds of trouble. Our idea is to notify him that his contract will not be renewed. No reason given. If he should ask, we'd just say we wanted a change. He'd have until his contract expired to look around for another job. We'd get a replacement as soon as possible."

"You mean while he was still here?"

"Why not? Look at it this way. Suppose we notify him that we're not renewing his contract, and he continues to serve until we get a replacement. So what kind of service would we get out of him? He'd be bitching all the time every chance he got. Say there's a funeral, God forbid. He might say he can't make it. Or a Bar Mitzvah, or a wedding. Can you imagine what it would be like if there was a wedding and the rabbi didn't show, the bride and groom standing around with all their family and friends, and the rabbi nowhere in sight? And he could do it because it's no skin off his nose, since he turns in his fees to the temple. But if we have another rabbi ready, willing, and able to take over the day after we notify Small that he's out, then everything is fine."

"But he has a contract."

"So we continue paying him until his contract expires. Or we could even give him a lump sum."

"Yeah. That way he'd have no beef at all. Hey, that's all right."

38

Notice of paul kramer's arraignment appeared in the News of the Courts section of the local newspaper. The rabbi, who usually only leafed through the paper to check the Religious News column, missed it. But Miriam, who read the paper more thoroughly, spotted it and called it to her husband's attention.

"It says he was released on his personal recognizance. Does that mean that the judge thought he was probably innocent?"

The rabbi shook his head. "No, only that he assumed he wouldn't be apt to flee the jurisdiction."

"The poor boy. Don't you think you ought to see him, David? I mean, he's alone and his folks are away."

"Well, I suppose it would be neighborly to invite him to dinner one evening. I tell you what. I promised his mother that I'd drop by and leave a note for him to make sure he's home when his folks call again. Why don't I just add an invitation to Sabbath dinner?"

"But Friday night is when they call."

"All right, so I'll ask him to get in touch with me for dinner one night. I'll do it right now."

He immediately sat down and scrawled a note, and then put on his topcoat to go out to deliver it. "I'll be right back."

But it was some time later before he returned, for just as he reached the Kramer house, Paul came out. "Oh, I was just going to drop a note in your mail slot," he said. "Your mother asked me to tell you to be sure to be home for their call."

"Oh, thanks. I wasn't likely to forget."

"I also included an invitation to come to dinner one night."

"Well, gee, thanks, Rabbi."

"Perhaps Friday night, a Sabbath meal?"

"That's the night my folks call. Maybe if they call early enough . . ."

"Fine. You could come over immediately afterwards. Are you planning to tell them of your problem?"

"No, I wasn't. And if they should happen to call you, I hope you won't mention it."

"But they'll find out sooner or later," the rabbi insisted.

"No, they won't. I'm sure the whole thing will be like, you know, squashed in a couple of days. See, there's been some new evidence that definitely clears me."

"Oh?"

The young man was embarrassed, but he realized that there was no way he could avoid explaining. "Well, the fact is I wasn't alone at the house here that night. I was studying with someone. It was a girl and we worked kind of late, so she stayed on. I thought you kind of guessed it when we talked down at the station house."

"I see." The rabbi made a conscious effort not to appear shocked or even disapproving. In a matter-of-fact voice, he said, "And she's planning to come forward and—"

"She already did. When she heard I'd been arrested and all, she said she'd go to Lanigan and tell him. I tried to talk her out of it because, you know, of what people might think. And I didn't want my folks to think that as soon as they left, well, you know . . ."

"She went and told Chief Lanigan that she spent the night with you?"

"That's right." Paul smiled to cover his embarrassment.

"I see. Did she tell you what Chief Lanigan said?"

"He didn't say much of anything. Oh yeah, he had her tell him just how she got to my house, I mean, what route she took, and whether she had seen anyone she knew and if her mother knew, and how she kept her from knowing. See, when she got to my place she called this girl friend and gave her my number in case her mother should call and want to talk to her, she could say she'd just stepped out for a minute and would call right back. Then this girl would call my house, and she'd call from there like it was from this girl's house. And later she called her mother and told her she was staying overnight, but of course she said she was at the girl's house. You know what I mean?"

"Yes, I get the picture."

"So I figure that in the next day or two, I'll be hearing from the police or maybe from the court telling me I'm in the clear and to come down and get my car. And then my folks wouldn't have to know."

"And your lawyer, does he know about this new development?"

"I haven't told him yet. Maybe the police did."

"And what will you do when he presents you with a bill for his services?"

"Well, I'll explain it all to him and tell him I'll pay it out so much a week. He seemed a decent sort of guy, so I figure he'll go along." The young man looked anxiously at the rabbi and blurted out, "Look, Rabbi, if you would rather I didn't come, well, that's all right. I understand, you being a rabbi and all."

"No, I rather wish you would, if you can make it."

39

For the tenth time at least, Chief Lanigan read over the reports in the Paul Kramer folder, again nodding an amused approval at Sergeant Dunstable's meticulously detailed report—"Examined trash barrel, Glossop's Garage, 4:13 P.M. Notified superior (Lt. Jennings) by phone from garage office, keeping barrel in sight, 4:15 P.M.; awaited arrival of truck for removal of barrel. Truck arrived, 4:31 P.M. Located black Chevrolet, license number 937254, corner of Maple Street and Glen Lane, 4:52 P.M., Returned . . . Reported . . ."

There was something about the report that had puzzled him. Now it came to him. He pressed a switch and called out on the intercom to the desk sergeant, "Billy Dunstable anywhere around?"

"Yes, sir. He's in the wardroom."

"Have him come in." And a moment later, when the sergeant appeared, he said, "Sit down, Sergeant, sit down. I've been reading through your report on that hit-and-run. I notice that you were able to find the Kramer car about twenty minutes after you left Glossop's garage."

"Yes, sir."

"How'd you manage that?"

Dunstable smirked. "Just routine detective work."

"But, considering the traffic, that's just about the time it would take you to drive to Glen Lane from Glossop's."

"Yes, sir."

Lanigan leaned back, folded his hands over his belly, and smiling benignly at the sergeant, said, "That's not routine detective work. That's extraordinary detective work."

Dunstable reddened. "Well, I did get a tip."

Lanigan leaned forward in his seat. "You mean someone told you just where the car was parked."

Dunstable squirmed uncomfortably. "Well, not exactly. He thought it might be there, that was where it was usually parked."

"Who was it? Who told you?"

"It was Tom Blakely who works at the garage."

"You know him?"

"Sure. You must know him, too. Big Red? Don't you remember? He was fullback on the Barnard's Crossing team that just missed out on the state championship about five years back."

"Oh yes, I remember. Quite a hero he was. And he's working at Glossop's now? I didn't know. I don't get down that way much. I thought he went off to college after graduating, that he'd got all kinds of offers of scholarships."

"That's right. He went to one down south, but he left after the first semester. He broke his wrist and they cut him off at the pockets. They do that at some southern colleges."

"And he's been working for Glossop's ever since?"

"No, he did some lobstering. Still does, along with working at Glossop's."

"And how did he know where Paul Kramer parked his car?"

"He sees Aggie Desmond who lives on Maple Street.

212

I expect he's seen the car when he goes calling on her."

"You seem to know a lot about him."

"Yeah, well, my kid brother was in his class at high and he's still kind of friendly with him."

Lanigan took a stab in the dark. "Was there a Fran Kimball in that class?"

"Yeah. She was a cheerleader."

"And Beth McAllister?"

"Yeah. She was in that class, too."

"So they must know Tom Blakely."

"Oh sure. Fran Kimball used to go with Tom."

"Did she now?"

"Oh yes. They were a pair."

"And then they split up? They quarreled?"

"I don't guess so. At least I never heard of any quarrel. But he went down south to college, and she went on to college in Boston. I suppose she met some other people and lost interest in him."

Lanigan thought for a moment. "You know what I'd like?" He leveled keen, blue eyes on the sergeant. "I'd like to know what this Tom Blakely was doing that Wednesday night."

Sergeant Dunstable laughed. "I can tell you that. You know, I had to be at the selectmen's meeting that night on that liquor store case. I was the one that caught the kid with the phony I.D. card who bought the beer. So when I was through testifying, I went down to the Ship's Galley, around half-past nine, it was, and Tom Blakely was there tying one on."

"Tying one on?"

"Yeah, you know, getting drunk. He said something about his girl having stood him up. I guess he'd been there for some time. Then, it must have been after ten, they refused to serve him, and he left, I suppose to go home and go to bed."

"That would be the sensible thing to do," Lanigan agreed. "Do you know what kind of car he drives?"

Dunstable shook his head. "I could find out easy enough."

"Never mind. It's not important. You've been very helpful, Sergeant."

40

Rabbi small leaned back in the visitor's chair in Chief Lanigan's office. "I met Paul Kramer and he told me that someone had come to see you—"

"That's right. A girl who said she'd been with him all night."

"So what are you going to do now?"

"Not a damn thing. Why should I? It's out of my hands now. It's up to the D.A."

"You reported it to him?"

"Of course. And he's supposed to notify the defense attorney. I presume he did."

"And now what happens?"

Lanigan shook his head. "That depends on the defense attorney, how he wants to play it. He might try to get the D.A. to quash it. Or he might save it for the trial and spring it then."

"But I don't understand. It clears him, doesn't it? If she's prepared to testify that she was with him all night and that they didn't leave the house—"

"But the D.A. might not believe her, David," said Lanigan patiently. "And Paul's lawyer might not, either, in which case, he'd do better holding it until the trial in the hope of befuddling the jury enough to acquit."

"Would a girl risk her reputation to admit she had spent the night with a young man if it were for anything less than a conviction for a felony?" the rabbi demanded.

"Yes, David, she would. You just don't know young people. They're not like you when you were their age. It's a different breed."

"I've had dealings with them," said the rabbi. "I've held postconfirmation classes and—"

"That's entirely different. They come to these classes for religious purposes. You are a rabbi, so they're on good behavior and careful not to say anything that you would disapprove of. But I see them when they get into trouble. You assume the girl would be ashamed to admit that she has been with a boy all night—"

"Paul was, too," the rabbi observed.

"Sure, because boys, especially young boys still in their teens, tend to be conservative. At least, about sex. But young women have changed. They're not shy about admitting that they have slept with a man. On the contrary, they're apt to be shy about admitting they're virgins. In their friends' eyes, that means they're square and probably unattractive. It was no sacrifice for the girl to come to me with that story, any more than it would have been if she had come to tell me that she had spent the night with her friend, Beth McAllister. It didn't mean a thing to her."

He put both hands on the desk and continued, "All right, so what do we have? We have an uncorroborated story. She says she spent the night with him. But you can't ask her mother if it's true because her mother thinks she was at Beth McAllister's. You ask McAllister and what do you get? When you finally get her to admit she was covering for Fran? Only that she was given a phone number which she was to call if Fran's mother wanted to talk to her.

What number? She can't remember. She wrote it down on a piece of paper, but of course she didn't bother to save it. Or she could have Paul's number, but how do we know it wasn't given to her when Fran and Paul cooked up their story? As for Fran Kimball herself, she says no one saw her go into Paul's house, or leave it the next morning.

"But even if we believe her story that she was with Paul all night, that still doesn't let him off the hook. It doesn't prove that they didn't go out at all. Here's a scenario. She goes to his house to study. Around ten o'clock, one of them suggests that they knock off for an hour. Go someplace for a beer, or for a hamburger and coffee. On the way back they come by way of Glen Lane and they have the accident. And then—" He broke off as a thought occurred to him. He smiled broadly. "Even better. Suppose *she* was driving and *she* had the accident. Naturally, she's in a panic and is afraid to report it to the police. She begs him not to squeal on her, and he agrees, providing she spends the night with him. Then when he's arrested, he makes her come to see me. What do you think of it?"

"I think your 'even better' makes them both much worse," said the rabbi dryly. "Have you considered the possibility that they both might be telling the truth? Whether Paul did it, or the girl, or both together, would he then have parked his car out in the open on Glen Road when he could have parked it in his own garage?"

"He might if he was drunk, or high on pot."

"Even if he were drunk that night, would he then have had his headlight replaced at a local garage? That was in the afternoon of the following day. He would have been cold sober by then."

"Not necessarily," said Lanigan. "If it was alcohol, I guess he would have got over it. But if it were drugs, it could very well have carried over to the next day. But question for question, would anyone in his right mind have

217

gone to the trouble of framing someone else for a road accident when all he had to do was ride off and no one the wiser? And, mind you, his own headlight wouldn't have been broken. What's more, think of the chances he would be taking. He might be seen while he was breaking the headlight, and then again when he drove back and dropped the glass near the body. Why would anyone take all those risks?"

"He could have—"

"And don't tell me he could have been drunk or high, David, because I used those."

"I was going to say that he could have hated Paul," said the rabbi primly.

"And wanted to avenge himself for some hurt he had suffered? Possible, but just barely. That would really be stretching the long arm of coincidence. Right after he has a serious road accident, he comes across the automobile of his enemy a few hundred yards beyond, and it's out in the open instead of being parked in a garage, and the owner is not around, and it's dark and late at night. It would have to be someone local or the chances are they wouldn't be using Glen Lane. But the Kramers are new here. They've been here only a couple of months. No chance of any terrible feud having developed. And wouldn't Paul have known about it? Yet when you went to see him, he suggested that he had been framed by the police. If he had so great an enemy, why didn't he mention *him* as a possibility instead of the police? Framing someone for a homicide is a pretty reprehensible thing, or don't you think so?"

"Of course it is," said the rabbi. "We probably regard it as more serious than you do. It's a breach of the commandment 'Thou shalt not bear false witness' and we punished it more severely."

"Oh yeah?"

"In biblical law the principle was if someone bore false

witness, 'then shall ye do unto him, as he purposed to do unto his brother.' "

Lanigan nodded. "Sounds reasonable. Of course, we're not easy on a perjurer, either. But I think it applies only to sworn testimony in a court. In the present case now, there isn't much that we could charge the culprit with, except willful destruction of property."

"And bringing the glass to the body on the road?"

"Ah, I suppose we could charge him with interfering with the police in the performance of their duty. But I don't think either one is likely."

"Can't you check it out?"

Lanigan shook his head slowly. "It's out of my hands now, David. It's the D.A.'s baby. Of course, if new evidence were to come along, I'd look into it before passing it on to the D.A. But I can't just go looking on the chance that I might find something, not with the iron-clad case we've got against Kramer. I don't have the manpower for that."

"Will you at least keep an open mind?"

"I always try to."

The rabbi rose and made for the door, when Lanigan called out, "How's Jonathon these days?"

"All right. Why do you ask?"

"Just that I've seen him downtown a lot in the afternoon."

"Oh, he's been going down to Republican headquarters after school. He does little odd jobs, runs errands, that sort of thing for extra pocket money." He smiled broadly. "He thinks now he wants to go into politics."

"Gave up on brain surgery, did he? Well, let's hope it doesn't last long."

"You and me both," said the rabbi.

41

HALPERIN CHUCKLED as from the other end of the phone he heard, in deep, solemn, liturgical tones, "Rabbi Halperin speaking."

"Hey, Herb," he called out gleefully. "Come off it. It's me."

"Morris!" And this time, the better part of an octave higher, "How are you?" And with sudden concern, "Nothing wrong, is there?"

"What's wrong is that I'm here and my kid brother is way out there in a hick town that nobody believes exists and you can't even find on a map. Look, Herbie, listen to me. I've got a proposition for you." He explained the situation in the temple.

His brother listened patiently and then said, "Gee, Morris, I'd love to take it, but I just can't. I can't be a party to a plot to kick a guy out of his job. And this Rabbi Small of yours, he's supposed to be kind of special. He's a real scholar. He had a piece in the last *Quarterly*—"

"Look, kiddo, his leaving has nothing to do with you. We're getting rid of him because we don't want him. Maybe he's special and all that, but he just doesn't get along with the congregation. He hasn't practically from the beginning. Half a dozen times he's managed to stay on just by the skin of his teeth. If you don't take it someone else will, so why not you?"

"Well, there's also this business of the wedding."

"So we've all got to make little adjustments in our thinking every now and then. And didn't you once do the same thing when you were a Hillel director? When the dean's daughter married the professor—"

"That was entirely different. Her grandmother was Jewish, so her mother was Jewish—"

"Yeah, like I'm Irish."

"I mean, according to Halacha—"

"I know all about Halacha and all that jazz. You were cutting corners there and you know it. So all I'm asking is, you do the same here. Nobody's going to know about it. If there's a newspaper announcement, your name won't be mentioned, or we'll spell it wrong. It's going to be done at the guy's house. Let me talk to Dolly—"

"I'm on the extension, Morris," said the rabbi's wife.

"Fine, so you know what this is all about. Now you've got to work on Herbie. It's his big chance. This guy, the president of our congregation, you know who he is? He's Howard Magnuson. *The* Howard Magnuson of Magnuson and Beck. I'll tell you the kind of guy he is. He gave me three cases, just three cases so far, and I made more than I made on my entire practice all last year. He warned me, he actually warned me, not to charge too little because it might make him look bad. That's the kind of guy Herbie would be connected with."

"Yes, but you said it was only temporary. How long is temporary?"

"You know how these things are, Dolly. It's not so much temporary as a trial period, because we're not sending the Ritual Committee to hear him and size him up. I'm going to show them that videotape you sent, but he'll still be coming here sight unseen. But if he doesn't mess things up, if he just keeps his nose clean, then he's in like Flynn, believe me. It's Herbie's big chance. He may not get another for a long time."

"We've got some leads, Morris."

"Leads, shmeads. You're in Kansas and Kansas leads to Arkansas. This is the East Coast I'm talking about. You're half an hour from Boston and Cambridge. There's the theater and concerts and all the universities."

"Well, suppose we think it over and let you know by the end of the week, say."

"No sirree. Look, it's ten o'clock now. You ring me by eleven tonight. No later. I'll be waiting right here by the telephone."

When the phone rang at eleven, it was Dolly Halperin who spoke, "All right, Morris, we'll go along. Now what do we do?"

"You don't do anything, Sweetheart. For the present you just sit tight. Then Sunday night if we can get things rolling by then, or the following Sunday night, I'll call you. My idea is that Herbie should come alone first. He'll stay with us. Then if all goes well, you'll come out with the kids and look for a house. But don't say anything until you hear from us. Okay?"

"You're the boss, Morris."

Morris glanced at his watch and decided that it was not too late to call Magnuson. "It's all set," he announced. "I had to do quite a selling job, and I don't think I could have done it without an assist from my sister-in-law, but he finally agreed."

"And my little problem?"

"Oh yeah, I explained that that was part of the deal. I told him there would be no publicity for him, although there might be on the marriage. I mean, it's going to be done in your house. So if your daughter sends a notice to the papers, she doesn't have to say who actually officiated. Or she could even say it was the Reverend Halperin, which might suggest a Protestant minister. I mean, having a rabbi is to fulfill her promise to her grandmother who's not around anymore. Right? So there's no reason for her to publicize it, is there?"

"I guess that would be all right," said Magnuson. "I've run the tape, and he looks good to me. In fact, I think he's just the kind of man we want for the job. Of course, I realize I can't act alone and that we're going to need a consensus of members of the board. So I thought if you could round up a bunch of the boys and have them come here tomorrow night, or the next day maybe for a light supper—nothing elaborate, just sandwiches and drinks— we could show them the tape, and if they approve of what they see, we can bring the matter up at the next board meeting."

"You don't want the whole board, do you?"

"No-o. I think it would be better if we just have those who are likely to react favorably. That would give us a majority, wouldn't it?"

"I think so. I'm sure of it. And for the others, we could have another showing the next day or—"

"Nothing doing, Morris. Let me tell you something about corporate management. If you have the votes, you railroad it through. It's not democracy, but it's the only way that works."

42

SEEING THE RABBI roll up his left sleeve and remove his phylacteries from the blue velvet bag in which he kept them, Miriam asked, "Aren't you going to the temple, David?"

"No, not this morning."

She watched wide-eyed for a moment as he put on the phylacteries and the prayer shawl, and then facing the east, began his morning prayers. Then she went into the kitchen to prepare breakfast. It was not raining. In fact, it was a crisp, clear Sunday morning, just the sort of day when he would be likely to enjoy the short walk to the temple. Once or twice she peered through the kitchen door, trying to discern from his appearance and attitude whether he was upset or disturbed.

When they were seated at the breakfast table, she said, "It's the board meeting again, isn't it?"

"That's right. The president asked me not to come."

With a brave little smile, she managed, "Another raise?"

"I doubt it. Quite the reverse. This time our president made it plain that I was not to attend meetings from now on."

"Why, what happened?"

"I told him that he ought to resign."

"David! You didn't!"

"Yes, I did." He proceeded to tell what had led up to it.

She shook her head wonderingly. "You do manage to get into rows, don't you?"

"No, I don't think so," he said easily. "Although I admit that over the years various presidents have managed to get into, er—differences with me. It always works out, though."

"But Magnuson is different."

"Is he? In what way?"

"You remember what Morton Brooks said. Magnuson doesn't realize what a rabbi is. From his point of view, you're just an employee of the temple organization."

"Well, some of the others thought so, too."

"But Magnuson has been dealing with employees all his life. His natural reaction to one who is recalcitrant or obstreperous, or who just plain disagrees with him, is to fire him."

"All right."

"Well, then . . ."

The rabbi put down his coffee cup and touched his napkin to his lips. "I can't live that way. I can't admit to myself that my livelihood, my well-being, is dependent on the whim of one man, and that I must concentrate my energies on pleasing him, or even avoid offending him. If that's the nature of my relations with Howard Magnuson, then I'd just as soon break it off now."

"But what if he asks you to resign?"

"I'll refuse, of course. If the board votes to ask for my resignation, I'll demand the reason, and I'll demand the right to argue my case before the general membership, and—"

"Oh, David, Howard Magnuson would never let him-

225

self get sucked into an open confrontation with you before the congregation. He'll simply persuade a majority of the board not to renew your contract when it expires. Then what would you do?"

He shrugged. "I'd probably notify the seminary that I was at liberty and to look around for another job for me. Or I might decide to try something else, teaching, or maybe I could get some kind of editorial job with a publishing house, or maybe a job as a correspondent on Jewish affairs with some newspaper, or—"

"But all of those involve being beholden to one man usually, a principal or a dean, an editor or a publisher, who could turn out to be another Magnuson."

"Then I'll use my savings to start my own business."

"What kind of business could you start?"

"Oh, I don't know. Maybe I could start a school of my own, a Hebrew school for adults, or—or any kind of business, a shoestore or a candy store, or—or—"

"A rabbi running a candy store?"

He grinned. "Sure, why not? Well, perhaps not a candy store because with my sweet tooth I'd eat up all the profits. The point is that unlike a Catholic priest or a Protestant minister, I am not dedicated to things religious. As a rabbi, I'm a secular figure. And earning a living in a trade or a business or a profession is quite within the tradition. Many of the great rabbis in the old days earned their livings as carpenters, blacksmiths, wood gatherers. More recently in the ghetto towns of Russia and Poland, some of the rabbis had to earn their livings in some sort of secular enterprise. My own grandfather, when he served as a rabbi in a shtetl, before he came to this country, operated a store, albeit the town gave him preferential treatment by limiting his competition.

"In a sense, it's even the more proper way, since our tradition dictates that one should not use one's learning as a spade to dig with. The present system of remunerating a rabbi is based on a fine bit of pilpulistic casuistry in which the contention is that the congregation is not paying him for his learning and knowledge, but for the time that he is prevented from earning a living by functioning as a rabbi."

"Tell me, David, are you tired of being a rabbi?"

"Why do you ask?"

"Because you've been a rabbi for twenty years. If you had gone into something else, law or business, I'm sure we would have been a lot better off financially. So if you were to give it up now, I'd always have the feeling that that twenty years was somehow wasted."

"No, Miriam, I'm not tired of being a rabbi. Taking one thing with another, it's been a very pleasant twenty years." He rubbed his jaws to aid cerebration. "But if the rabbi really cares about his congregation, and if they are not just a flock of sheep who think of him as their pastor, then there has to be an occasional fight. Just as in a good marriage," he added.

She giggled. "Men's or women's shoes?" she asked.

"What?"

"In this store, would you be selling men's shoes or women's shoes?"

"Oh, women's, of course, and I'd limit my trade to small sizes so as to attract the young and pretty ones."

They heard the clumping of feet on the stairs, and Jonathon came in, yawning and stretching. "Hey, Dad, are we riding or walking?"

Before the rabbi could answer, Miriam said, "Your father is not going to the minyan today, Jonathon, and I think it would be better if you said the morning prayers at home, too."

"Okay. I'll go upstairs." Jonathon said his prayers at home except on Saturdays and Sundays—that is, when he had no school—and would accompany his father to the minyan. And of course he preferred to pray at home, since it was quicker and there was no need to wait to complete the ten needed for the minyan.

When he had gone, the rabbi said, "You know, Miriam, it just struck me that Jonathon is not much younger than the Kramer boy."

"So?"

"So if he got caught up in something—" He stopped and was silent for a while. Then he said, "I think I'll take a little ride along Glen Lane."

Rabbi Small drove the length of Glen Lane all the way to High Street, and then turned around and started back, going very slowly. When he came to the clearing where D'Angelo had left his car, he parked and got out. Although he was not unfamiliar with the road, he realized as he walked that it was longer than he had previously thought. Also, there was a considerable rise about halfway to Maple Street that he had not noticed when driving. When he reached the top of the rise, he was able to see all the way down to Maple Street. He turned and walked back to where he had left his car, counting the paces as he walked.

43

"GOT THE LAB REPORT ON HALPERIN'S CAR," Lieutenant Jennings announced as he took the visitor's chair.

"And?" Lanigan asked eagerly.

"Well, one of the prints is a possible."

"What's that mean?"

"It means that if you got other prints that are positive, you can use this one, too."

"What for?"

"Oh, you know, for its position on the hood to indicate how he might have fallen."

"But without a positive?"

Jennings shook his head. "Nothing. Ah, here's something. One of the fibers taken from the headlight rim on Halperin's car matches fibers taken from the rim of Kramer's car." He looked up from the report. "See, we got two chances, the action on the top of the hill in Glen Lane where the guy was hit, and the action involved in the breaking of Kramer's headlight. Obviously, the same guy did both, so if we can pin the headlight thing on him, it would mean that he was the one who did the hit-and-run. It says here: 'Possible source—Turkish toweling.'"

"Swell," said Lanigan in disgust. "You wipe your head-light with a bit of Turkish toweling, or a gas station attendant does, and you get some fibers in the crack where it joins the fender. I'll bet you'll find some on my car or yours."

"Yeah, guess so," said Jennings despondently. "So do we forget about Morris Halperin?"

"Well, let's say we put him on the back burner for a while. Right now I've been kind of concentrating on Tom Blakely."

"Oh yeah?"

"I went down to Maple Street last evening and stopped in front of the Desmond house. And, you know, sitting there in my car I could see all the way to the Kramer house in my rearview mirror."

"So?"

"So, let's say Tom Blakely goes calling on Aggie Desmond. We know he did because he said so at the Ship's Galley that night. Billy Dunstable heard him. He parks his car just about where I did. He's waiting for her to come out, see. Now, while he's sitting in his car waiting, along comes the Kimball gal. Maybe he hails her. He used to be sweet on her. Maybe she waves back. Or maybe she just kind of tosses her head and walks on. So he follows her in his rearview mirror and sees her go into the Kramer house."

"Okay."

"The Desmond girl stands him up, or she comes out and tells him she can't go out with him. He gets sore at the Desmond girl, or maybe he's sore at the Kimball girl for passing him by like that. When I asked her if she'd seen anyone who knew her on her way to Kramer's, she kind of hesitated before she said no."

"All right."

"He stays down at the Ship's Galley until around ten o'clock, according to Dunstable, and then he leaves because they refuse to serve him. Dunstable thought he probably

230

went on home. But if he did, he's not like any drunk I know. I figure, more likely he'd get in his car and go looking for someplace where he could get served. That wouldn't be anyplace in Barnard's Crossing because we're pretty careful here. But in Lynn or Revere they have all those dinky little nightclubs where you wouldn't have any trouble getting a drink unless you were lying on the floor."

"Hell, some of these places are so dark, you wouldn't know anyone was lying on the floor unless you fell over them."

"Well, anyway, I thought it was worthwhile checking it out. So I had one of the boys go around to some of these places with a picture of Blakely."

"Where'd you get the picture?"

"From his yearbook. They keep them at the town library. And we made some photocopies from the machine they have. The pictures aren't very good, and he was five years younger when it was taken, but they're good enough."

"And?"

"And bingo. In one of the places there was positive identification. They were a little hazy about time, but they thought he came in around ten and left around eleven."

"All right, so you can prove that Tom Blakely got drunk in Lynn and started for home around eleven o'clock. Where does that get you, Hugh?"

"It gives me the basis for some guessing."

"Like what?"

"I'm guessing that Blakely came home by way of Glen Lane. If he was drunk, he'd want to avoid the main road as much as possible. Besides, it's a short cut."

"All right. I'll go along with that."

"And that he hit the guy on the hill—"

"Just a minute."

"The time is about right. He'd accelerate going up the

hill, and then suddenly there's a man on the road where you don't expect to see a pedestrian. He's drunk and his reactions are slow."

"All right. It's possible."

"Okay, so he's scared. And he can't report it in the normal way, even if he could prove that it was the pedestrian's fault, not even if he had a moving picture of the guy throwing himself in front of his car, because he's drunk and so is automatically presumed guilty. At the very least he'd lose his driver's license. How can someone work in a garage without a driver's license? He might not care very much about the job, although they're kind of scarce these days, but—"

"Okay, you mean that he would be likely to run rather than report it to the police. I'll buy that."

"So he drives along Glen Lane, and just as he approaches the corner, I'm guessing he saw a light." Lanigan leaned back in his seat and folded his hands over his belly, obviously much pleased with himself.

"What light?"

"A light in the Kramer house, upstairs, probably in a bedroom that faces Glen Lane. Maybe he saw her shadow on the blind, or maybe the blinds weren't even down, since there are no houses on that side and he actually saw her, or maybe he just assumed she was up there—"

"So he gets sore and—"

Lanigan nodded. "And decides to take revenge. He breaks Kramer's headlight because in the state he's in, he thinks of him as having stolen his girl. So he turns around and drives back to the scene of the accident and drops the broken glass there. The next day, he's lucky enough to be in a position to tell Billy Dunstable where the car is."

"Of course, you don't have the slightest proof, Hugh."

"No, I don't. But I've got a good story, and if I piece it out, and then call in Tom Blakely and spring it on him, it might work. There are a lot of angles we can work on. We can take a look at his car. It might have a dented fender. He'd say it's an old dent, but maybe Glossop would remember that it wasn't. The chances are that he washed his car the next day, and maybe Glossop would remember that."

"He wouldn't remember that. They must wash lots of cars in that garage. At least, they have one of those machines that steam cleans your engine, so the chances are they wash and wax, too."

"He might remember it if it were unusual. Then I could talk to this Aggie Desmond and find out just when Blakely came calling that night. I intend to talk to the Kimball girl again. I'd like to know what time she went to bed, and which bedroom they used, and whether the lights were on when they undressed, and if the shades were up."

"You could ask Kramer."

"No, he's under indictment. I can't question him unless his lawyer agrees."

"Well, maybe Scofield would agree if you explained that it wasn't his client you were interested in, or that you were trying to clear him."

"Possible," Lanigan admitted. "The point is to get as good a story as I can, with all kinds of little details pinned down by testimony from one person or another, and then I'd have Dunstable bring in Blakely to make a statement."

"A statement about what?"

"Oh, as to how he came to know where Kramer's car was," said Lanigan airily. "Just a matter of form for possible use in the trial. I'd have him hang around for a while until he got kind of restless, and maybe a little nervous, and then I'd call him in and ask him how he happened to break Kramer's headlight. You remember we used the same technique a couple of years back on that guy Slocumb in the breaking and entering when we didn't actually have a thing."

"How about Miranda?"

Lanigan looked at his lieutenant in innocent surprise. "Why, I wouldn't be accusing him of anything, merely asking him how he happened to break someone's headlight."

44

AT THE DINNER TABLE, Rabbi Small looked at the empty place on his right and asked, "Where's Jonathon?"

"Oh, he called up and said they'd asked him to work late at the Republican headquarters. They're very busy there right now."

"He thinks he's a big shot," said Hepsibah spitefully.

"Sibah!"

"I don't like the idea of his missing dinner—"

"He said he'd get a sandwich and some milk," Miriam explained.

"I mean I don't like him missing dinner with the family. I'm not sure I care to have him work there," said the rabbi.

"Why not? It pays better than baby-sitting and he feels it's more dignified. He also says he's learning a lot, and that he is now the shark of his Political Process class."

"Well, I suppose it's only for another two or three weeks until the election. How is he planning to get home? Did he take his bike?"

"No, he went there right from school. He'll walk, or maybe take the bus—"

"Or maybe call and ask me to come down and get him," said the rabbi.

"He might get a lift from somebody there."

"Did he say when he'd be through?" asked the rabbi.

"About eight or half past, he said. You seem overly concerned, David. After all, he's seventeen."

"And very impressionable. There are always a lot of loafers hanging around the Republican Committee headquarters, talking and drinking, especially in the evening, and I don't think it's a good influence on a young boy."

"Well, you can tell him that you don't want him working late there and that he is to be home for dinner every night," said Miriam reasonably.

"Yes, I think I will."

But Jonathon did not come home at eight, nor even at half past. When the clock struck nine, Miriam, uneasy, went to the telephone to call the Republican Committee headquarters. She returned to the living room a few minutes later to say, "I spoke to the man in charge. He says he sent Jonathon on an errand down the street about an hour ago, before eight. He's probably walking home. Do you think you ought to drive down and see if you can pick him up?"

"No. If he left before eight, he should be along pretty soon."

Chief Lanigan raised his whiskey in a perfunctory and automatic toast to his wife, who had just handed it to him, and drank deeply. He had dined well—Amy had a way with spareribs—then relaxed with the evening paper and watched television for a while. Now, at nine o'clock, he was planning to get into pajamas and go to bed and read, but Amy was inclined to conversation.

"Anything happen today?"

"Nothing special. Just the usual." Then, out of politeness, "And with you?"

"I bumped into Mary Hagerstrom this afternoon."

"Uh-huh."

"You remember her."

"Hagerstrom?"

"She's the housekeeper and cook for the Magnusons."

"Oh yes."

"I asked her why she didn't come to the sodality the other night. And she said Mr. Magnuson asked her to stay on because he was having some men over and he wanted her to prepare a bunch of sandwiches for them."

"Is that so?"

"Have you seen David Small lately, Hugh?"

This sudden change of subject, while exasperating at times, did not surprise Lanigan. He was used to it. What is more, he was sure that sooner or later Amy would make a connection between the Magnusons, Mary Hagerstrom, and Rabbi Small. So he said, "No, not lately."

"Is he in any trouble?"

"Who? David Small? Not that I know of. Certainly nothing that involves the police."

"I mean with his congregation."

"Well, I hear rumors. I've been hearing them ever since he came here. Jews do a lot of bitching about their rabbis, I guess."

"I mean a plot to get rid of him."

"No, I can't say I've heard anything lately. Why?" He put his paper down and gave her his full attention.

"Well, according to Mary Hagerstrom, the reason for that party with the sandwiches, you know, there were just men—"

"Come to the point, woman."

"It was to show one of those videotape things about a rabbi."

"They had a videotape of Rabbi Small?"

"Not Rabbi Small. Another rabbi, a younger man. It showed him in a robe and a kind of scarf, and one of those little caps that bishops wear, only it was black. And it showed him standing at a lectern, I guess, delivering a sermon. Mary only got a glimpse when she'd be in and out with sandwiches and coffee. And she heard comments about how good he was, and what a nice appearance he made."

"Mary Hagerstrom told you all this? Why?"

"Well, she just happened to mention it, and I kept pressing her."

"What are you getting at, Amy?"

"I think those men at the party are the big shots in the temple. Mr. Magnuson is the president, you know. And I think they were planning to get rid of the rabbi and hire this one in his place. Mary Hagerstrom said that when they were leaving, Mr. Magnuson kept telling them to keep it under their hats, not to mention it even to their wives."

"It could be they're getting Small an assistant, a sort of curate," he suggested, but his tone lacked conviction.

"Then Rabbi Small would know about it, wouldn't he?"

"Yeah, I suppose so."

"Why not call and ask him?"

"Yeah, maybe I will." He went to the telephone and dialed. When Miriam answered, he announced, "Hugh Lanigan."

"Oh, hello. Did you want to talk to David?"

"Yes. No, look, Miriam. Just tell me, are you folks alone and planning to be in?"

"Yes, Chief. Would you like to come over?"

He changed from house slippers to loafers and put on a sweater. "I'll be back in a little while, Amy. I couldn't ask him something like that over the phone."

He drove to Maple Street, and Miriam opened the door for him as soon as she heard him turn into the driveway. "We were just going to have tea when you called," she said, "so we waited for you."

"Thanks, Miriam, I could use a cup."

It was only after the tea had been poured and they were nibbling on cookies that Lanigan asked, "Are you in trouble with the congregation, David?"

"Oh, David is always in trouble with the congregation," said Miriam lightly. "It goes with the territory."

And from the rabbi, "Why do you ask?"

Glancing from one to the other, Lanigan told them what he had learned. He could see by the frozen smile on her face that Miriam was upset. Her husband, however, merely nodded and smiled, saying, "It proves the importance of having a high-powered executive in the top position. There have been attempts before to get me out. Usually the dissidents start by trying to get a majority on the board, and by the time they do, a sizable opposition to them has also developed, some of them because they approve of me, I suppose, and some because they don't like those who are trying to oust me, and the greatest number, perhaps, because it means avoiding trouble. It means doing without a rabbi until they find another, and how can they be certain that the new one will be any better? But with an executive type like Howard Magnuson, we have efficiency. They line up another rabbi first, and then they get a majority, and they keep it all secret so that an opposition can't get started."

"And can't you do anything about it?" asked Lanigan.

"I'm not sure I want to."

"You don't?"

"No. I can't admit that my livelihood and the general welfare of my family is entirely dependent on the goodwill of one man. Once I think that, then I'm no longer my own man. I'll spend the rest of my life worrying about whether what I say or do will please him. And I can't live that way."

"The one man is Magnuson?"

"Of course."

"But he can't do it alone. Doesn't he have to have a majority of your board?"

"Oh, that's no problem for him. He's a tycoon, a millionaire."

"You don't mean that he'd bribe them or that they'd sell their votes—"

"Not their votes, just their souls. Here's a small businessman who needs a bank loan, or access to a particular wholesaler. Magnuson can arrange that with a phone call. Or say, he's a professional man, a doctor, or a dentist, or a lawyer—they all have stock portfolios. 'What do you think, Mr. Magnuson? Shall I sell? Any truth to the rumor that ABC is going to merge with XYZ?' Even if you don't ever come to him for a favor, it's nice to have a friend who's a millionaire if only to brag to your friends about. No, it's entirely his doing. You see, I know what it's all about. His daughter—"

He stopped as he heard a car drive up in front of the house. "That's probably Jonathon," he said. "He must have gotten a ride home."

Miriam and the rabbi both went to the door, and Lanigan, wondering at their uneasiness, joined them.

"He said he'd be home at eight o'clock and he hasn't had dinner yet," Miriam explained.

In the light from the living room, they saw Scofield's pink car with the sign on top at the curb. They watched as Jonathon got out, circled the car, and said to the driver, "Gee, thanks, Mr. Scofield."

"Thank *you*," said Scofield and put the car in motion.

As Jonathon came up the walk, Miriam asked, "Why were you so late? What did you do to your hand?"

Jonathon held up his right hand, which had a handkerchief wrapped around it. "I scratched it. It's nothing."

"Let me see."

"Aw, Ma, it's nothing, I tell you. Mr. Scofield was fixing

a flat outside his headquarters. Mr. Chisholm had sent me down there with some campaign stuff they wanted. So naturally I helped him. I must've scraped it when I reached in the trunk for the wrench. There was a lot of junk in there."

"Let me see it."

"Aw, Ma." But he unwound the handkerchief.

"That's not a scrape. That's a cut. Now you go right upstairs and wash your hands with lots of soap and hot water. Then you put some Mercurochrome on it and a Band-Aid. Then you can come down and have your dinner in the kitchen."

"Okay, okay. But I'm not hungry. I had a couple of cheese sandwiches."

"Well, it's there if you want it. Or you can take some milk and cookies."

"Was that Scofield's car? I mean, the one he uses regularly? Or is it just for campaign purposes?" Rabbi Small asked Lanigan after Jonathon had galloped upstairs.

"No, that's his car. It's the only one he owns as far as I know."

"But the color!"

Lanigan chuckled. "Yeah, it's the only one I've ever seen."

"Then that could be it," the rabbi exclaimed.

"What could be it?" asked Lanigan. "What are you talking about?"

"That could be the reason for smashing Kramer's headlight and bringing the shards back to the scene of the accident," said the rabbi quietly.

Lanigan stared, and Miriam, who had risen to remove the tea tray, sat down again. "If you hit someone with your car on a dark, lonely road like Glen Lane," the rabbi continued, "and you didn't want to report it for fear of the consequences, what would you do?"

"Why, I suppose—"

"You'd get away from there as fast as you could," said the rabbi. "That would be the obvious and sensible thing to do," the rabbi went on. "But my guess is you would slow down as you approached Maple Street, because there are houses there, and someone might see you coming out of Glen Lane and remember that when the body was found. You might even stop and get out and look at the front of your car to check if there was anything incriminating like a dented fender or a bit of the victim's clothing caught on the fender or the bumper. You might notice that where there was some rust on the fender, perhaps some paint had chipped off. It might have flaked off before, but you can't be sure that there isn't a chip of paint on the ground near the body of the victim. And if it's the bright, shocking pink of your car, then you're the one the police will go to immediately because yours is the only car around in that color. But you can't go back to where the victim is lying to look for little chips of paint. It could take hours. However, you see a car parked right on the corner, as though placed there by Providence."

"So you give the police an obvious clue like a shattered headlight," said Lanigan. "Yes, that would make it worthwhile going to the trouble of turning around and—"

"Precisely. You've opened your trunk perhaps, to get your flashlight—no, that you'd be apt to keep in your glove compartment—"

"It could be one of those big lanterns like the electrician had who came the other day," Miriam suggested.

"Right, an electric lantern," said her husband. "And there's sure to be a wrench or the handle of the jack—"

"And you get a newspaper or a magazine to catch the pieces of glass," suggested Lanigan.

"Or if he kept an old sweater in the trunk the way you do, David—" Miriam offered.

"Or an old rag or piece of Turkish towel for grease or dirt," said the rabbi. "It would also serve to muffle the sound. He'd wrap it around the headlight, then whack it with the wrench, and just gather it up and put it on the passenger seat. Then he'd turn around and drive back to the body. He'd shake out the towel and drive on to High Street, and circle back to Barnard's Crossing that way. Then when the police arrive on the scene, they have all this lovely glass as a clue."

"But he was still taking a chance, wasn't he, David?" said Miriam. "What if Paul Kramer had gone off to a movie with a bunch of friends? Then the police would know it was a false clue."

"Not right away," said the rabbi with a glance at the police chief. "They would first check on his alibi with his friends. 'Where were you sitting with respect to Paul? Did he get up at any time during the course of the movie? To buy popcorn? He's a close friend of yours and you'd do anything to help him out of a jam, wouldn't you?' Then if the alibi held, they'd start checking Paul's enemies, those who might conceivably want to do him a mischief. Suppose it had been the car of that Samuel Perkins, you know the one who writes all those critical letters that appear in the *Courier.*"

"Sam'l Perkins? Gosh, we'd have to check out half the town," said Lanigan, chuckling.

"Jonathon's hand!" exclaimed Miriam.

Both men looked at her in puzzlement. "What about Jonathon's hand?" asked Lanigan. "What's it got to do—"

"He cut it. He cut it helping Scofield change a tire this evening," she said, obviously excited. "What would Scofield do with the towel? Why would he throw it away? I'll bet he just dropped it back in the trunk. And when Jonathon was trying to find the wrench, he cut himself."

"I'm going back to the station house," said Lanigan,

rising abruptly. "I've got a lot of work to do. I want to get a look at Scofield's car."

"But how will you—"

"He parks it on the street. I'm going to have it towed in. Starting in November, it's illegal to park on the streets overnight during the winter months."

He started for the door. With his hand on the doorknob, he said, "It was seeing that pink car that gave you the idea?"

"Well, I had been thinking about it from the time I saw Paul Kramer. You see, *I* believed him. And for a while I thought it might be Morris Halperin."

"Morris Halperin? Why him?"

"Because he was the one who reported it to the police. But when I learned that Scofield had undertaken Kramer's defense, and that without a retainer, I began to think of *him.*"

Lanigan grinned. "Maybe that's the difference between a policeman and a rabbi. I tend to think well of my fellow-men. I put it down to his being a good guy."

45

THE RABBI HAD JUST FINISHED his breakfast when the call came from Lanigan. He sounded jubilant. "I thought you deserved to know. We took Scofield into custody this morning. That was a lucky guess on your part."

"It wasn't just a guess. You see, I started at the other end."

"What do you mean, the other end? Never mind. Not over the phone. I'm coming down to see you. Things will be breaking loose here pretty soon, and I'd rather not be around answering a million questions."

Very well pleased with himself, Lanigan began talking as soon as he entered the house. "I picked up the car at one o'clock in the morning. I opened the trunk—"

"You forced it?"

"No, didn't have to. There's a release lever that you can operate from the inside. Well, the towel was there and I could see right away it had some specks of glass in it. I had a patrolman take it in to Boston. I had already got hold of the Forensic people and asked them to stand by. My man waited for the results. They found fourteen bits of glass, one of them a sliver almost an inch long and an eighth of an inch wide—" He stopped abruptly to ask, "What blood type is Jonathon?"

"Same as mine. AB."

"It figures. There was type AB blood on the sliver, which fit the neck of that broken sealed beam that we picked up at the garage but perfectly." He chuckled. "In the morning Scofield called up to report his car had been stolen. I got on the line and explained that a rookie officer had had it towed because of the ordinance on winter parking. I asked him to wait around for a few minutes." He cocked an eye at the ceiling. "I suppose he thought we were going to tow it back and apologize for inconveniencing him. But instead I sent Eban Jennings down to take him in. Now, what did you mean that you started at the other end?"

"Well, the police started with the accident—"

"Naturally."

"But that was the end, the culmination. I was interested in what the man, D'Angelo, was doing there in the first place. What was he doing walking along in the middle of the road late at night?"

"Well, he drove there. His car was in the little clearing just beyond High Street."

"All right, then why did he drive there? Why did he turn into Glen Lane? It's barely noticeable from the highway."

"We assumed he had to take a"—a glance at Miriam, and he cleared his throat—"that he had to relieve himself."

"So why would he be in the middle of the road a hundred yards beyond where he had parked his car? I made a point of pacing it out last Sunday. It's a good hundred yards. If he wanted to relieve himself, he could have gone anywhere. The road is lined with bushes and trees on either side all the way from High Street to Maple "

"Well . . ."

"I assumed he went there to meet someone," the rabbi said.

"He could have gone there to nap for a few minutes. Say, he'd been driving and was falling asleep—"

"Then what would he be doing on foot a hundred yards beyond?" the rabbi challenged.

"All right, say he was going to meet someone," Lanigan conceded.

"Then obviously it was a secret meeting, one in which it was dangerous, or at least impolitic, for the two to be seen together. So I asked myself who the other man could be."

"It could be almost anyone, couldn't it?"

"We can narrow it down quite a bit," said the rabbi. "First of all, what was the purpose of the meeting? It couldn't have been just to talk because that could be done just as well and more secretly by telephone, by public telephone if there was any fear that a line might be tapped. My guess was that something had to be passed from one to the other. The most likely thing was money, a packet of hard cash."

"A payoff?"

"That's right. Something that could not be entrusted to the mails or to a messenger. So then I began to wonder what kind of man would have to pay off in hard cash in secret."

"I suppose you mean it was some sort of blackmail. Well, that could happen to anyone, I suppose."

"I'm not thinking of who might be blackmailed, but rather who might have to make his payment in secret." He got up and began to pace the floor. His voice took on the Talmudic singsong into which he lapsed occasionally. "It couldn't be a doctor. Anyone can come to see a doctor and it would be no problem for him to pass the money in the privacy of his office. And it couldn't be a lawyer because he sees all kinds of people in the way of his normal practice,

247

either as clients or as possible witnesses to some suit he's engaged in. And the same would be true of the businessman in his office or in his store. The only one who might have to be careful about whom he's seen with is a politician, someone holding or running for office. Even if the politician is a lawyer, he would have to be careful about who might be seen coming into his office. And when I read in the newspaper account that the victim, whatsisname?"

"D'Angelo. Tony D'Angelo."

"That's right. When I read in the newspaper account that he had been active in Boston political circles, I was sure I was right. He held no office, either elective or appointive, or they would have mentioned it. Even if he had been a lowly clerk in a government office, it would have been mentioned. But 'active in political circles' suggests someone who has no official position and acts as a go-between, or is a hanger-on of a political boss, someone with no regular job, who would be paid for bits of information or little services rendered."

"Yeah, I guess that would fit D'Angelo," said Lanigan.

"From here on, I've got to use my imagination," said the rabbi.

"My God, what have you been using up till now?"

"Up till now, I've been using inferential logic," said the rabbi severely. "I see D'Angelo waiting in his car, smoking cigarette after cigarette. Then perhaps it occurs to him that he was expected to wait at the other end of Glen Lane. That's why I think he walked to the top of the rise. If it was only to stretch his legs, I don't think he would have gone that far. But if he wanted to see if the other was parked at the other end of Glen Lane, he would have had to go to the top of the hill. I see Scofield, with a packet of bills in an envelope, turning into Glen Lane from High Street. Maybe he doesn't see the car parked in the clearing. Or maybe he does, and he slows down or stops and, seeing it's empty, drives on. He probably had his high beams on. It would be only natural. I assume he was driving slowly so as not to miss seeing his man. Then he spies him at the top of the hill, and he speeds up to reach him, give him the money, and drive off as quickly as possible."

"But wouldn't it have involved a swap of some kind, an incriminating letter, or a photo. And then he would have had to stop."

"Obviously not, since nothing of the sort was found on the dead man, and it's most unlikely that Scofield would have stopped to search him. No, this must have been what you called a payoff, in which he pays and hopes that's the end of it."

"Yeah, all right."

"He notices that his headlights had blinded D'Angelo. Maybe he threw his hand up against the glare, and it suddenly occurred to Scofield that if he rammed him, he would be free of him and not have to pay. So he pressed down on the accelerator."

"But, still, it could have been an accident."

"Of course, but he'd have a hard time proving it that he had made an appointment with him. My guess is that he didn't even stop to see how badly he had hurt him. It would be dangerous because if the man was conscious, he would recognize him—"

"But in any case, he'd know it was Scofield who had hit him." Lanigan objected.

"How would he know? How could he see the car with those headlights glaring at him out of the darkness?"

"Yeah, I suppose not."

"But—but if Scofield knew who it was, and was there to meet him, isn't that murder?" Miriam ventured timidly.

"Second degree, anyway," said Lanigan. "I don't know if we can prove it. And I'm sure the defense attorneys will try to get some of our evidence thrown out on the basis of the Miranda ruling, but I expect the D.A. will consider it a strong case." He rose to go and said, "You know, David, I'll be sorry when the new man comes to replace you and you leave town."

"Thanks. It's good of you to say so, but I think I might be staying on for a while."

"You mean because of this?"

"That's right."

"This man, Magnuson, was somehow involved with Scofield?"

"He wanted me to officiate at his daughter's marriage to him. That was what all the fuss was about."

"And you people don't sanction marriage outside your faith any more than we do. Although we've loosened up a bit in recent years."

"Well, we haven't."

"And that's what it's all about, eh?" He shook his head admiringly and said, "All I can say is you're a lucky guy."

The rabbi smiled. "Well, we believe in luck."

"I guess everybody does, don't they?"

"No, it's different with us. We believe in luck, good and bad, as a matter of practical philosophy. You might even say, it's a matter of religion with us."

"Is that so? How do you mean?"

"Well, when a person is sick or poor, or miserable, we don't assume that he is wicked and a sinner. We just consider him unlucky."

"Well, of course, but—"

"I can turn on the TV any Sunday morning, and other times as well, and hear a preacher say that if you repent of your sins and give your heart to Jesus, you will be relieved of your sickness and your misery. And usually there are testimonials to that effect, people telling of terrible ailments that they were cured of through prayer, or how giving their hearts to Jesus made them prosperous. The implication is, of course, that disease and misery in general are the result of sin or lack of faith."

"Ah, those are the evangelical sects," said Lanigan with a wave of the hand, dismissing them.

"Yes, but the Catholic Church has ventured into that area lately, too. How about the various saints to whom you can pray to intercede for you. Presumably, the act of prayer, with the repentance that's implied, removes the sin which is the cause of the condition. The basic difference between the Catholic Church and the Protestant evangelical churches in that respect would seem to be that in the Catholic Church, the work is largely delegated to the saints. I suppose it's logical in the light of the elaborate bookkeeping system involved in balancing sin and grace to determine one's eventual destination—heaven, hell, or purgatory. We don't believe in any of that, so we can be realistic."

"Well, what if you had been fired?" suggested Lanigan.

"Then it would be because I was unlucky. Not that I had sinned, or was even wrong. Just unlucky."

Lanigan smiled broadly. "Well, I'm glad you were lucky," He chuckled. "They say it rubs off."

46

LAURA PUT DOWN the receiver and said in bewilderment, "They've arrested him. They arrested Jack."

"Who arrested him? What are you talking about?" her father demanded. "Who were you talking to?"

"I called Jack's office and I spoke to the girl there. She said he'd called to say he'd been arrested and he wanted J. J. Mulcahey—he's the sort of senior lawyer there—to come and see him at the Barnard's Crossing Police Station. Mulcahey hadn't got in yet, but it sounded urgent, so she called him at home, and he said he'd go right over. He hasn't got to the office *yet*, and here it is almost eleven."

"Did she say why he'd been arrested?"

"She didn't know. Oh, I've got to go down there right away."

"No, Laura. I'll go. I can get more out of the police than you can."

"Why?" She was suspicious of her father. She felt he had no great enthusiasm for Scofield.

"Because I make a sizable contribution to the Policeman's Association every year."

"When would you go?" she asked, still suspicious.

"I'll leave right now. And I'll come right back as soon as I find out anything."

At the station house, Magnuson had no difficulty in seeing Lanigan. In fact, he was at the front desk talking to the sergeant. When he saw Magnuson enter, he said, "Hello, Mr. Magnuson. What brings you down here?"

"You know me?" asked Magnuson, surprised and a little flattered. "Can I talk to you—er—"

"Sure, let's go into my office, we can talk there. Coffee?"

"Er—no thanks." When they were seated, he said. "Look here, I'd like to know what you've got on Jack Scofield."

Lanigan spread his hands and shrugged. "That's in the hands of the D.A."

"I'm not asking just out of curiosity. My daughter is involved with this man."

"Yes, I know. She managed his campaign."

"It's more than that. She's almost engaged to him. Now, if you arrested him because of violation of some minor regulation, something that he did or didn't do, maybe in connection with the campaign, that's one thing. But if it's something serious, something reprehensible, then I've got to know that for Laura—for my daughter's sake. I assume it will be on the radio or in the newspapers before the day is over, so why not give me that much of a head start? I may even be able to help you."

Lanigan pursed his lips and then nodded. "All right. There was a hit-and-run on Glen Lane a little while back, and the victim was killed. Scofield was the driver. Is that serious?"

Magnuson nodded. It was a terrible thing not to stop after an accident, to see how badly the victim was hurt and go for aid. On the other hand, he could also understand Scofield's panicking, considering all he had at stake. "Is that it?" he asked.

"There's more. In order to misdirect the police, he broke a headlight on a parked car and brought back the bits of glass and scattered them near the body. Now, that might qualify as reprehensible, I think."

"You know for a fact that he did that?"

"Uh-huh. You see, he gathered up the glass in an old towel that he kept in the trunk of his car. Some fragments adhered to the towel. And they match up perfectly with the glass near the body."

"This parked car, it belonged to someone he had a grudge against?"

"No, it's just that it was there, available, you might say."

"I see. So that's it. A hit-and-run, and then misdirecting the police."

"That's all we can prove at the moment. But we have reason to believe that Scofield knew the man he killed, that he drove there to meet him, and that it was no accident, that he did it on purpose."

"You mean—"

"M-hm. We think the victim perpetrated some kind of dirty political trick for him, that he had arranged to meet him in Glen Lane to pay him off."

"But that's murder."

"That's the way it looks to us."

Magnuson nodded. "I see." He thought about Laura, and how she would take the news. She was a sensible girl, but if she loved the man, she might feel that she had to be loyal to him. She might be able to rationalize the hit-and-run on the grounds that he was weak and had panicked. Maybe even the business of misdirecting the police. But murder? He was sure she could not accept that. Still . . . He came to a decision.

"When Laura told me she was interested in Scofield, I checked his bank account," he said quietly. "I'm a director of the main bank in Boston. One day right after the election, Scofield withdrew three thousand dollars in cash, half his total capital."

"Is that so?"

"And redeposited it the next day."

"Very interesting. We'll subpoena the records and check it out. Thank you very much, Mr. Magnuson."

Telling Laura was not as hard as he thought it would be. At first, she was aghast, and then weepy, whether for Scofield or for herself, he could not be sure.

"I'm responsible," she insisted. "Maybe if I hadn't encouraged him to win ... If I hadn't pushed him ... I thought he didn't have enough drive, but I thought the two of us would make a first-rate team. You see, he's weak ..."

"Well, you know weak people aren't just weak in one thing; they're usually weak in everything."

"I've got to see him."

"No, Laura. That's one thing you mustn't do. I don't want you to get within a mile of him. As far as we're concerned, he's poison."

"But I've got to. Even if it's just—. There are things to be done in connection with the campaign—bills to pay, letters to answer—"

"I don't want you to have anything to do with them. It could be dangerous for you. I'll get Morris Halperin to handle it. He'll get in touch with this Mulcahey who's acting for Scofield, and between the two of them, they'll work out what has to be done."

"Oh, Dad, it's like rats deserting a sinking ship."

"No, Laura. It's more like taking care to walk around a mud puddle."

"But what will I do all the time that he's—"

"I suggest you go to Paris with your mother. And I might come, too. It's been some time since I've seen my brother."

255

47

"Look, kiddo," said Mulcahey, "if you want another lawyer, it's okay with me. But if you want me, then you've got to give me all of it."

"I'd like you to handle it, but—"

"Look, kid, I've defended in cases of rape, murder, even incest. I don't sit in judgment. Talking to me is like talking to a tape recorder, no matter what you did. All I'm interested in is what I have to play up and what I have to play down to get an acquittal. But I can't stand surprises in court. So either give it all to me or get yourself another lawyer."

"Sure, J.J., I understand. See, the campaign wasn't going so good, and I didn't think I had a chance. I was running up a lot of bills, and I wasn't getting any of that free advertising you spoke about. At least, it wasn't bringing in any business. Then this guy came to see me."

"D'Angelo?"

"Yeah. He seemed to know his way around. He talked as if he knew all the big shots in Boston. And he said they had their eye on me because I was a new figure while Baggio and Cash were just ordinary pols. We talked about the campaign, and he said Baggio was the man I had to beat, that I didn't have to worry about Cash because he couldn't win. They wouldn't let him. Then he told me he had a way for me to beat Baggio, but it would cost me a little money.

"I asked him how much money and he said a couple of thousand. I told him I didn't have that kind of dough, and he explained I wouldn't have to pay it all at once, that I could give him a couple of hundred now and the rest after the election. But I figured I'd still be paying out money for nothing if I lost, and it would just add to all the bills I was going to have to pay. Anyway, we finally agreed I'd give him a couple of hundred for expenses, and then if I won the nomination I'd give him three thousand. And if I lost I wouldn't owe him anything. That seemed like a good bet. I got the feeling that he could deliver."

"What were you getting for your money?"

"He had this picture, a snapshot, of a bunch of gangsters in tuxedos. And right there with them was Baggio. He was going to get out like a leaflet, naming each of these guys and what they were charged with, and underneath he'd have in big print, 'Is this the sort of company you want your senator to keep?' You understand, he wouldn't get out the leaflet personally. It would be like from a special association, The Committee of Concerned Citizens."

"Ah, so *he* was the committee. But then you repudiated it just before the election."

"Yeah, Laura insisted. She thought it was a dirty trick. I guess it was at that, but you know it's like they say, all's fair—"

"All's fair in love and war is the way that reads. These days that doesn't include politics," said Mulcahey.

"Yeah, well, you could say it was for love because by that time I was pretty hung up on Laura and I got the feeling that if I lost I didn't have a chance with her."

"All right, but it wasn't very smart of you."

"It won me the nomination," said Scofield.

"Maybe. But if it ever got out, you'd be poison for the rest of your life. You're not supposed to play dirty tricks on the members of your own party. If you win the nomination, you count on them to help you win the election. You work dirty tricks only on the other party. All right, so then what happened? He called you and asked you to pay up?"

"Not right away. It wasn't quite clear whether I was to pay him after the nomination or after the final election. But Baggio was good and sore about it, because you see that wasn't his picture actually. It was somebody else. He'd never been at the party where this picture was supposed to have been taken, and he could prove it. He was out of the state at the time. He complained to the Election Commission, and I guess he had some friends there because they got onto it right away."

"He's got a brother-in-law on the commission."

"Oh yeah? That accounts for it. Then I got a call from D'Angelo. He said that the detectives from the commission were nosing around among printers and he was afraid that sooner or later they'd get to him. He thought he ought to go away for a while, maybe until after the election when he figured it would all blow over. Naturally I agreed. He said he was planning to leave the next morning early, but he needed going-away money. That's what he called it. He wanted me to get the money and come over to the office or to my apartment to collect it that day. Well, under the circumstances I naturally didn't want to be seen with him, so I said I'd meet him someplace, and I suggested Glen Lane. He was to get there around ten and wait because I was due over at Laura's house for dinner—I'd been eating there practically every night—and I didn't know how soon I could get away.

"You see, I was a little bothered because I had given him a check for the two hundred, not him, you understand, but the committee—"

"Your own check, or one from your campaign fund?"

"I couldn't give him one from the campaign fund because Laura checked the statement, and I didn't want her to know. But when my own statement came from the bank, he hadn't cashed it yet, so I was a little worried. See, what with finding out that the picture was a fake and the investigation by the Election Commission, I was beginning to think I'd got myself into something of a mess. So, naturally I was pleased that he was going to get out of town. I went down to the bank and withdrew three thousand dollars in cash. When I went to Laura's that night, I told them that I'd have to leave early. Usually I stayed until about eleven, but I managed to get away just after ten.

"As I drove out to Glen Lane, I began thinking about my situation, thinking all kinds of things. Maybe he'd have a photographer there who would snap a picture of me just as I was passing money. Because now that I knew the kind of guy he was, I figured there was no telling what he could arrange."

"I understand."

"So I got to Glen from the Salem end, and I was going pretty slow because I didn't want to miss him. And then I see his car in this little clearing, and at the same time I see him up ahead in the middle of the road, on foot. Then I don't know what happened. It crossed my mind that even after paying him, he'd still have a hold on me even after the election because of that check I gave him. Anyway, I stepped on the gas—"

"And you rammed him. So then what did you do? Did you stop?"

"I must have. At least, I'm sure I slowed down, because I looked back and saw him lying there in the road face down. I was going to report it to the police. I really was. I mean, report it as an accident. I could say that he came out of the woods suddenly and that I hadn't seen him. But you know how the police are about motor accidents. You can imagine what effect that would have on the election. And if I lost the election, then I'd lose Laura, and—everything. So I thought I'd just stop off and make an anonymous phone call. That would take care of D'Angelo, and I wouldn't get hurt. Because after all, he was blackmailing me. I stopped at the foot of the hill, just where Glen Lane turns into Maple Street to check my car—"

"Check it for what?"

"Well, did you see that movie on TV where the medical examiner cracked a hit-and-run case by a chemical analysis of some little paint chips found at the scene? He was able to prove that they came from the car that did it. So I wanted to see if any of the paint had chipped off my fender, and if it was dented."

"And?"

Scofield shook his head sorrowfully. "I couldn't tell. See, the fender had rusted some and I couldn't tell. But I have this pink car, and it's the only one in town so far as I know, and I was worried. And then I noticed a car parked just a little beyond. I thought maybe I could get the police to look in another direction. Well, all the houses were dark, so I thought I'd take a chance. I got a wrench out of the car and an old towel that I leave in the trunk. I sort of wrapped the towel around the headlight and then whacked it with the wrench. Then I kind of gathered up the glass that had fallen into the towel and brought it back to my car. Then I turned around and drove back to where—to where he was lying and dropped the glass on the road. And then I went home."

"And how did they catch up with you?"

"They picked up my car for parking on the street. You're not supposed to park overnight in Barnard's Crossing during the winter months. On account of it might interfere with snow plowing. But the weather has been so mild—"

"Was the car locked?"

Scofield shook his head. "No, I don't think so. I don't usually lock it. I figure nobody is going to pinch it around there. And it being pink, and easily recognized—"

"Okay, go on."

"So then I guess they found the towel in the trunk—"

"You kept it?"

"Well, sure, it didn't occur to me that there might still be bits of glass in it."

"But surely the trunk was locked."

"Of course."

"Then they must have forced the lock."

"No, there's a doohickey under the dash that releases it. What difference does it make?"

"We might claim illegal search. Okay, I'll check it out. Who picked you up this morning?"

"Lieutenant Jennings came, with another cop. He said they had found glass fragments in my trunk and that they matched the glass on the road near the body."

"I see. And what did you do with the money?"

"What money?"

"The three thousand that you didn't give to D'Angelo?"

"I deposited it the next day."

"Was that all the money you had?"

"No, I had another three thousand in the bank. Why?"

"So that makes six thousand. All right, that will do for starters."

"What do you mean for starters?"

"Look, kid, I'm planning to shave my own fees, but there'll be costs, lots of costs—detectives, experts of one kind or another, psychiatrists. Your six thousand won't go far, not these days. What other money can you raise?"

"Well, if the Magnusons stick by me—"

"They won't. You can just about forget them. If the D.A. goes for murder, a guy like Magnuson is not going to let his name be associated with yours."

"Then I don't know. Maybe my sister—"

"Well, you think about it. You'll have plenty of time. I'm going to see the assistant D.A. who'll be handling this case. If they don't know about your connection with D'Angelo, he may elect to go for the hit-and-run. Then our strategy is to plead guilty to that. You panicked. That's all."

"How about the business of my smashing the headlight?"

"I'm going to try to keep that separate from the hit-and-run. Two different trials if I can manage it."

"What's the point of that?"

"Because all you can be charged with there is misdirecting or maybe interfering with a police officer in the performance of duty. But if the D.A. gets onto your connection with D'Angelo, he'll be sure to go for murder, and then we may have to plead temporary insanity. I don't know. I'm giving it to you straight because, well, because you're a lawyer and if I tried to kid you, you'd know it. In the meantime, I think you better resign as nominee for senator. I'll get up a statement of some kind and you'll sign it. Something on the order of wanting to clear your name first. And whatever you do, don't talk, not to anyone, not even to Laura, or her old man. You understand?"

48

HOWARD MAGNUSON WAS GIVING Morris Halperin instructions before departing for Paris. "Here are Laura's keys to that store. She says the leases for the stuff they rented are all in the top drawer of her desk, and there's the key to that. You'll get in touch with the Mulcahey person and arrange with him to close the place down and return the furniture. Here's a power of attorney from Laura. That should enable you to draw on any money in the campaign fund to pay off whatever bills are due. She used to sign all the checks. But Mulcahey acting for Scofield may want a hand in it."

"He will."

"Then don't fight him. I want to wind it down as quickly as possible. If there isn't enough money in the campaign fund to cover, I'll make up the deficit for anything within reason. Notify my Boston office and they'll pay it. Let's see, anything else?"

"What about my brother, Mr. Magnuson?"

"Oh well, under the circumstances, you can understand that we can't go ahead with our original plan. Did he resign his job out in Kansas?"

"No, but—"

"Look, Morris, these things happen. You once told me your brother was unlucky. I suppose what it comes down to is that Rabbi Small is lucky. Why don't you call your brother, explain the situation, and tell him that I'm grateful to him for his willingness to cooperate, and I consider myself indebted to him and will help him anyway I can. And, who knows, maybe someday the rabbi will leave."